Also by Nancy Wood

THUNDERWOMAN

Thunderwoman

A MYTHIC NOVEL OF THE PUEBLOS

Nancy Wood

WITH ILLUSTRATIONS BY
RICHARD ERDOES

A DUTTON BOOK

Text copyright © 1999 by Nancy Wood
Illustrations copyright © 1999 by Richard Erdoes

Library of Congress Cataloging-in-Publication Data
Wood, Nancy C.
Thunderwoman: a mythic novel of the Pueblos/
prose and poetry by Nancy Wood; illustrated by Richard Erdoes.—1st ed.   p.   cm.
Summary: Follows the Pueblo Indians from creation and prehistory to bloody massacres
by the Spanish and others, ending with the testing of the atomic bomb.
ISBN 0-525-45498-5 (hc)
1. Pueblo Indians—Juvenile fiction. [1. Pueblo
Indians—Fiction. 2. Indians of North America—
Southwest, New—Fiction. 3. Southwest, New—Fiction.
4. Creation—Fiction.] I. Erdoes, Richard, ill. II. Title.
PZ7.W853th 1999
[Fic]—dc21 98-28373 CIP AC

Published in the United States 1999 by Dutton,
a member of Penguin Putnam Inc.
345 Hudson Street, New York, New York 10014
Designed by Ellen M. Lucaire
Printed in USA   First Edition
1 3 5 7 9 10 8 6 4 2

ACKNOWLEDGMENTS

For their loving support and generous reading of the manuscript, I thank Carolyn Johnston, Virginia Westray, Robert "Foxhole" Parker, Art Bachrach, and Anna Gidley. Tal Luther deserves special recognition, because the idea for a novel much like this originated with him. Richard Erdoes, Indian scholar, fellow writer, and dear friend, was generous with his love and suggestions. My son, Chris, patiently bailed me out of many a computer mess. Don Congdon was, as always, the perfect agent.

Karen Lotz, my editor, is like editors used to be. Realizing the difficulty of writing such a complex work, she edited at least three different versions, offered invaluable suggestions, and supported me throughout. Assistant editors Jamie Michalak and Amy Wick lavished care and attention on this book. For meticulous copyediting, thanks to Nora Reichard and Andrea Mosbacher. For inspired design, *abrazos* to Ellen M. Lucaire.

To all of them, I offer special thanks.

NANCY WOOD
Santa Fe, New Mexico
April 1998

For Karen Lotz,

MY FAVORITE EDITOR

CONTENTS

POETRY

PART ONE

The Time of
the Great Goodness

ARENAL 1522

The Original Beings

In the Beginning Time,
*   we were the Original Beings,*
*   sleeping under a molten tongue of lightning.*

In the Beginning Time,
*   we were newborn stars,*
*   expanding our thin shadows*
*   until they became worthy of substance.*

In the Beginning Time,
*   we were the dagger teeth of fire,*
*   lacerating the earth until seeds had a place to take hold.*

In the Beginning Time,
*   we were the fulfillment of raindrops,*
*   the invisible mouth of wind blowing potential*
*   to villages awakening from false dreams.*

We lived in a Circle of Power,
*   a Circle of Beauty,*
*   a Circle of Wisdom,*
*   as if we had forever to expand.*
*   Beneath the Sun's hot eye,*

We grew strong enough to marry animals.
*   We endured hardship, but on the horizon,*
*   our destiny was approaching.*

By the year 1522 on the Christian calendar, the palace of Moctezuma had been destroyed by the army of Cortés, the canals filled in, and the great city of Tenochtitlan leveled. The pagan idols of the Aztecs were smashed, the priests tortured, the temple at Tlatelolco burned. Three hundred thousand Aztecs were slaughtered during the final battle, when blood flowed knee-deep through the zócalo and the severed heads of children bobbed off on a tide of blood. The spirits of the massacred nation drifted in and out of the Spanish houses, along the cobbled streets, and into the viceroy's quarters, listening, listening. Who knows what will happen next, the spirits said, arranging themselves on the plush furniture hauled over the waves in ships filled with the king's own men, choking on anticipation.

Crude maps were drawn of the vast unexplored territory to the north. No one knew exactly where the oceans were, the rugged spine of mountains, the fabled cities of gold that would make the conquistadors rich. All that was needed was royal money for an expedition, a roster of mercenaries unafraid to risk their lives, strong horses, war dogs with polished fangs, an arsenal of lethal weapons, friars to offer salvation to the pagans, and enough Aztec slaves to make the perilous journey bearable.

The clock of conquest ticked on. It would take another eighteen years for Spain to march upon the peaceful pueblo villages to the north, where ancestral voices were strong and animals shared the same sacred blood with humans. In one of these villages, called Arenal, strange things began to happen even as the ashes of Tenochtitlan were cooling.

CHAPTER
One

An old man named Lizard-Goes-Forth was the first to notice something was wrong. He looked at his right foot and saw it wasn't a foot anymore, but a hoof, unlike anything he had ever seen before. It was as big around as his wrist, delicately shaped, and knife sharp. What is this? he cried, and got up from the bed of furs where he'd been lying with his wife, Turtle Woman. Another hoof replaced his left foot. Then two more where his hands had been. Fur sprouted in clumps on his legs, his belly, his face. Two gently curved horns formed on his head. He could not go up and down the ladders to his third-story house, so he was given a room on the first floor, which he entered through an opening covered with deer hide. He looked exactly the same as the animals who came to spend the winter. He was able to think like them.

People marveled at his appearance, and he was given a new name: Deer-He-Becomes. Far and wide, he was revered for his deer wisdom.

As word spread, people came to visit him. They brought him presents and asked for his advice. Look at what I've become, he said. Does that not tell you something? Deer-He-Becomes had the voice a deer might have, if one could talk. His children were half-deer, half-human. People wondered what it meant.

Shortly after the Man/Deer appeared, an unearthly moan blew in on the southwest wind. An enemy, ready to attack? The chief sent scouts to find out what was happening. The Wind Spirits, they said, upon returning. But the Clay People could not sleep. They had lived in Arenal since the Time That Fish Emerged. They had never felt this uneasy before.

One night, a green phosphorescent light surged through the village like a tide. Small eels were in it, also giant crabs and fish with feet. It awakened Deer-He-Becomes, who bounded over the wall. Turtle Woman dissolved in the light's green, probing tongue. Then an earthquake jarred people from their beds, and they ran outside, thinking the village was about to fall down. Beams fell and crushed two sleeping children. Walls collapsed on a couple making love. For many moons, women did not conceive. Others had babies with short little tails. A meteorite fell in the mountains and from it came the intoxicating smell of jungle flowers. Shaking their gourd rattles and dancing their energetic dances, the elders moaned prayers of solicitation and forgiveness. They bathed in the Great River, but one elder slipped and went under the water. He became a large, blue fish with long whiskers. Scorpions rose and became sun dogs.

These are signs from the spirits, the Memorizers said, sitting in a tight circle in the kiva, the underground chamber where the principles of authority and religion were taught. We are not living right. What should we do? An old man named Kobili nodded. I created the Universe together with a spirit called Thunderwoman, he wanted to tell them. We had an argument. She disappeared. Now she is coming back. I am sure of it. But he told them nothing. He waited to see what would happen next.

A giant, dressed in the moth-eaten skin of an elk, rampaged

through the village and kidnapped two women, one under each arm. He went north in long, easy strides while warriors ran after him, uselessly shooting their poison-tipped arrows. No one saw the women again, though two does appeared at the village wall, staring at their old families with a forlorn look. Then one man's eyeballs fell out. A boy grew the wings of a giant fly on his back. A huge black snake swallowed the war chief's baby son, sleeping in his cradle. Night and day the dry, chirping sound of locusts filled the air. People went crazy from the sound. Some ran away to the mountains and were never seen again. Others floated down the river in canoes, anxious to escape.

Mice scurried into the empty storerooms and inhaled the last of the corn dust, then they turned on their backs and expired.

The Memorizers climbed up the ladders to Kobili's house and confronted him, angrily. You are the chief shaman, they said. Yet you do nothing. You have powerful medicine. Use it, Old Man. Our people are sick. They are dying. Sun Mountain Shining, the headman of the Sun Clan, pounded his walking stick on the hard dirt floor. My grandson was borne away by a red-eyed Eagle, he said. Blossoms Falling, my favorite wife, is now a green lizard. Restore her!

Kobili shrugged. There is a reason for everything, he said. When Blossoms Falling is tired of her life as a lizard, she will return to you as a woman. At this, Deer-He-Becomes banged his antlers against the wall. You put a spell on me, Old Man. Restore me as well!

Go to the mountains, Kobili said. There you will find your answer. A procession of all the clan leaders made their way to the mountains to talk to Cougar and Elk, Bear and Eagle. They found the footprints of the giant and followed them to a cave, where they heard loud snoring. The ground shook. Leaves fell from the trees. They found the kidnapped women's clothing piled in front of the cave. They decided not to go in. They sat in a clearing, wondering what to do. One Fist looked down. He saw fish scales appearing on his arms, a split tail where his legs had been. There is no answer in the mountains, he said to Kobili after he slid into Arenal. Look at me.

The shaman had lived in the village as far back as anyone could remember. He had helped Arenal grow from the earth. Into the adobe mud he had stirred bat dung and frog bones and the blood of a rattlesnake to make the village strong. He had invented the first songs and taught the Clay People how to pray to the gods he brought with him. Around the campfire he had explained their origins and given them the stories they would need to carry them through many lifetimes. Now, raising his arms, he made One Fist's fish tail disappear. He blew on his fish scales, and they fell off. Go and purify yourself beyond the Three Big Rocks, Kobili said. Fast and pray for one moon. Fall to the ground and watch the path of the ants. When you learn their humility, you may come back to the village.

One Fist knew better than to argue. Kobili was the Ancient Revered One, the highest religious leader in the Seven Wise Villages of Tiguex, of which Arenal was one. It was said in the kivas that he had arrived on the back of a golden Eagle when the Sun Father was still trying to decide his course through the sky. Before that, he had wandered the Universe, picking out places for the stars to go. No one knew for certain who or what he was. Only that he had power beyond their comprehension.

Kobili watched One Fist climb down the ladders to the plaza. The shaman's house was on the fourth story, where no one else was allowed to live. From his terrace he could watch the Twin Bears shove the Sun Father into the sky each morning. He watched the Brotherhood of Eagles cover up the Sun Father's burning red face each night. He was able to see in all directions. To the east, mountains—just the way he'd hoped they'd turn out. Below him, the Great River curved where he'd pressed the palm of his hand against its grassy banks. The big animals were his: bears, buffalo, elk, eagles. Thunderwoman liked smaller ones like rabbits and beavers and foxes. Flowers so tiny you could hardly see them. Hummingbirds, insects, worms. Also clouds and grass.

The Old Man began to sing on his rooftop, enjoying the sun on his back. Wherever you are, I will find you. In a little while, we will be together again. His voice was not musical, but it had strength. He realized he had never told her she was beautiful, only that the things she made were beautiful. Waterfalls, turtles, anemones. Colored stones that she put in rivers. Rainbows, snow. The spirit of his mate was everywhere, which meant that she was everywhere. The shaman climbed down the ladder into the familiar darkness of his house. Raven was waiting for him. Brother Raven, he said, I miss Thunderwoman. It has been ten thousand years, and I cannot get her out of my mind.

Raven had not seen his own mate in nearly that long, either. She is on her way, Old Man, Raven said, fanning the fire with his wing. He brought water from the river in his beak and dropped it onto Kobili's face to cool him off. Then he flew out the small window and headed across the rosy desert. He had much on his mind.

The shaman was deep in thought. I can do many things, he said. But I cannot bring her back. I must be losing my power. Coyote rose from the shadows. Old Man, he said, your power is strong. Your patience is not. Coyote remembered the Time Before Time because he was God's Dog. During those days, the Old Man was not willing to let stars form slowly. He wanted them all at once. Kobili went to the window and pushed the hide covering aside. Where are you? he shouted. I'm sorry, do you hear? Thunder crashed down from the mountains. Her voice. Thunderwoman's voice. He was sure of it.

CHAPTER
Two

he Memorizers stared with melancholy eyes
into the yellow-tongued kiva fire. What was
happening to them as leaders without chosen
successors? As warriors feasting upon old victories? Once, they had
great power; now, they had none. Something or somebody was responsible. Kobili with his uneasy presence? Their great hereditary
chief, Elk Heart, whose arrows collapsed the moment they left his
bow? Were the deer responsible, refusing to die when they were reverently asked, thus creating a shortage of meat? Something was happening in the Seven Wise Villages that had not happened before. The
elders from the six other villages knew it, too. The Time of the Great
Goodness means we should not have to worry, they said when they
gathered during each full moon to share their knowledge and experience. Do you remember such strange events before?

The Memorizers, men of the highest position, descended in a di-
rect line from the First Wolf and the First Eagle, whose stories sus-

tained and instructed, could not remember anything. Their stories had slipped away. They fasted and prayed, sang until their hearts moved to their windpipes, but their stories receded into fog. They went down to the Great River, where the Fish People lived. They watched their rela-

tives from the upstream villages sweep past in canoes, shouting bits of news as the water bore them away. The Memo-rizers shouted back, We have nothing to tell you. They turned to the fish, who were their ancestors, which is why they never ate them. Help us, the Memorizers cried. The fish swam on.

Now, the elders had spent the whole night in the kiva, trying to remember the stories that had sustained them. Blue Water moistened his lips. The Winter of the Three Big Snows, deer came to the village in search of food, he said. We shared our dried corn with them. When they were full, they said— But he could not remember what the deer brothers had said. He scratched the stone walls with a knife. Soon a drawing of a deer appeared.

The Summer of Devouring Flames, fire ate trees and animals, Red Dog said, slowly. The river filled with ash. Fish were dying. We car-ried them downriver, and they swam away. They thanked us and then— But he could not remember what had happened next.

The Spring of White Ash, bears taught people to look inside themselves, said Bent Oak. Bears married the First Women. The First Children were half-bear. Remember how they— But he could not remember any more about bears, though his own son was a Bear Boy, hibernating all winter long. He had fur all the way down his back and claws instead of fingers. Peo-ple from all over revered him.

The Winter of Falling Stars, our enemies approached in the night, said Snow Eagle. They would have killed us, for they were great in number. But a shower of stars frightened them away. My grandfather said to the Star Beings— But he could not remember what his ancestor had said, though the story had been repeated to him many times.

Deer-He-Becomes pranced on four legs. His antlers had grown wide, so now they reached halfway across the kiva. The Memorizers had hung little rattling shells and colored stones from them. I remember nothing of my life as a man, he said. I live in the mountains now. I remember the sweetness of grass. The blue of the sky. The gentle song of water. These are things worth remembering. I am content to know them, my friends.

An old man opened his toothless mouth. I remember nothing, said Gray Wolf, bitterly. And I don't care. My wives and children are dead. My house sags under the weight of so much memory I gave it up.

Every time the Memorizers convened, Gray Wolf said the same thing. He was in his eighty-first year of amnesia.

Grandfather expresses our thoughts, said One Fist. Whenever I try to find the stories I used to know, smoke fills my head. Soon I will know nothing. They looked at one another and drew their blankets around their shoulders. Snow Eagle beat the blackened kiva drum. The elders rocked back and forth, singing softly. They prayed to understand the things that were upon them.

Our blood used to be mixed with that of the animals, Sun Mountain Shining said, thoughtfully, rubbing his chin. Bears. Deer. Elk. We were strong. We remembered everything without hesitation. The reason we can't remember our history is because women no longer mate with bears. Our blood needs freshness. The other villages say the same thing. Except for Deer-He-Becomes, who among us is part animal anymore?

I no longer remember my purpose, mourned Red Dog.

I no longer remember how to plant corn, said Bent Oak.

I no longer remember the names of my ancestors, said Blue Water.

Why have our stories disappeared? asked Gray Wolf.

Why do bad things happen? asked Snow Eagle, putting his drum aside.

No one answered, then Feather Keeper spoke up. The Time of the Great Goodness is coming to an end. I had a dream about it.

One Fist said, the Time of the Great Goodness cannot last forever.

Not forever here, only a little while here, said Blue Water. The Memorizers stared morosely into the fire. Snow Eagle beat his drum in a slow, rhythmic song. It comforted them.

How will it end?

Why will it end?

What can we do?

CHAPTER
Three

y this time, which was the year 1522 on a
Christian calendar that no one in that part of
the world had ever seen, Kobili had dreamed
the same dream seven nights in a row. In this dream his beloved had
come to him as a red and squalling infant, although she had not been
an infant before. He looked into his dream self, hoping for a change
in message. An infant? he said. A voice from the other side of the
Universe said: Why not, Old Man? You are too set in your ways. You
need something different.

But an infant? he protested. What will I do with an infant?
Nonetheless, he prepared potions from roots and leaves and berries.
He made a cradle and decorated it with porcupine quills. He traded a
bear claw for a buffalo robe. He caught a red-tailed hawk and trained
it to do diving tricks. She had always enjoyed bird tricks before. Then
he looked around Arenal to see which women were carrying a child.
Twenty-six in all, from the Seven Wise Villages, from the Hopi, from

the sky village of Acoma, from invincible Pecos, and even one from a Plains tribe he detested. There was one particular woman he observed closely. No Name was coarse-featured, broad-hipped, sharp-tongued, with a mind Kobili thought too wild. The other women did not like her; the men were wary of her. Some said she was a witch. When she was twelve years old, her father had traded her for a sack of salt to Elk Heart. She had cut her hair as a sign of resistance and had run away toward the place she remembered as home. Elk Heart had found her weeping by the river. The chieftain liked her fire, the way she pummeled him with her small fists. He called her No Name because she would not tell him her real one; in fact, she would not speak at all.

Kobili saw No Name as a life-size ear of corn, her stoical face protruding from the tassels. When she carried water in two magical gourds to the parched fields and covered them, saving the corn, he smiled. He spoke to her about where she had come from and what she was doing there. She did not deny what he said, but she did not confirm his suspicions, either. Then one day he noticed she was carrying a child. He knew it was no ordinary child. Whenever he passed close, it spoke. Not gurgling baby sounds, but an old language he thought he had forgotten. He answered in the same tongue. Is it you? he cried. What are you doing in there? No Name pushed him away and gave him a dark look. If she could have spoken, she would have told him to stop. Kobili never spoke directly to unborn children. It would bring bad luck.

As the child within No Name's womb grew, strange sounds were heard. The cry of a wolf. The roar of a mountain lion. People stopped what they were doing and listened. The Bird Women said to their husbands: No Name is a witch. At night she flies across the rooftops. We have seen her. When we put our ears to her belly, the unborn child *speaks*. It says all manner of things. The Bird Women made up stories that their husbands liked. Their husbands were the Memorizers, who were trying to find an excuse to take action against the unfamiliar.

Now, on a crisp cold morning during Ash Moon, Kobili hurried across the plaza, stopping to pick up a smooth white stone, knowing how much his beloved liked stones. Any moment now, she would be born. He had had a dream about it. She would not know who she was, or where she had come from. But he would know.

CHAPTER
Four

Coyote had been waiting along the river all night. As the Sun rose, something within him knew it was time. He slipped past the people in the plaza and raced up the ladder to No Name's house, then stood in the shadows of the small, musty room, watching with his intelligent yellow eyes. No Name was writhing on her bed of wild goose down. She motioned him to her side. Brother Coyote, you've come at last, she whispered, speaking for the first time in years. She was drenched in perspiration. He licked her face tenderly. Her swollen belly heaved and contracted. She reached for him. Brother Coyote, my child is ready to emerge. Help me expel her from my womb. Do not leave me now. She grabbed his fur. You always helped me before.

I don't know what to do, Sister, Coyote said. He climbed to the roof and called for Raven, who flew in the small window and landed on a ledge. Raven's beak was filled with water, which he let drip into No Name's dry mouth. Again and again he brought her water, until at last her thirst was quenched. As No Name's cries pierced the air, Snake Sister slithered down the ladder and across the floor. With her thin tongue darting in and out, she wrapped herself around the woman's contracting belly and squeezed. Push, Snake Sister said. Raven fanned the flames in the fire pit with his wing, watching nervously.

Harder, Snake Sister hissed. No Name's Birthing Circle was small, and for a while it seemed the infant would never be born. Then a tiny foot appeared, a knee, an elbow. Help me, Snake Sister said. With his paws, Coyote gently pulled out a foot. The rest of the infant burst forth. A tiny girl with bark-colored skin, Raven's hair, and Coyote's enigmatic expression. The Sign of the Jaguar blazed on one cheek. Coyote knew what the sign meant, though he had not seen it in many years. Raven likewise knew.

Raven stared at the wrinkled creature lying on her mother's contracting belly. His children had all been hatched from eggs, so he was unaccustomed to the sight of a human, all slimy and dissatisfied. Snake Sister's green scaly skin shone in the firelight. Her black eyes were impassive. Lick her off, Snake Sister said to Coyote. Bite the navel cord in two. Coyote bit off the umbilical cord and dropped it on the floor. He cleaned the baby's face of blood and mucus. Raven ate the placenta, though it took a while. Above them on the rooftop, Kobili was nervously waiting, turning the white stone over and over in his hands. May I see her? he called down. Not yet, Coyote said. We are busy.

Snake Sister slithered across the floor. Above her, the Grandmother Spiders hung from the ceiling beams on fine silver threads. They had been watching. Come down and feed her, Snake Sister said. No Name's milk is dried up. The child is hungry. The spiders had more than a million children among them, and they knew what to do,

though it took all day to feed the infant a few drops of milk from some magical part of themselves. No Name opened her eyes. The spiders were working furiously. They were nurturing creatures who overcame their smallness to contribute what they could. Thank you, Grandmother Spiders, No Name said. She saw Snake Sister crawling up the ladder. Thank you, Snake Sister. With a shake of her rattle, the snake disappeared.

Coyote gazed at the fretful child, all red and wrinkled. I will show you how to travel fast across the earth, he said. Someday you'll become a Coyote Girl.

Raven fluttered closer. She was rather ugly, with that red mark on her face. He remembered the first human born of fish and human parents. It had looked watery, like this one. I will introduce you to the sky, he said. Someday you'll become a Raven Girl.

No Name held her daughter close. Many years from now, you will know my true name. It's a name repeated throughout the world. I gave you life, as I have given life to everything on Earth. Her eyes grew dim. Now I must die in order that you may live. Before I go, I will name you Sayah, the Woman-Who-Can-Stop-the-Sun.

Don't leave me, Mama. The baby wailed hysterically. The whole village heard her, including Kobili, waiting outside, frantic with worry. Why was the birth of his beloved taking so long? Why could he not see her? No Name ran her fingers over the baby's soft black hair. She touched her perfumed skin. And noted the special mark on her cheek. You will have many good mothers, she said. A wise man will guide you. Animals will help you. No Name's eyes drifted closed. The Grandmother Spiders quickly walked on No Name's eyelids and gave her stories to take to the World Beyond.

Then a strange thing happened. Out of the eastern sky a bright object came hurtling toward the village so fast that those who saw it coming thought they would be struck dead. The object became brighter and brighter until it blinded all who watched. The villagers covered their eyes and ran toward their houses. The Whirlwind People generated a strong wind, trying to keep the thing from arriving.

Their wind sucked up dust and fire sticks, cornmeal and ashes. It sucked up the village dogs. Faster and faster it whirled, but the object sailed right through the powerful whirlwind and landed in the plaza with a dreadful hissing sound. Dawn Giver's dress caught on fire. She ran to the river and jumped in. The Memorizers gathered around the object, which was hissing in a patch of snow, and poked it with their sticks. *It is a star!* Very small, no bigger than a good-sized rock. But it had the searing brilliance of the Sun. When they saw it breaking into many sparkling pieces, the Memorizers jumped back. Beneath their moccasined feet, the Earth trembled. They ran to the kiva, noticing Snake Sister coiled on the hearth. You will not believe what I am about to tell you, she said.

As the snake told what had happened, two star pieces flew off like fast birds, circling the village before they whistled through the rooftop opening of No Name's house. They illuminated the room with an eerie, bluish light. Coyote shrank against the wall. Raven flapped his wings to keep from getting scorched. The star pieces whirled above the bed, then suddenly embedded themselves in the infant's eyes. She tore at them with her tiny fingers and howled in pain. Coyote tried to dislodge the pieces with his tongue. They burned him. Raven tried to pick them out with his beak. Coyote looked helplessly at Raven. She will be blinded, he said. Coyote released his animal energy into her mouth. Raven fanned her with his wing. We are not succeeding, Coyote said. Kobili is waiting. He will know what to do. They called to him. The shaman nearly tripped coming down the ladder. He hurried to the shrieking infant lying on top of No Name, by now barely conscious. He pressed his lips to the child's eyelids and whispered: Do not cry, little baby. In these star pieces lies your power. Now, see, it no longer hurts, does it? He made a soft cooing sound.

At last, she fell quiet. As Kobili looked at her, a flood of memories came back. She was so tiny! So newborn! So *his*, though the last time she was an extra-tall woman, with her head above the clouds. Do you remember me? Kobili said softly.

Wah, the infant cried again.

CHAPTER
Five

*T*he shaman had little time to waste. No Name, the intractable Plains girl who had captured the chieftain's heart, was almost to the World Beyond. Her skin was becoming transparent; her bones showed through. I did not know you, strange girl, he said, yet I did know you. We walked a common path. Singing loudly, shaking his gourd rattle, Kobili danced a fast circle around the room. Coyote and Raven danced with him, weeping as a bird or an animal might do. Then the shaman laid two pieces of turquoise on No Name's eyelids and brushed her cheeks with an eagle wing. The infant lay in the crook of her mother's limp arms, eyes wide open. She seemed to be trying to tell him something. He willed into her brain the memory of their time together and touched the Sign of the Jaguar on her cheek. This proves you are my mate, he said. She screamed in response. The shaman drew back. He was not used to the shrill sounds of an infant. He wondered how long it would take for her to grow up.

I am leaving you, but I am never leaving you, No Name whispered, and handed the child to Kobili with the last of her strength. The infant smelled like wild roses, the beautiful bush she had created the day he made thorny cactus because it could grow without water. The breath went out of No Name's body in a sudden, wild rush. The Grandmother Spiders swung down on their threads from the ceiling beams, where they had been resting after their ordeal of trying to feed the infant what little nourishment they possessed. There were thousands of them. Here, they said, move aside. We know what to do. Around No Name's motionless body they spun a beautiful silver blanket. It covered her from head to toe, shining in the firelight like the Moon itself. The Grandmother Spiders worked diligently, spinning and turning, stopping only to let Kobili turn No Name over. At last they were done. They scooted up their threads to admire their work from above. It is satisfactory, they said. No Name is clothed in finery for her long journey.

Within the spider-thread blanket Kobili tucked a bear fetish, along with white cornmeal and water, so No Name would have something to eat and drink as she traveled. He blessed her from head to toe with prayers that he, as chief shaman of the Seven Wise Villages for twenty generations, had repeated many times before. Go with the Sun Father to his House in the Sky, dear Sister of Wisdom and Beauty, he said. Our blessings go with you. He lifted her from the bed and tenderly carried her a short distance up the river and laid her on its grassy banks. She weighed almost nothing, no more than the weight of the spider-thread blanket. At last No Name and her blanket sank into the earth. A red flower burst forth. Kobili looked at it with pleasure. It was a new kind that Thunderwoman had not created. It came from somewhere else.

Though you have gone to the Other World, you will watch your daughter grow up, he said to the flower. From the sky. From the earth. From everywhere, you will be watching. She will not disappoint you. You know who she is. He looked toward the village. The screams of the baby pierced the air. Did babies, even mystical babies such as this one, ever cry themselves to death? He ran down the path as fast as his arthritic legs would carry him.

CHAPTER
Six

The shaman felt ridiculous, holding the infant in his arms. Thunderwoman had returned, no bigger than a rabbit, shrieking her heart out. He held her close and tried to soothe her, hoping she would suddenly become a woman. The spider milk had only made her hungrier. Her mouth hung open like a bird's. What am I to do with you? he said. You have never been an infant before. You could have come full grown. I know nothing about babies. What they eat. What they wear. He rocked her gently and sang a song he hoped she'd remember. He had sung it to her the day she made her first waterfall. The years I searched for you will soon fall away. When last we parted, we were halves, yet whole. The baby made a fussing noise. Ah, you understand. You left on a tongue of lightning and never came back. I have not seen you again until now. He kissed her tiny fingers. Tell me you recognize me. The sight of him only made her cry harder. Kobili's face fell. He looked around. The house smelled of birthing. The imprint of No Name's body was on the bed. Butterflies rose from it and fluttered out the small window.

Raven circled overhead, then landed on the terrace. He was exhausted, having done his little raven dance all day to amuse the child. All is well, he said. All is *not* well, Coyote said. He was lying on the hard surface, licking his paws. Fatigue overcame him, and he wished only for the dark comfort of his den. We will have to spend all our time feeding it. What will it eat? The spiders took all morning to give it a little mouthful. It's hard work taking care of a human baby. From where he waited on the terrace, there was no sign of any kind of food she might enjoy.

Mice, Raven said. I will find dead mice and feed them to her myself.

Coyote thought about it. Raven, he said, if she eats mice she will become like you. She needs to learn to kill rabbits, like me. First, she has to wait by their holes and pounce on them when they come out. Coyote and Raven entered the house and looked dubiously at the baby. She would not be able to eat mice or rabbits for a long time.

The shaman sat cross-legged on the floor, pushing the cradle back and forth. It hung by leather thongs from the ceiling beams. The infant had fallen asleep at last. He looked at her tenderly. Her hair was as black as the universe before they had created light. Her skin reminded him of the flower petals he had brought along for a pillow that time they visited the soft-edged Moon. You are as beautiful as I remember you, he whispered. Because he had magical powers, he saw her as the woman she would become, which was the same woman she had been long ago. Raven saw her as Raven Woman. Coyote saw her as Coyote Woman. To Kobili she was the Womanheart spirit who had helped him create the Universe.

Her energy was soft and delicate, while his was harsh and overwhelming. It took both of us to create beauty, he thought. Both to create balance. He pressed his face closer. Why have you returned like this? Though his knowledge was vast, and his stories without equal, the shaman did not understand why she had come to Arenal as a human so small he could have stuffed her in his pouch and carried her away. Coyote looked at Raven. The shaman loves her, he thought. Raven looked at Coyote. The infant loves him, he thought. But she does not know it yet. They promised each other they would never leave the shaman or the infant, who someday was bound to grow up.

CHAPTER

Seven

The Memorizers built up the fire in the kiva, trying to hide their excitement. Into each man's mind came a picture of what the newborn Jaguar Girl could do if she wanted to. Snake Sister had described her perfectly, sacred mark and all. Blue Water spoke up. The last time such a child appeared, our village turned to dust. When there was nothing left, new life appeared, said One Fist. Hawk brought seeds in his mouth. Bear provided blood. Bison provided bones. Eagle gave vision to warriors. Perhaps she is here to tell us we will be destroyed.

The elders had been watching the patterns of life for a long time. They'd inherited the superstitions of their ancestors, mixed with a natural fear of what lay beyond the horizon. A solar eclipse, a streaking comet, an earthquake, a tornado were all warnings. So was the Sign of the Jaguar. The child would cause illness. Crops would fail. Game would disappear. What should they do? They stared into the fire until they saw the brooding yellow eyes of Iatiku, the Corn Mother, staring back. She looked familiar, a little like No Name. Between her teeth she held a sword, a weapon that was unknown to them, though it looked somewhat like a spear, only shorter and made of shiny material.

What does it mean? they wondered. Iatiku was powerful. She appeared only when catastrophe was upon them. Blue Water and One Fist ran to cleanse themselves in the icy river. Sun Mountain Shining said it was not Iatiku in the flames, but the six-point buck he had missed last year. No Name is to blame, Red Dog said. She was never one of us. The elders agreed. They had heard of No Name's death, and they were worried. The Bird Women had not prepared her body, nor buried the placenta, according to custom. In fact, both had disappeared. We will pay for these mistakes, the elders said, fearfully.

No Name put a spell on Elk Heart, Blue Cedar went on. She made our chieftain fall in love with her. He was like a young buck, prancing and pawing the earth. The Memorizers laughed uneasily. The child had started out wrong. Did Snake Sister bless her? Did Turquoise Woman? There, you see. No Name was responsible for their inability to remember their stories, too. She was blamed for drought. For sickness. For the Sun Father turning black at noon. A witch, as Snake Sister said. They brooded and sang, brooded and discussed what to do. The child will bring more trouble, said Gray Wolf. She has No Name's blood and No Name's disposition. She will destroy us. Who is more powerful, she or us?

One of us must drown the child in the river, Sun Mountain Shining said. The fish will welcome her. Who will it be? He looked around. He was the headman, though when he was gone for long periods of time, Gray Wolf took over. No one offered to do the work. They stared into the fire, waiting for a vision. A feeling of apprehension engulfed them. The elders fell silent, listening to the tender voices of the night. Each man tamed his own wild thoughts.

From a secret part of the kiva, they brought out a jug of the Elixir of Dreams, a powerful potion that enabled them to hear the watery voices of ancestral fish trapped in the underground lake. Voices of long-ago hunters who had forgotten to ask permission of the deer to take its life. The piercing whistle of an escaping elk. The complaining roar of a mountain lion. The Elixir of Dreams was sweet and comforting. On certain nights, when the Moon was ascending and Long Sash was directly overhead, the Memorizers were able to fly on the wings of the Eagle with Red Eyes, up to the highest cloud, to see how the world looked from there. From brown earthenware cups, they drank the Elixir of Dreams until there was no more left. They dozed peacefully. Their dreams were pleasant.

When the last few stars left the sky and the first pink glow of dawn appeared, they climbed a ladder made from the Moon's huge tears. They tasted them. Quite salty and good. As they climbed higher into the sky, they saw the beautiful continent spread out below. They called it Turtle Island. Many hundreds of tribes lived there. They were rumored to live in harmony, though as they passed overhead, the Memorizers saw much conflict. Warriors marched against enemy villages and killed them. They scalped their enemies and cut them open. They impaled their hearts on trees. They dropped virgins into lakes. They tied enemies to anthills. They peeled their skin. Here and there they ate one another. As the Memorizers sailed past, they dropped all sorts of feathers down. There, take comfort in our feathered brothers, they said. But the dead warriors had already passed beyond. War is necessary, they thought. How else could a man become brave or a warrior pass on his skills to his sons? Long ago the elders had been warriors themselves. Now, they were too old. As they rolled from one end of the sky to the other, they felt happy. Their journey through the heavens gave them the reassurance of experience, as old as their ancestral days in the Underworld.

Kobili had not slept in several nights. His body ached. His brain no longer functioned. The unhappy infant was driving him to distraction.

Coyote and Raven had dropped of exhaustion. The Bird Women had done their best to care for her, but it was no use. The infant could not be satisfied with spider's milk or dry clothing. She wanted something else. The Old Man rubbed his eyes and dragged himself up the ladder. He turned his face to the East and called for the women who would raise her.

PART TWO

*The Six Grandmothers
Explain the World of Being*

WOMANHEART SPIRIT

Womanheart spirit, rising from dry grass,
sea foam, earth muscle, and sky sinew,
we are rejoining you as women

Who hold up our half of the sky. We are
certain that what the world lacks is us,
uncomplicated as dust, beautiful as
cactus plants. We have been waiting to see you again

Since the time you drew a star curtain across the sky
and made Earth out of your menstrual blood
and the Old Man's sperm and saliva. Wait,

We are coming to you, now, when
you are as unformed as corn bursting
from the mystery of the underground.

The suffering of women becomes you, the rage
of the Sun as it pursues the Moon strengthens you,
the wisdom of old women seeps into your skin,
even when you are sleeping.

CHAPTER

Eight

*T*he Six Grandmothers had been everywhere, for all time. They were present in the Beginning Time with Thunderman and Thunderwoman, yet separate from them. They had watched the fish struggle up the cornstalk from the Underground lake and exchange their fins for feet, scales for skin. When the Fish People complained they were hungry, the Grandmothers made deep gashes in the earth with their fingernails. They taught the Fish People how to plant the corn seeds Thunderwoman had saved from the roots of her hair. They instructed the Fish People on the difficulties of becoming human. The Grandmothers formed a young girl's inheritance, given to her at birth. They stayed as long as they were needed, teaching, comforting, and cajoling. People saw them or not, depending upon whether they believed in them.

The Grandmothers were the Six Cleansing Winds, the Six Sacred Directions, the Six Cardinal Rules. There was a necessary quality to each of them. The Presence in the Void. The Shadow in the Water. The Voice above the Fire. The Energy within a Leaf. They moved as one idea. They were young women who had grown old, though sometimes they were old women still in their youth. They were the Blue Corn Mothers, the Women Who Married Light. They could make brooms dance. They lifted the edge of the sea like a blanket and walked under it in order to better understand mystery. When girls came into the world, the Grandmothers taught them how to love unappreciative men. They taught them the meaning of patience.

When they heard Kobili's voice, the Six Grandmothers rose from the river and stepped ashore. They looked like fish, though arms and legs quickly sprouted from their bodies. They had not been seen in a long time. As their clothing materialized, their hair grew long. They became old women, faces as wrinkled as ancestral rock. Their white hair flowed like fine thread, nearly to the ground. Their song was so familiar that mountains woke up to listen to the same music that had accompanied their own fiery birth when the Earth was still contracting from its creation. The old women walked in a stately procession across the plaza, taking in the beauty of Arenal. The village was the same color as the earth, for it was made of earth. How strong it looked, how timeless! They inhaled the clear air and felt their lungs expand. They loved the sigh of wind, the gentle lapping of the river against the shore, the cheerful voices of birds who flew past to greet them. There was a bluejay! A cardinal! A yellow warbler! A hawk!

One Grandmother carried a blanket woven of precious ermine. Another an ear of yellow corn. Another a jar of bee pollen. Another had a pouch of sacred tobacco. The Fifth Grandmother carried an offering of carved buffalo bone. The Sixth carried the feathers of Bluejay, Cardinal, Dove, and Raven. When they reached the house where the newborn infant lay, they rubbed her with pollen and cornmeal. They fed her their own milk, extracted from their aged breasts. When they were finished, they breathed into her mouth and smeared their blood over her body to make it strong. They rubbed saliva onto her tongue and told her that a woman's job was greater than a man's. Without nurture, there is nothing, they said. Life needs softness.

The baby's eyes flew open. Who are you? she asked.

The first generation and the last, said the Grandmother-from-the-West, placing an eagle bone beside the baby's head. We carry life's lessons in our hearts. She was known as Learning Woman. She had spent a lifetime gathering the knowledge of dust and bone, blood and sinew. She passed along this knowledge to all the tribes of the world.

One half of your body shelters life, the other death, said the Grandmother-from-the-East, wrapping the infant in softest corn husks. She was known as Listening Woman. No sound escaped her ears, not even the imperceptible song of a butterfly.

The lessons of the past are with you, said the Grandmother-from-Above, brushing the baby's fine hair with the snow white wing of a dove. Because you created the past, the future is up to you as well. She was known as Changing Woman, for she was the foundation for and the measure of time. All tribes had originated with her.

The Grandmother-from-the-North leaned closer. A long time ago, you swallowed the Moon to keep it safe from Sun, who wanted to devour it. You made a separate path for the Moon to follow through the sky. Then you blew it out between your lips. That's why moonlight makes women seem more beautiful. This Grandmother was known as Praising Woman. It was up to her to offer encouragement during the worst of times.

The Grandmother-from-the-South spoke up. You are the daughter of the Corn Mother, though you came before her, she said. When the first star fell, you returned it to the sky. This Grandmother was called Healing Woman. She could cure illness as well as pain.

The child looks like our ancestors, clucked the Grandmother-from-Below. The star pieces are there, to give knowledge later on. She pressed her wrinkled face against the infant's neck and kissed her. This Grandmother was known as Walks-with-Earthquakes Woman, for it was her job to destroy the world in order to make it whole again.

Sayah is the Jaguar Girl, said the Grandmother-from-the-West, running her fingers over the red jaguar mark on her cheek. She will travel farther than anyone has ever gone before. Jaguars run like the wind. Nothing can catch them. The infant yawned.

The Grandmother-from-the-East held the baby close and made cooing sounds. With amazing strength, Sayah squirmed loose and slid to the floor, crawling toward Kobili. Grandfather, Sayah said, raising her fat little arms to him, make me a bear.

Kobili stared. I made you a bear once, he said. You liked it. He scooped her into his arms and whispered the old names he used to call her, as if she would remember them. I am not your Grandfather, he said. Then he realized he was an old man. He would always be an old man. She would always be younger than he in earth years. Of course she would look upon him as Grandfather. What else could she think?

I cannot make anything more here on Earth, he said bitterly. When I left the world I shared with you, I left my power behind. He handed her to the Grandmothers, then made his way quickly up the ladder. The shaman walked alone along the river, deep in thought. Sayah is a spirit trapped in an infant's body, he said to himself. Does she know beyond her infant's mind? Does she have the wisdom that came with her in the Beginning Time? No, Earth makes spirits bend. Not the other way around. Kobili's heart was heavy. All his plans for a new life with her were shattered.

Raven flew overhead, calling excitedly. Old Man, there is much talk about what to do with the child. The elders say the Sign of the

Jaguar means she brings trouble. I heard them talking in the kiva about throwing her into the river. Raven swooped lower and flew across the shaman's path. Sayah comes at the wrong time, he said.

Kobili frowned. She comes at exactly the time she was meant to, he said. He knew, in his shaman's heart, why she had come now, and he wondered how he could protect her. Patience, he said to Raven. I must have patience, dear bird. Raven flew up. And I must learn to fly higher and better than I used to, Old Man.

CHAPTER
Nine

Sun Mountain Shining clung to Feather Keeper's arm as he tottered across the plaza. He was exhausted, having slept with two of his wives the night before. They were younger and they wore him out, though he did his best to make them happy. Sun Mountain Shining loved making love to women almost as much as he loved to hunt. He had thirty-nine children, scattered in various villages along the Great River. Though he was more than one hundred winters old, he was not finished making children yet. He cleared his throat and addressed the Memorizers, who gathered around him. Yesterday a big elk jumped the wall and walked up the ladder to my terrace. Our arrows could not touch him. He left when he was ready. He made the dogs go crazy. He was a spirit animal. He gave me this advice: Do not listen to Kobili. The chief shaman is under a spell. He has not made any right decisions in a long time. He is with No Name's child every single day. It is not right for a man to do this. I say we go against him.

We cannot go against Kobili, One Fist said. He is the highest among us.

There are exceptions, Sun Mountain Shining said. My grandfather killed a shaman in order to save himself from rot. It ate his feet and then his arms and was starting on his head. When he killed the shaman, the rot stopped. But something else set in.

Wise and Experienced One, you cannot believe what is happening, said Feather Keeper, walking on the other side of the Sun Clan leader. Ever since the child was born, things have gone badly. I discovered a thistle growing in my ear.

I am no longer able to make love to my wife, said Blue Water.

I am no longer able to dream, said One Fist.

The child stole our stories, said Brave Bear. Even before she was born, she stole them. Remember how we heard her speaking from the womb? Making all sorts of animal noises. The last time that happened, it did not rain for many moons. Our corn died. We had to go around begging for food. We ate our dogs and the bark from trees.

We are the esteemed Memorizers, said Blue Water. We have a great responsibility. But we remember nothing now. If we were to steal the child from the old women, we could examine it. Perhaps there are horns. Two heads and a tail, as Snake Sister said. That's all we'll do, examine it. If there's nothing wrong, we'll give it back. If something is wrong, we'll kill it.

Kobili will kill me, then, said Sun Mountain Shining. We have never been friends, though I depend on him in times of need. He healed my oldest son.

Too much power, said Gray Wolf, blinking in the sunlight. He preferred the darkness of the kiva. Suppose Kobili is not our Ancient Revered Elder? Suppose he is losing his power as Brave Bear says? He is disregarding the message of our ancestors.

They moved to the edge of the river, where the Six Grandmothers were bathing the infant. There was something strange about them. Faces that kept changing. Bodies they could see through. Witches, they thought. We will get rid of them. See how the child's eyes blaze?

They moved closer. The spirit of the river is in you, the Grand-mother-from-the-North said to Sayah, squirming to get free so she could see for herself the way fish swam. May you have the silence of fish, the wisdom of the four-legged animals, the freedom of the winged creatures. Yah-yah-yah, the other Grandmothers sang. The river goes up and down. The wind goes up and down. The birds go up and down. Baby goes up and down. Laughing, they threw her into the air. She seemed almost weightless.

I am a baby bird, the child giggled. Teach me to fly, Grand-mothers. She flapped her arms. It seemed to them she flew across the river and back. They clapped to encourage her. Ah, the old women thought, she is learning quickly.

Coyote stood on the riverbank, watching intently. He was never far away. Raven circled overhead. He was never far away, either. They had promised to be her spirit guardians for the rest of her life. The Grandmothers moved away from the river, the infant wrapped in a little rabbit-fur robe. The Memorizers followed at a short distance, trying to become invisible. As One Fist made a sudden move to grab the baby, Raven swooped down and made a deep gash across his high, rounded cheekbone. Do not even think such thoughts, Raven said. One Fist recoiled in pain. Coyote bit Red Dog on the leg. He collapsed on the ground, screaming. Do not try to harm this child, Raven said. She has come to help us.

The Six Grandmothers fell upon those men and dragged them to the river by their hair. That will teach you, they said as they threw them into the water, even old Sun Mountain Shining, who grabbed hold of a tree limb as he floated away, too shocked to speak. His three wives caught him as he swept over a little waterfall. They hauled him ashore and comforted him in the ways they knew best.

CHAPTER

Ten

lk Heart moved quietly into the village, exhausted from his long journey to the sea. He
was a great chieftain, revered throughout the
Seven Wise Villages for his hunting skills and his warrior's abilities.
He was a handsome man, with features that looked as if they had been
chipped from stone. He had been gone for six moons with thirty hand-
picked warriors from his Eagle Clan. They had crossed snow-capped
mountains, burning deserts, and swift rivers. He had spoken to chieftains greater than himself, had hunted bears and lions, caribou and
seals. In the far Northwest, a whale had taken him on its back out into
the sea. A Turtle Woman had taught him how to dance close to the
ground. His feet were sore from his long walk. After he was purified
in the kiva, with smoke and sage and cedar, No Name would bathe his
feet in warm water and rub them gently with fresh juniper berries. She
would press her brown body against his, and he would gladly take it.
He had dreamed of her every night. She was his favorite wife.

The chieftain had seen what the Grandmothers had done to the Memorizers and he laughed. They deserve to be thrown into the river, he thought. Especially that old fool, Sun Mountain Shining, his uncle, not as high in the kiva hierarchy as himself, but causing plenty of trouble. The Memorizers had crossed him often; they could not remember the stories they were supposed to; they plotted and spoke against everyone, himself included. The chieftain headed toward the kiva with its ladder sticking up into the turquoise blue sky. He was covered with blood. Enemy blood, shed during an ambush early that morning beyond the red hills to the west. He would recount to his Eagle Clan his exploits, and they would praise his valor. He had killed four of the enemy. Until he purified himself, he would see their faces, smell their rotten flesh, hear the last words they spoke, begging for an opening to the Sky World. His bones ached. His mouth felt dry. Soon he would rest and eat, though he would stay away from salt and meat and women until he was cleansed. Those were the kiva rules he lived by.

He walked quickly past the Grandmothers and stopped. They were looking at him strangely. Your daughter, said the Grandmother-from-the-West, pulling the blanket away from the baby's face. He bent closer. How unearthly her eyes were. They seemed on fire. The Sign of the Jaguar disturbed him. He had not seen it since he met the god-king Moctezuma, the year he spent in Tenochtitlan, learning the ways of the stone gods. Where is the son I prayed for? he said, trying to hide his disappointment. His dreams had given him many sons, but in reality he had none.

Her name is Sayah, said the Grandmother-from-the-North. The-Woman-Who-Can-Stop-the-Sun. She is a Sacred Being, not the baby you see, but something more. The chieftain drew back. What of No Name? he asked. He had brought her a special present made of walrus tusk.

No Name is in her Original World, they said. She died peacefully. Elk Heart turned away. He had loved the spirited Plains girl best of all. She made him forget about the responsibilities of his office, the treachery of men who despised him. She taught him to smell the fresh earth and to grasp the Moon between his fingers. He often pulled it down and gave it to her as a present. His eyes suddenly filled with tears. But he must not show his sorrow in front of the old women.

Nothing lasts long except earth and sky and water, he said. He was suddenly exhausted. He turned from his daughter and began to walk away.

Sayah cried out, Father, I am Wind. Embrace me. Father, I am Fire. Embrace me. Father, I am Earth. Embrace me. Father, I am Water. Embrace me. Elk Heart turned. A strange thing happened. The infant grew to maturity before his very eyes. A tall, beautiful woman walked toward him, wearing a white beaded dress. In her hands she carried four ears of corn—red, white, blue, and yellow. She motioned him toward her.

The chieftain drew in his breath. Welcome, daughter, he said, raising his arms above his head. Walk with the blessings of our ancestors. He turned to the Memorizers. Hear me! You will teach her and protect her. One hand raised against her will bring death. The Memorizers turned away. They knew, by now, Elk Heart meant what he said.

Elk Heart looked around at the village. It had grown to more than six hundred rooms, layer upon layer of generation and struggle. Where he stood, his great-grandfathers had once stood, and before them, their great-grandfathers, back to a time when animals tended human children. Fires burned in the plaza. On them, women were cooking stews in clay pots. Drying racks held strips of buffalo meat from the last big kill. Women went back and forth to the river, carrying water jars on their heads. One man was making a flute, another a drum, another a pair of moccasins. They were singing softly. Somewhere, a drumbeat sounded. Elders stood on the rooftops, calling back and forth. Is the rain coming? Are the deer east of the big rock? We are having an Eagle Dance. You are welcome to be our guests. They took turns singing, beating their well-worn drums, stopping to notice the shapes of clouds. Life was like concentric rings formed by pebbles tossed in water. The religion of the Clay People was simply circles, ritual, and generation. It would last as long as the Earth lasted.

Elk Heart was content to see the fabric of his life stretched out before him. He did not want to live anyplace else. He went into the smoky interior of the kiva and stared into the blue-ribbed fire, thinking about the time he'd spent in Moctezuma's golden palace, accompanied by Kobili. Elk Heart remembered how he had killed his first enemy in Mexico, a ferocious Tlaxcallan warrior, and how he had made love to Moctezuma's favorite daughter as part of his passage into manhood. With her he developed a fondness for parrots, macaws, and monkeys; with her he visited the bustling market of Tlalteloco, with its vast array of treasures from throughout the Aztec Empire. He had witnessed human sacrifice at the Teocalli. Fighting nausea, he had tasted his first human heart, freshly severed from its chest cavity. He had drunk the blood of a man sacrificed to the gods. The priests had terrified him, with their knee-length hair, foreheads smeared with their own blood, chanting incantations that he knew brought death to all who opposed them. While Elk Heart lived in the golden palace at Tenochtitlan and became like a son to Moctezuma, Kobili had lived with the priests and learned their medicine. Kobili and Elk Heart came back wiser, stronger men, the shaman carrying the ingredients necessary to make the Elixir of Dreams, plus various jungle medicines, poison darts, and snake venom that he carried with him at all times. Elk Heart had never returned to that land of sweet decay and complexity, though he missed Moctezuma greatly.

Just before the Sun Father emerged from his nighttime journey, the chieftain went out into the pale silvery stillness and turned his face to the sky. The Twin Bears were trying to push the Sun up from the Underworld. The Magpie Sisters stood on either side, lifting the Sky Curtain. The Bears pushed and pushed until at last the Sun Father burst forth in a great orange ball, then began his journey to his home in the West. The chieftain closed his eyes and prayed. There are signs of unrest, he said. What must I do? The Sun Father never answered directly, but made his great power known in other ways.

The chieftain looked across the river to the mountains. He could not believe his eyes. There, taller than the tallest tree, stood Moctezuma, in buckskin leggings and shirt. A large bow was slung across his back, and he had a quiver of gold-tipped arrows. He raised his arm and in one quick movement cut open the mountains with the side of his hand. He struck the mountains again. Buffalo poured out and ran to the Four Directions, making a noise like thunder. A huge cloud of dust arose, gathering Moctezuma with it.

Elk Heart hurried back to the kiva to tell them all he had seen. Kobili, because he was chief shaman, was allowed into all the kivas. He listened intently, then he said: Moctezuma comes with a message. In the Beginning Time, the child you know as Sayah was the breath of the Universe. Whatever she breathed upon came to life. Sun. Moon. Stars. Earth. The elders stirred uneasily. The mythic history of the Universe had been revealed to them by their grandfathers. It was the same as Kobili said. Go on, they whispered. Remember what Brother Hawk told us many moons ago? the shaman said. They nodded. Great change is coming. Sayah is part of the change. Kobili looked at Elk Heart. Moctezuma comes with a warning. We must learn to live right. The Memorizers had drawn and worried faces. When memory dies, the purpose of a people is obliterated, Kobili said. The elders stared into the fire, wondering if his prophecy would come true.

PART THREE

The Time of
Running with Deer

ARENAL

When memory dies, the purpose of a people is obliterated.

Long ago, at Arenal, Earth and Sky were mysteries, joined
 at the heart, male to female, fortified
 by holiness. Elders honored the fossilized remains
 of oceans, the kinship of snakes with birds,
And the power of bears, who were once human grandfathers.

No one revealed their knowledge of the sacred ways
 or why rock drawings contained the secret to survival.
 The Clay People listened to birdsong for inspiration
 and to stories of the elders in order to reaffirm
 their connection to rain clouds. Their birthplace

Lay beneath their feet, nurturing dreams and lifetimes,
Uninterrupted for the time it took to create fireflies.

Whenever they danced, people renewed their belief
 in corn mothers and in spiders, in eagles
 and in turtles. They were consumed by correctness
 and they never laughed at animals for fear
 the animals would despise them.

The Clay People tied a rope to stars and dragged them home
 for companionship and wisdom.
 They slid down rainbows before
 they had a chance to fade and they absorbed

the indestructibility of rock
into their bloodstream.

The drums never stopped beating, memory
never stopped expanding, and the heart connection
went on, unbroken, until the time came. The elders
believed they would forget nothing, not even names
of animals entrusted with innermost secrets.

When memory dies, the purpose of a people is obliterated.

CHAPTER
Eleven

obili was the wisest man who ever lived. His knowledge was of lifetimes beyond lifetimes, of why leaves had veins, how animals acquired fur, and reptiles, skin. He alone knew the entire history of Arenal. One day, to ensure its safekeeping, he divided it among the six kivas. In this way, an enemy would have a hard time learning all the secrets of the Clay People. He buried the oldest fetishes and clay figures; he began to change language so that people from one tribe could not understand another tribe. The stories became different, too, with at least six versions of Creation in the Seven Wise Villages alone.

The elders watched Sayah closely. One Fist, unable to forget the time that he nearly turned into a fish, said: The star pieces fell from her eyes and made huge holes in the ground. Children fell into them. Feather Keeper said, The Mark of the Jaguar jumped from her face and became real. It ate two old women gathering berries. Sun Mountain Shining trembled. When my wife had a fever, the girl cured her, he said. My youngest son was crippled. She made him walk again. I gave her an elk-tooth necklace as a gift.

Sayah grew in knowledge and in magic power. Stories about her spread throughout the land. At the wedding of a man who married a Badger Woman, she summoned fire from a ponderosa tree. She reversed the flow of the river so she could float backward to its source high in the mountains. She went with Elk Heart to look for the buffalo freed by Moctezuma. She found them in a valley, and she turned them completely white. From now on, she said, the white buffalo will be the highest among the Four-Legged Creatures. She was still small, coming barely to his waist. Do not move so fast, Sayah, he said.

I must do these things, Father, she said. They are part of a circle. At the center of this circle is me and an old man. Elk Heart asked if she remembered her life in the sky. No, Father, she said. I have always been here among you. And here I will stay. He smiled. He knew she would not stay long.

Sayah amazed them. She could move objects merely by looking at them with her fiery eyes. She made a cooking pot slide across the plaza. A tortoise rose from the ground to the mesa. When she stared at the Sun Father, an eagle came forth. Reaching up, she grabbed hold of his powerful legs and sailed through the air. The elders became used to seeing her dangling from the great clawed feet of this mystical bird. They noticed how fond the girl and the eagle were of one another as they soared high above the mountains. The eagle revealed his secrets of the Sky World. It sounds familiar, she told him. She made the clouds into shapes she liked: coyotes, ravens, and old men.

Deep in the forest, where the heartbeat of every living creature was a continuous affirmation of life, she learned how Coyote and Raven breathed. She was able to read minds. When Sun Mountain Shining was thinking of making love to his niece, she knew it. When Red Dog was dreaming of making a new pathway through the sky, she knew it. She knew the secrets of the kiva long before they happened. The Memorizers discussed how best to keep their position as esteemed men, at the same time being careful not to offend her.

She is Moctezuma's daughter, Red Dog said. I had a dream about it.

Deer-He-Becomes shook his great antlered head. She is something more, he said. When I was in the forest, she appeared to me as a lightning bolt. I was blinded for a time. When I opened my eyes, there was Sayah, as tall as a ponderosa tree. Corn seeds fell from her scalp. She had corn tassels instead of hair. The Four-Legged Creatures gathered to protect her.

Elk Heart taught her to throw a spear and how to make obsidian points and how to hunt game. Soon she was better than any hunter in the Seven Wise Villages of Tiguex. *We* are the hunters, the men said. Women skin the animals. Tan the hides. Make tools from bone. Why her? Because she is meant to, Elk Heart said. By then she could kill a deer with one arrow from a distance of sixty paces.

Are you willing to die for me, Brother Deer? Sayah would ask. We need your meat for food. Your hide for clothing. Your bones for needles and whistles. Your sinew for thread. Your antlers for tools. Nothing will go to waste. Deer would think it over. Very well, he'd say and turn himself around so she had a clear shot. Her arrow was true. It pierced his heart. As he fell, a great rush of blood spurted out.

Sayah peered down the hole where the Fish People had emerged and threw wildflowers into it. She climbed to the top of a tree and jumped, thinking she could fly. Coyote caught her with his front paws before she hurt herself. She loved the world. So much color. So many new things to see. She spoke to animals in a language they understood. The river let her borrow its song. So did the wind. She went about her healing tasks. She extracted two star slivers from her eyes and inserted them in a blind woman's eyes to give her sight. She fixed

Feather Keeper's broken leg as good as new and removed a tumor from Gray Wolf's back. She breathed into the mouth of One Fist's grandson after he had fallen into the river, and brought him back to life. She set the broken bones of animals who came to her from great distances, having heard of her power. She bandaged Bear's neck after Cougar attacked him. She soothed birds about to hatch their eggs and gave to bats the vision they needed at night. The children of Arenal listened to her stories. What happened after that? they'd say. Kobili was always nearby, watching, listening, wondering when she'd recognize him. The Grandmothers taught her something new every day. Coyote and Raven whispered their own stories.

When Sayah danced in the forest, aspen trees swayed and followed her as far as their roots allowed. She crawled inside a hollow tree to see what it felt like to be without an inner life. She noticed the energy of streams splashing over rocks, twisting between two grassy banks. If she closed her eyes, she saw how the strong male arteries of lightning struck the weak parts of land and strengthened it. The female voice of Thunder rolled across the land, awakening birds and animals. When the Whirlwind People sucked her into their vortex, she saw the Time Beyond.

Every moment of past and future is here, Kobili said. You can go backward and forward, whenever you like. Up. Down. If you want to talk to the Underground People, go there. How is it possible? she said. Anything is possible, he said. Life exists in the mind. But you do not remember me, he thought sadly.

She is part of you, Old Man, Raven and Coyote said, trying to comfort Kobili when he lay with his head on a rock. Sooner or later she will grow up. You must learn to wait.

Wait? Kobili said irritably. I am tired of waiting. I have been waiting for ten thousand years.

CHAPTER

Twelve

The Six Grandmothers had much to teach Sayah. Their lessons were different from those of Kobili or Elk Heart. Mostly, they sang to her, hundreds of verses about girls loving boys, about birthing babies, about creating a good home. Their job was to teach about a young girl's inheritance. In the kivas men passed knowledge on to sons. But not to daughters. That was a woman's job. Daughters took the pulse of morning. They never abandoned their children. The houses belonged to them. So did the knowledge of bloodlines. With the wisdom of countless generations, the Grandmothers taught Sayah how to cook cornmeal mush, venison stew, and flat bread, wash clothing in the river, scrape hides, make dresses out of buckskin, sweep the house with a broom that wanted to dance, dig yucca roots for soap, make pottery from the earth and decorate it with a fine hand. She learned to replaster the mud houses, leaving a small stone fetish in the walls to give them strength and unity. She was proud of her work.

The Grandmothers explained how a man's body was different from her own. Children start like corn, they said. The female seed lies in fertile ground, waiting for rain to make it grow. A man provides rain. Nourishment for the seed. Sayah listened closely. Even Grandfather? she asked.

Especially him, they said.

But he is old.

Old men have their uses, said the Grandmother-from-the-North, remembering her experience with a man eight hundred years old. She had loved him, gruff as he was, clumsy at lovemaking, unable to express his thoughts, silent for days at a time. Sayah touched her flat belly. Would children grow there? The Grandmother-from-the-East said, your children will grow everywhere. Like seeds of corn. Her own children had sprung from piñon nuts. Millions, all over the Earth. She kept in touch with them through the wind.

Grandfather says in a long-ago time, I was fire, then ash, then bone. He says I have tree sap flowing in my veins. He says he and I were in the sky together. Imagine.

Ah, Kobili, said the Grandmother-from-the-East. What does he know?

He knows how the Earth began, Sayah said. He was there when it happened. Grandfather says he is twenty thousand winters old.

Ah, what stories, said the Grandmother-from-Above. No one lives that long.

Sayah wondered what age people lived to be. How old are you? she asked.

As old as the mountains, but older, said the Grandmother-from-the-West.

As old as the Sun Father, but younger, said the Grandmother-from-the-East.

As old as an embryo, but more fully formed, said the Grandmother-from-the-North.

As old as the backbone of the sky, said the Grandmother-from-the-South.

As old as turtles, said the Grandmother-from-Below. But less willing to travel slowly.

As old as stars, said the Grandmother-from-Above. But we are able to touch one another. The Grandmothers put their arms around her. They loved this small inquisitive being. Sayah looked at her Grandmothers fondly. I am not a real girl, am I? she said. You are not my real Grandmothers, either. At this, they laughed. The Grandmother-from-the-East said, Everything is real. It depends whether or not you believe in it.

Sayah examined her hands, her feet; she lifted her long skirt and examined her strong, brown legs. Did I always have this body? No, the Grandmothers said, a different body. Think of oceans. Mountains. Limitless sky. That's the sort of body we mean.

They began walking toward the Great River, where the ancestor fish would help answer the girl's persistent questions. Sayah hurried along. Were you always old women? No, they said, walking faster. We were young, like you. We were girls when rocks began. She ran after them. Where did I come from, Grandmothers?

No one knew what to say. They were uncomfortable with questions that went too deeply, questions best answered by Kobili. With a sigh, the Grandmother-from-the-West picked up a handful of dust and threw it into the air. From there, she said. The Grandmother-from-Above grabbed a handful of sunbeams and threw them at her. From there, she said. The Grandmother-from-the-South ran to the river and scooped up a handful of water. She splashed it on Sayah. From there, she said. The Grandmother-from-Below cut her finger with her sewing needle. Blood oozed out. She squeezed two drops into Sayah's hands. From there, she said. The Grandmother-from-the-

North waited until she was back at the village, then she grabbed an ember from the hot fire. From there, she said. Now it was the turn of the Grandmother-from-the-East. She pressed her mouth up against Sayah's and pushed her breath into it. From there, she said.

At last Sayah became all the things her Grandmothers were: Learning Woman, Listening Woman, Changing Woman, Praising Woman, Healing Woman, and Walks-with-Earthquakes Woman. They taught her how to observe the world. She watched the path that ants took and crawled after them to learn how life was lived close to the ground. Earthworms gave her the opportunity to touch their smooth, purplish skin. Dimly she remembered how they came about, but she could not quite form a picture in her mind. She stared at the Sun Father until her head began to hurt. In his deep, encompassing voice he said: When you and Thunderman made love, you created me from your heat. The full Moon said: When the Sun Father tried to devour me, you put me in your mouth for safekeeping. At this, Sayah fled to the river and threw herself onto the ground. I don't want to be *that*, she sobbed. Dawn Giver sat beside her. When my mother swallowed a bone and almost choked to death, you brought her back to life, she said. When an enemy sneaked into the village one night and tried to kill Juniper Branch, you put a spell on that enemy, and he died. You have great power, Sayah. We love you. You are here for a purpose. Don't you know who you are?

Sayah wiped her eyes on the hem of her dress. She looked at Dawn Giver, a pretty girl, with a round, full face, long lashes, and white teeth. She was betrothed to a warrior from the Sun Clan. Who do *you* say I am, Sayah asked her. Dawn Giver laughed. A lizard, she said. Perhaps a little mouse. Don't be so serious about yourself. With that, she shoved Sayah into the river, amazed at how well she swam, almost as well as the fish who nibbled playfully at her feet.

CHAPTER

Thirteen

hen Sayah passed into womanhood and came out of her house to show the bloody cloth to the Bird Women, who were the guardians of female rituals, they led a procession across the plaza, having chased away all the men first. They painted her cheeks with two bright spots of color, right over the Sign of the Jaguar. They dressed her in a white doeskin dress, decorated with tiny white shells. With a feather wand, they pulled songs from the sky and sang them to her. When they prepared a feast in her honor, men withdrew from sight. They believed they would be struck dead if they gazed upon her. During five days in the menstrual hut, the Grandmothers instructed her on becoming a woman. They rubbed her with sage and purifying smoke, wove flowers into her hair and rubbed sacred herbs into her limbs to give her strength. They sang outside the menstrual hut until her bleeding stopped, then they scooped up the mess with a clamshell and put it in a basket. They told her about those times when a woman answered the call of the Moon and how her body became sacred during Moon Time.

Now you are a woman, the Grandmothers said, aware that many boys had taken notice of her beauty. Soon you will marry a boy from the village. Someone will pay handsomely for you. You are Elk Heart's daughter.

Sayah made a face. I am never going to marry anyone. The Grandmothers said, Listen closely. Spiderwoman migrated through your bones before you were born and made you who you are. She sleeps inside your pelvic arch. She is an even line gliding through each day. Spiderwoman will pick out your husband for you. Listen to what she says. Sayah turned her head. No, she said. I will make up my own mind.

Deep in the forest, the Grandmothers gathered the Plant People and put them in a basket. They showed Sayah which ones were strong medicine and which were allies and which were deadly poison. The bank of willow trees, pine resin, piñon nuts, yucca roots, and juniper berries were all-important medicines. Sayah learned their uses, especially a plant from the gentian family, said to cause men to fall in love. She hung the leaves upside down to dry, singing softly to herself. She had a certain man in mind.

The women of Arenal honored her. They combed and brushed and fixed her hair in two sleek coils on either side of her head. Dawn Giver, by now married to Fire Dog, made her a shiny coat of bluebird feathers. Bird Wing made her a necklace from eagle bones. High Cloud braided her hair with red flowers. Bent Twig gave her a turquoise necklace. These daughters of the Bird Women walked up into the mountains with Sayah. They talked openly about what lay deepest in their hearts. They shared their secrets. Our men speak of hunting, but not our beauty. When we lie together, our men fall asleep. Teach them to say I love you, Sayah said, blushing.

When women complained about being unable to conceive, she helped them. First, gather a big clot of blood and boil it, she said.

Take the child that results and drown it in the river. When a fish appears, eat it. The women were horrified. We can't drown our children, they said. We never eat fish. They are our ancestors. Sayah shrugged. Then no more babies will be born. It's up to you.

After no babies were conceived for several moons, women started boiling blood clots. And drowning the Blood Clot Children in the river, and eating the ancestor fish. The following spring a hundred babies were born in the Seven Wise Villages of Tiguex. They were the strongest children anywhere, with a deep and comprehending look that no other babies had. The women loved them. Looking around at the Place of Dreams, their babies strapped into cradleboards on their backs, they inhaled the dry desert air and rejoiced at the purity of the deep blue sky and the peacefulness of the vast and rosy land.

Our children's heritage is here, they said happily. Above their heads drifted a wispy plume called the Thread. It was part of their ancestry, passed on through belief. Sometimes they saw it; sometimes they did not. It appeared out of the clouds, connecting the Clay People to the vast and shimmering land, to the mysteries of the sky, to animals and birds. The Thread was the most powerful force in life, present at birth and death and in between. The new mothers of Arenal, their babies at their breasts, reached up. They caught the Thread between their fingers and wrapped it around themselves, marveling at its resilience. They snipped off pieces of it to make blankets for their children. The Thread satisfied their hunger and thirst and need for warmth. Sayah pulled the Thread around her shoulders, noticing it felt like the softness of the sky.

The Memorizers stirred inside the roots of ancestry. Each elder had had a dream about Sayah. In these dreams she blinded them. A woman with so much power frightens me, said Sun Mountain Shining. Deer-He-Becomes looked down at his fine, strong hooves. He believed Sayah was responsible for his transformation. A woman with so much power has great possibility, he said. The Memorizers began to love her the way they loved whatever made them better men.

CHAPTER
Fourteen

he rain fell with the steadiness of tears, pelting the Earth with its life-renewing force. Sayah ran across the plaza, her hair wet, her moccasins ruined. She had something important to say to Elk Heart. She stormed into his house, unannounced by the toothless old man who stood outside, dreaming of the days when four women loved him. The chieftain looked up in surprise. His daughter had never come in unannounced before. What do you want? he said. I want you to leave the choice of a husband up to me, Father. The chieftain shrugged. It is the custom of our people, he said. A lump rose in his throat. How beautiful she was, with her blazing eyes, reminding him of No Name.

Customs change, she said, moving closer to the fire to dry herself off. In the last several moons, she had become quite popular in Arenal. Young warriors came courting with presents they thought she might like. They sang songs for her. They played their red cedar flutes.

They waited for a chance to walk with her along the river, where they would tell her of the gifts their fathers had offered Elk Heart on their behalf. She did not love them. She did not want their gifts. She let them kiss her, to find out what it was like, but afterward she would wash her mouth with river water.

Antelope Water wants to marry you, the chieftain said. His father has offered six buffalo robes, three sacks of turquoise, and a handful of porcupine quills. His father is the headman of the Bow Clan, and I am headman of the Eagle Clan. It would make our bloodlines strong. I am considering it.

She threw back her head. I will never marry him, Father. Coyote says he is untrustworthy. Raven says he saw him steal a fetish from the kiva.

He is a fine warrior, Elk Heart said. Already he has six kiva names.

I have more than that, she said. The Grandmothers gave them to me. With the power of her gaze she moved a buffalo head from one wall to the opposite wall. She made a green snake materialize from the fire pit. Don't do these things, Sayah, he said. You are here on Earth, not there. Her eyes were defiant. There is much talk of you, he said.

Let them talk, she said. He took a deep breath. There is unrest in Arenal. Your marriage to Antelope Water will bring peace. Is that not what you are meant to do?

No, she said. With a cry she was out of the house, running through the gooey mud of the plaza. The rain had stopped. Women called to her as she stumbled past. Do not marry Antelope Water, Dawn Giver said. She was heavy with child. I know who you really love, Rain Flower whispered. Go ahead and marry him. High Cloud touched her sleeve. I married a man I did not love. My life is miserable. And I, said an emaciated woman called White Bird, I am a Keres. I dishonored my father, so he sold me to an old man at Arenal. I can never go home. I refuse to eat as long as I'm here. You must do what is right.

Antelope Water was standing by the wall, waiting for her. She went up to him, but she did not look directly into his eyes. It was forbidden until after they were married. I greet the highest in you, Antelope Water, she said. Her hands were at her sides.

I greet the highest in you, Sayah, he said. His hands were clenched into fists.

I do not want to marry you, Antelope Water. Though I like your character.

I do not want to marry you, Sayah. Though I like your character as well. Antelope Water felt foolish, having a conversation like this, especially with the Memorizers watching. The news would be all over the village. People would laugh.

I will ask my father to give the gifts back to your father.

Give the gifts back, then. In all of Arenal's long history, no girl had refused to marry a boy of such important bloodlines. It was an insult to his heritage. He backed away from her, his arms folded across his chest. With a sense of relief, he ran through the gate and up into the hills. He threw himself down on the ground and laughed. He would marry the beautiful Bird Wing of the Feather Clan. He had loved her since he was six years old.

The Grandmothers made a clucking sound when Kobili told them how Sayah had defied Elk Heart. Standing outside the chieftain's house, the shaman had heard everything. The Grandmother-from-the-South said: You must take your time, Ancient Revered One. If you move too fast, you will lose her. You see, she does not quite believe who she is, though she is learning.

Kobili scowled. She remembers nothing, he fumed.

She remembers everything, said the Grandmother-from-Above. She chooses to forget, that's all.

CHAPTER
Fifteen

obili was sitting in the tall grass beside a stream, watching the dark water flow past. Small fish poked their heads up to have a look. Coyote and Raven watched. The shaman was deep in thought. Sayah was nearly at the end of what he had to teach her and soon she would not need him anymore. The thought sickened him. She sat with her back against the chalk white trunk of an aspen tree, her eyes turned toward the Sun. He picked a bouquet of wildflowers and gave them to her. Long ago I gave you wildflowers. You put them in your hair. Between your toes. Remember? She shook her head.

Will we be here forever, Grandfather? She dropped the wildflowers. He reached up and touched her face. How beautiful she was! More so now than before, when all she had was the magic of creation. Now she had experience to define her beauty.

Not forever, Kobili said. Only a little while longer.

Why?

Nothing is forever. Except love. Did you love Antelope Water?

No, Grandfather. I told him I wouldn't marry him.

That's what I heard. Everyone is talking about it. Antelope Water will be a powerful leader someday. He could give you many fine children.

I don't care. I don't love him. I hear Bird Wing has become his wife.

Don't marry a man you don't love, he said. Wait until the right one comes along. He drew in his breath. I wish it could be me, he thought. He had tried to make himself look younger, but none of his potions had worked. He was still old, with white hair, wrinkled skin, and an old man's infirmities. No wonder she wasn't interested. He got up abruptly and walked into the forest, leaving her by herself. There was rumored to be a certain root which, when ground into a fine white powder, made a man look young enough to become his own son. He wondered where to find it among the Plant People he depended upon for his magic. Deep in the forest, he began to dig. There were many roots, of various kinds, and he chewed on them, thoughtfully. He would do anything for her, even this.

The Grandmother-from-the-West stepped out from behind the trees and sat beside Sayah. Men need women, she said. Women need men. It has been that way forever.

When men learned what tenderness was all about, women let them enter them, said the Grandmother-from-the-South. That's how children began.

Women taught men how to be brave, said the Grandmother-from-the-North. Not the other way around. Sayah stared into the water. She seemed not to be listening.

Men taught women how to fight, said the Grandmother-from-Above. It was against their nature, but when their children were involved, women went to war.

Sometimes it's better to give in, said the Grandmother-from-the-South. If you don't like argument, cut out your tongue. Sayah shook her head. Is it possible to love a very old man?

The Grandmothers looked at one another, knowingly. Ah, so that was what was happening. You can love anyone, said the Grandmother-from-the-North. I once loved a polar bear. We had children together.

I once loved a javelina, said the Grandmother-from-the-South. He taught me the ways of the jungle. I learned how to wait, very patiently, for flowers to open.

I once loved two men at the same time, said the Grandmother-from-the-East. I married them both. Then one killed the other. The one who was left gave me the Twin Stars. You can see them up in the Sky at certain times of the year.

Sayah and the Grandmothers joined hands and made a circle on the grass. Her heart was filled with love. Grandmothers, will you ever die?

Everything dies, yet nothing dies, they said.

Even I?

You will experience a change of worlds.

Do you ever feel pain, Grandmothers?

That's what women feel the most. Only they don't talk about it.

Why is there pain?

So you appreciate the times when there's not.

The Grandmothers said good-bye and walked down the path, singing their familiar songs. Sayah took off her moccasins and sat with her feet in the stream. If I am them, then they are me, she said to Coyote, who looked at her with his intelligent yellow eyes. A part of them *is* you, he said. But not all. Some of me is you as well. Raven perched in a tree. Those Grandmothers were here when I was young, he said. So were you. That makes me part of you.

But the Grandmothers are old, and I am young, she said. How can they be part of me? Kobili dropped down beside her. He was chewing a root that he thought had brought about an immediate change in his appearance. He waited for her to notice. He took her hand.

The old have young hearts, he said. You place too much importance on how people look. She glanced at his eagle nose. The firmness of his jaw. The mysterious eyes. The knotted veins in his hands. The Grandmothers say you are a spirit, Grandfather.

Ah, he said, I am many different things. As you are.

Am I a spirit as well?

He looked away. You are whatever you need to be.

An eagle?

Yes.

A bear?

Yes.

A butterfly?

With such beauty in your wings, what else could you be?

She closed her eyes, remembering a long ago time, when she had been a young and curious bear living in a cave high in the mountains. A man had danced with her in the forest amidst wildflowers, tall grass, and stately aspen trees. He had not minded if she was a bear and she had not minded if he was an old man. His legs became young again and when he stopped dancing, he made love with the bear until the seasons changed. Then the bear had sent him away. Bears cannot love people, she'd said then.

As Sayah looked at Kobili, her voice grew soft. She took his hand in hers.

Were you the man I met in the forest? she asked. That time I was a bear?

He turned his head away. I was, he said.

His tears fell onto the grass and became white mice. They scampered away.

PART FOUR

When the Battle of the Spirits Began

ARENAL 1538

The Snake

Spain was moving,
like an uncoiled snake it moved, slowly
devouring, hungry for possession,
for dominance,
for submission to Jesus and the rights of Kings.

The fearless Son of Italy,
Admiral of Castile, embraced the Ptolemaic earth and
announced he had discovered India's green bounty.
In his frenzy, he created new bloodlines, created supremacy,
created misery among the innocents. So began
the downward spiral toward obedience,
toward a new religion,
toward oblivion. Stone jaguars and war gods
                    screamed,

macaws spoke in new voices, and whales became
messengers of destruction. Los Indios
fretted about their unborn children,
about rain-giving Tlaloc, about how
Huitzilopochtli would be remembered.

Saturated in despair
were the jungles, the high mountains,
and death-scented shores where human blood
mixed with salt water and crested waves
bore the corpses of Los Indios
to sanctuary among multicolored fish.

The future had already been determined
when Quetzalcoatl's prophecy was fulfilled
in the year One Reed,
the year that Tenochtitlan fell
and the spirits of mutilated Aztecs
went into the ground for safekeeping.
In the Valley of Mexico, monkeys became human,
the ocean receded,

volcanoes stirred,
and across the great, sweet land
     a sourness descended.
Eyes upward, dead Aztecs released their stories
to the wind, while in ruined Tenochtitlan
enormous war dogs,
eyes flashing fire, looked northward.
The Spaniards coiled themselves like snakes
around the fallen city.
In the name of our Holy Mother,
our Holy King, and the Holy Gold that drives us,

    we are lord and master, they said, loaded
with so much treasure they walked like iron men.
As the Bat God shattered,
Tortoise set out on a long journey to warn his relatives
about what was happening. After a time,
Jaguar and Javelina followed, and Monkey
with a golden cup, traveling on two legs,
tail curled up like a spiral. Macaw had already started
from the ruins, and in his mind, the history
of Tenochtitlan began unfolding.

CHAPTER

Sixteen

ne day, during the Sun House Moon, four Aztec traders dragged themselves into Arenal. Their bodies bore many wounds. One man's thumbs were amputated. Another had a ragged stump of a foot. A third limped along on a wooden leg decorated with the ducks and jaguars of his old religion. The Aztecs were hungry. They ate and drank for two days before they felt satisfied. As they lazed happily in the sun, they offered shells, clay effigies of bats, cats, warriors, and snakes, brightly colored feathers, and cotton cloth. In return they wanted turquoise, salt, tallow, and women. The enemy destroyed our people, the Aztecs said. Elk Heart and the Memorizers stood motionless in front of them, listening. The traders went on. They leveled our great city. The temples. The market. They filled in the canals. Nothing is left. *Conquistadors*, they call themselves. Spanish invaders who crossed the ocean in big ships.

The traders drank the Elixir of Dreams and felt better in no time.

Their stories spilled from their lips quite naturally. They scratched their lice-ridden bodies. Soon they would bathe in the river and the women would help them. When they were pleasantly intoxicated, they offered Kobili a magnificent scarlet macaw with bright eyes and long tail feathers of blue and orange and yellow that nearly touched the ground. The shaman was pleased. He had loved tropical birds ever since he lived at Tenochtitlan and enjoyed a macaw like this one.

The bird perched on the shaman's arm, taking in his new surroundings. Too dry, he thought. Too hot. Too much sky. Not enough trees and flowering plants. In a shrill voice he said, all my friends died. He looked around as if he expected a siege. I lost my home. The bird trembled. How did he know he would not meet the same fate here?

Do not worry, Kobili said, stroking his back. This is your home now. You are safe. Macaw shuddered. I was Moctezuma's favorite bird. I don't like it here.

The Aztec without thumbs rose unsteadily to his feet. Moctezuma is dead, he said. Killed by his own men. Elk Heart stepped forward, thinking of his vision where Moctezuma had cut open the mountain with his hand and the sacred buffalo poured out. Moctezuma is truly dead? The trader nodded, slowly.

The bird looked away. The goddess of death fell off her pedestal, he said. Some of my relatives got cooked in a stew pot. He stared at the people who reached out boldly to touch him. The bird did not like the look of them, like the dreaded leaders of Tlaxcallan, who tried to pull his tail feathers out. He hopped to Kobili's other shoulder.

Do not be afraid, the shaman said. I am always afraid, the bird replied.

The Aztecs gave wet kisses to their gift women and helped themselves to more cornmeal cakes and roasted venison. They drained the last of the Elixir of Dreams from the jug. When Tenochtitlan fell, some of us saw possibility, said the man who had lost a foot. No more tax collectors. No more children sacrificed to the gods. But Cortés was worse than our old leaders. War dogs ate our children. Soldiers pierced women's bellies with sharp lances. Babies fell out. Then there was smallpox. So dreadful no one could walk or move. The sick were so helpless they could only lie on their beds like corpses, unable to move their heads or hands or feet. They could not get up to search for food, so they starved to death in their beds. The Memorizers pressed closer. Truly, these were amazing stories, worth repeating often in the kiva.

The traders sat up. We pretended to be dead as human blood flowed over us and the stench of rotting flesh filled our nostrils. When night fell, we swam across the lake. Macaw rode on my back because he is afraid of water. We hid for many days, eating insects and toads. We were so hungry we almost ate him, but he is our friend. And he does not contain much meat. The traders had traveled a great distance, enduring every discomfort. They had shared their stories with Macaw and he, in turn, spoke to them of his life with Moctezuma Xocoyotzin, of his own little bed of gold, and the mangoes, bananas, and chayote that formed his diet.

We went northeast, spreading news of disaster, the trader with the religious leg said. We crossed rivers and mountains, telling people what to expect. Now we are telling you. The Spanish snake is coming. On its belly it is coming. Prepare yourselves. Elk Heart remembered Kobili's prophecy. Now it was coming true. When will they arrive? he said. The traders shook their heads. When snakes are hungry, they move quickly. When they are full, they sleep. This particular snake may not come for many moons. On the other hand, it may arrive tomorrow.

Moctezuma found out Cortés was not his friend, Macaw ventured. Soldiers everywhere. Taking things. Destroying where I lived. The bird looked around. Everyone was listening attentively, a bigger audience than he had ever had before. He walked the length of Kobili's outstretched arm and back to his shoulder. I said to Moctezuma, Attack them before they attack you. But nobody listens to me. The Memorizers shook their heads, amazed at the bird's vocabulary. Here was a storyteller to rival the best of their own. A talking bird who knew history!

Remember what he says, Sun Mountain Shining whispered to his nephew. If Kobili doesn't want him, we will give him a place of honor in the kiva. And I, he thought to himself, will have some of his tail feathers to wear in my hair.

Coyote and Raven liked the colorful bird who spoke so eloquently. Coyote offered to take him for a ride on his back. Raven offered to show him the sky. Macaw shuddered. I hate sky, he said. Besides, I cannot fly. Moctezuma clipped my wings.

Kobili carefully listened to the traders. They proved his dreams were real. What did these intruders look like? he said.

They have the white skin of Quetzalcoatl, the traders said. Eyes like milk. Hair, on some it was yellow, on some it was black. They shot death from long firesticks. They wore metal clothing inside of which they roasted like meat. *Metal.* Remember that word also, our friends. The traders took sticks and drew pictures in the dirt. *Conquistadors.* Little men, our size, with pointed beards. They ride animals bigger than an elk. *Horse,* the Aztecs said, drawing a huge creature with a big head and long legs. With a horse you can go like the wind. In one day you can cover many times the distance you can with feet. *Conquistadors. Horse. Metal.* Kobili rolled the words around on his tongue and stared at the pictures until they wore an imprint in his brain.

Horses are the new gods, the man with no thumbs said. On them an ordinary man becomes king. *Horse.* Remember that word, our friends. It will change the world. The traders sprawled on the ground, content with the women they had traded for a conch shell and a clay effigy of the Bat God. Raven and Coyote moved closer, interested in what the traders said. Coyote perked up his ears. Can a horse go faster than me? Twice as fast, the traders said. Faster than me? Raven said. If you want to race, Horse will win, the Aztecs said.

Sayah stood quietly at the edge of the circle. She too had memorized the drawings and listened to everything Macaw and the traders had said. She moved closer to the Grandmothers, who said, Gather cornmeal, woman. Develop a strong stomach. Make sure your feet are aligned so you can walk faster. Pray for the Earth to be strong. She went to the Center Place and began to pray. Not long here, but forever here. Not to spill blood, but to clean it from the Earth.

Elk Heart also studied the pictures intently. He touched them lightly. I would like a horse, he said. With a horse I could defeat my enemies that much faster. His mouth watered. The Memorizers wanted horses, too. We will become the best warriors around, they said. Old men on horses can go faster than old men on foot. We will trade all our turquoise for these magical beasts. Take us to them. The Aztecs shook their heads. The conquistadors trade nothing, they said. They take what they want.

Before the wind blew the pictures away, Kobili knew how conquistadors and horses looked. He gently stroked the bird. From hair like yours, they made strong ropes, Macaw said shrilly. From the fat of dead Aztecs, they dressed their wounds. They will kill you too, Old Man. The shaman was unafraid, having survived poison, spears, and a fall from a cliff into the river, not to mention when an enemy warrior tried to scalp him, and when he was stabbed by one of his own men. He listened to the visitors, asking many questions. Were these men kind? Did they respect women? Were children spared? Did they show mercy toward the Aztecs?

No to everything, the traders said, weeping for their slaughtered wives and children. One man played a flute. Another recited a poem. They lay in the dry grass, listening to the songs of the women. How beautiful they were! The Aztecs would never forget their wives, but with these new women, they were becoming happy again. Come with us, Brother Macaw, they said, taking the bird from Kobili's shoulder. The one-legged man stretched out an arm for a perch. We have something we must do. You can help us. Two men carried a hide sack between them, as they had done all the way from Mexico. The sack was nearly worn out. From a hole, several round, bright objects dropped in the dirt. The children of Arenal ran to pick them up and, because they saw no value to them, tossed them in a corner of their houses.

The Aztecs were gone all day. When they returned, the shaman never asked the bird where they'd been. Because his back was turned, he had not seen the gold coins drop out nor the children pick them up. The Aztecs gave the bird to his new owner. We will be back for you, they said. You know our secret. Promise you will never tell. Macaw bent his head so he could look into Kobili's face. I promise, he said. He had never made a promise before. He wondered what a promise was.

In time, Macaw learned to imitate the shaman's reedy voice so cleverly that people could scarcely tell one from the other. Prepare to die! the bird would cry and bury his sleek feathered head beneath his large wing. The shaman took the bird with him wherever he went.

Listen, the shaman would say. Fortify your houses.

Listen, the bird would repeat. Fortify your houses.

Do not waste any more time, the shaman would say. Prepare your poison arrows.

Do not waste any more time, the bird would repeat. Prepare your poison arrows.

I am so glad you have come, Brother Macaw, Sayah said, feeding him wild strawberries she had gathered along the river. They were his favorite food.

I did not want to come, Macaw said. This is not my kind of place. He rolled his gray tongue out of his beak.

We have need of you. With your knowledge you can help us.

I only know about jungles and god-kings and bad men who ate my friends.

You have seen things none of us have seen, Sayah said. You must tell your stories.

I don't know, Macaw said. Suppose I forget?

Sayah put her face close to the bird's curved beak. He nipped playfully at her ear. You won't forget, she said. I won't let you. Macaw loved her from that day on.

CHAPTER

Seventeen

*T*he medicine man hurried up the steep trail to the Cave of History, Macaw clinging to his shoulder, taking in the view. Not that he liked it much. The vast, nearly treeless land was ugly. He missed the moist and teeming jungle, laden with exotic blossoms, and macaws like himself with whom to exchange news. He missed his old life with Moctezuma, his golden bed, the women who did nothing but polish his beak. We are here, Kobili said, sprinkling cornmeal and pollen across the entrance to the cave. Once a year he did this, on the first full Moon following the vernal equinox. At no other time did the laws of his Medicine Society permit it. They went in, inhaling the musty odor of mouse habitation and the stronger smell of Bear, snoring loudly on a pile of leaves. The Cave of History was where the First People left cryptic messages about their lives: spirals of emergence, the arrows of direction, the spirit of animals, the hump-backed flute player, a map to the inner world, zigzag lightning, and war chiefs. The walls were so crowded with visual history that Kobili had to look for space to say what he wanted. He found room above Bear's softly rounded ears and stood on the animal's furry back, balancing himself with care. He ran his fingers over the rock. With the tip of his deer antler, he scratched a picture of a conquistador as the Aztecs had drawn it in the dirt.

When he saw the shaman's efforts, Macaw fluffed his feathers. He had been in this cave once before, and he didn't like the looks of it. Bad men pulled my tail feathers out, he said. If it hadn't been for a woman who loved me, I'd be dead. The bird cocked his head. Before those bad men came, a fire burned at Tenochtitlan every night for a year. The temple of Huitzilopochtli burst into flame and could not be saved. He paused. Do you want to hear more, Old Man? Later, Kobili said. I am busy. Kobili had become his greatest friend. Macaw felt he could tell him anything. Make a horse, Old Man, Macaw said. With four legs and a big head. I will help you.

Horse. Kobili repeated the word the traders had taught him. He did not want horses in the Place of Dreams. He did not want men with fire sticks. What of the other word? *Religion.* Not the religion of natural cycles and all living things the Clay People were used to. A religion of terror and authority. So he'd heard from the footsore Aztec traders. We would rather have died than give up Quetzalcoatl, the deity who gave the arts and maize to humans, they'd said. Quetzalcoatl remained in their hearts as they trudged across the desert with the borrowed women from Arenal. Quetzalcoatl was the last thing the traders thought about when enemy arrows pierced their bodies and they fell, facedown, in the prickly pear near the village of Oraibi, far to the west. Two sisters escaped and were already on their way back to Arenal, carrying a gift of six rattlesnakes from the Hopi.

While the shaman worked, Macaw perched on Bear's furry brown head. He liked the sensuous feel of his thick fur, the rhythmic heaving of his body as he slept. Moctezuma had many wives, he said. One hundred and fifty children. The bird hopped up and down, remembering how he had been entrusted with the education of Moctezuma's

children. He was anxious to see whether any of his old students had survived, but the longer he stayed at Arenal, the more he realized that, like it or not, this was to be his home. I taught those children to speak graciously, the bird said. I prepared them for the inevitable.

Kobili was intent on his work. I do not know how to prepare my people, he said sadly. Elk Heart has sent scouts to see if the Spaniards are coming. The scouts have not yet returned. In his corner, Bear rolled over with a yawn. Macaw rolled with him. I had a golden cage filled with rose petals, he said. Slaves played music for me. One day Moctezuma and I went down to the sea. We caught a half-woman, half-fish. He made love to her. Then I made love to her. She gave birth to one human and one macaw. I don't suppose you believe me.

I believe everything, Kobili said.

The shaman worked until the sun cast deep blue shadows across the gaping mouth of the cave. A family of mice scampered in to spend the night. Kobili put aside his deer antler and stood back. His drawing was made from memory, for the pictures the traders had drawn in the dirt had long since blown away. Is this how they looked? he asked.

They wore parrot feathers in their hats, the bird said. Some of my friends became quite naked. They died of shame. He nibbled on his ration of dried cactus fruit. He much preferred the bananas of the jungle, but he was never to see bananas again.

Kobili added feathers where Macaw told him to place them.

Beards, the bird said. Those men had pointed beards. Full of food.

The medicine man carefully added beards. The bird studied the drawings. Something was wrong. Horses have bigger heads, he said. Long teeth. Round eyes. The shaman made bigger horses. He drew the sun with an arrow through the middle. The moon with a piece chewed out. When he was finished Kobili sat on a rock, talking to the mice who listened intently. It was the Time of the Great Goodness, he began. People thought it would last forever. Nothing lasts forever, my friends. The little gray mice stared at him. They blinked their beady eyes. They understood everything the shaman said because they were connected to him.

He turned to Bear and poked him with his foot. Bear groaned and turned over. He opened one sleepy eye. Brother Bear, you must tell the animal kingdom about these conquistadors. Tell them about horses. They are bigger and stronger than you. They can run faster. Bear yawned. What makes you think so? What makes me think your four legs are attached to your body? Kobili retorted. He left the cave and hurried down the path. It was already quite late. A full moon was rising. Macaw complained he was cold. Kobili wrapped him in a fine weasel pelt. Only his head poked out.

Bear got up and shook himself. Beneath his warm belly was a hide sack. It contained greenstone beads. A jade fetish of Tlaloc, the Rain God. And many gold coins. Bear was guardian of these treasures, for he had given his word to the Aztecs. He had slept all winter on top of a fortune great enough to buy much of the unexplored world, if land had been for sale at that point in time. With his powerful claws, Bear dug a hole and buried the sack. Then he headed through the forest to a cave on the other side of the mountains where a beautiful she-bear was just waking up.

When they neared the village, Kobili looked up. Stars and moon made him nostalgic. Those stars in the shape of a dog I made, Brother Macaw. She made the Hunter. Gave him his own belt, too. The Milky Way we created together. Is it not beautiful?

Stars are the oldest beings, Macaw said thoughtfully. They visited Moctezuma whenever one of his children was born. So many stars fell out of the sky they left huge holes where they used to be.

Kobili resumed walking. The village was quiet. Dogs barked. Owl greeted him from a nearby tree. I will tell you a secret, Brother Macaw. Sayah is a woman I knew long ago when we lived in the Sky World. She is called Thunderwoman.

The bird pressed closer to the shaman's neck. I never heard of her, he said.

The shaman smiled. I am still in love with her, he went on. We used to argue about silly things. Whether Moon should have a happy face. Or sad. She liked flowers. I liked mountains. She liked turtles. I liked snakes. Grass was her idea. I came up with rocks. Kobili hurried across the plaza. I wanted to do something large. So I made whales.

The bird whistled. Too big, Old Man. A whale took Moctezuma out in the ocean. He never wanted to come back.

Kobili laughed. First I made condors. Albatrosses. Eagles. Birds with power. She liked canaries and finches and bluebirds.

What about macaws? the bird said.

I'm sure they were her idea, the shaman said as he climbed the three ladders to his house. He stood on his terrace for a while before he went in, speaking to the Star Beings, whom he loved. They were his children, as well as hers.

A fire burned low in the fire pit inside Kobili's house. When it came time to make people, we had a disagreement, the shaman said, helping himself to a plate of cornmeal cakes High Cloud had left. I wanted to do it gradually. She wanted to put them in various places right away and let them live with the animals. I said people should start out as fish, in a big underground lake. She got angry and left. For ten thousand years she's been gone. She doesn't remember our time together. She calls me Grandfather.

Macaw was not easily impressed. He had lived with Moctezuma and seen what the god-king could do. Do you expect me to believe you're the Creator, Old Man? He nipped him playfully on the ear.

I'm not the Creator *now*, Kobili said. If I were, I'd make Sayah love me. And I'd make you a banana tree right there in the plaza. I love her, Brother Macaw. If I were young, perhaps she'd notice me. But I am old, and she does not care for me.

Love requires persistence, Macaw said. Leave everything to me.

CHAPTER

Eighteen

nside the tiny pouch Macaw wore around his neck were several treasures Moctezuma had given him. One was four black smooth stones. Every day Macaw chewed on the hard surface of one of these until at last the stone cracked open. Inside was a fine, white powder with a pungent, musty odor. The bird was delighted. He knew exactly what it was. Moctezuma had taken this powder every day until at last he looked younger than his children. The bird took a pinch of powder in his beak and dropped it into a mug of water. He stirred it with a stick he held between his beak. Then he hopped along the upper terraces until he reached a dark house. He heard the beating of a drum and a deep, anguished song. He hopped down the ladder. The shaman was sucking magical darts from Brave Bear's motionless body, to cure him of a spell put on him by an enemy. The warrior appeared dead, but the shaman worked and worked until at last Brave Bear expelled his breath. Macaw tugged at the Old Man's sleeve. Come, he whispered. I have found a way to make you young again. The shaman put away his medicines, his knives, his darts, the magical snake, the gourd rattles, and all his salves and ointments. Then he followed the bird to a place where he often went to think.

Drink it, Macaw said. The potion tasted terrible, but it did its work. Kobili drank it every day until the full moon, though it was hard to swallow. It burned his throat. But after a while a change took place. People noticed that their shaman seemed to be growing unaccountably younger. His snow white hair had turned the color of a raven's wing. His face had become that of a young man's. He no longer walked on bowed legs but straight ones. Even his voice had changed. Look, they said, our shaman has become young and handsome. How did he do it? The Elixir of Dreams? No. The seeds of a milkweed pod? No. The berries of a juniper tree? No. Three old men, Sun Mountain Shining, Snow Eagle, and One Fist, begged to know his secret, for they had recently acquired young wives who expected them to do a young man's contortions. Sun Mountain Shining trembled from fatigue. Ancient Revered One, you have done what none of us can do. We want to know your secret. Learn to live right, Kobili said. Don't speak against your brother. Pray often. Eat worms.

Sayah noticed the change, too. She watched him walking across the plaza with a light and easy step. He looked at her with hopeful confidence, waiting for her to say something. Grandfather, she said at last, I look at you and think you are as young as Antelope Water.

I am. He turned his head so she could admire his youthful profile. I am a young man again, he said. I can run as fast as a deer. I am capable of having children.

She laughed. Grandfather, if I did not know you were as old as the mountains, I might fall in love with you. As he reached out to touch her, she ran away. But at his feet was a huge piece of shiny black obsidian, many times bigger than he was. She had moved it all the way from the Jemez Mountains with the power of her gaze. It was too big for him to carry, so he left it where it was. The arrow makers chipped away, but a long time later, the obsidian was still the same size.

Kobili looked down at his hands. They were no longer covered with old-age spots, with wormlike blue veins showing through the skin. He pulled his long hair around to where he could see it. As black as a sick man's teeth. He felt his neck, his face, his shoulders. No more flabby skin of an old man. Now he had a young warrior's firm flesh. People said he was handsome. Macaw said the younger women wanted to sleep with him. I do not want them, Kobili said. I want *her*. Well, *she* is busy making herself a dress for the Corn Dance, Macaw said. What does she want? Kobili said. She wants to make up her own mind, Macaw said. He hated the difficulties that love presented. The great love of his life had been captured by Cortés and shipped back to Spain for the amusement of the King. He would never love anyone else again. His bird heart had been broken.

Kobili went to Coyote and Raven, Sayah's constant companions. You helped her into the world, he said. Don't you want to see her happy? Then go to her and tell her I am a young man now and I have a young man's desires. Coyote lay down, enjoying the hot sun on his back. He had recently found a beautiful Coyote Girl to share his life and he was busy preparing a den for her, with a fine view of the river. I never interfere in such matters, Old Man, Coyote said. Raven landed in a tree. Old Man, he said. You look young and you act young, but it's what's in your heart that counts. If you really love her, the sky will fall. He flew away. He had recently found a raven like himself, but different enough to make him remember her all the rest of his days. Raven was busy helping her to build a nest in which to hatch their young.

You know what it's like to wait, Ancient Revered One, the Grandmothers told him when they saw him pacing along the river. Sayah is a headstrong girl. Some day she'll come to you, not now. Be patient.

I have never been patient, he said crossly. I thought it took her much too long to make stars. Each one had to be perfect. Not too big. Not too small. Able to move on their own. Willing to live by themselves. *I* could have done the same thing in half the time.

The Grandmother-from-the-South spoke up. But you didn't, she said.

He watched Sayah walking arm in arm across the plaza with Bird Wing and High Cloud, her two best friends, both married to kiva leaders, with children of their own. He smiled at her with wry affection, remembering the attention she had lavished on the making of every living thing. She had agonized over whether to give sea clams arms and legs. She worried about alligators and their sharp teeth. She regretted making reptiles so ugly. She thought some birds, like the roadrunner, should have had bigger wings to enable them to fly. She had disguised the usefulness of cacti with thorns, the deadliness of oleander with a pleasant smell, the lowliness of ants with diligence.

I liked everything you made except persimmons, he whispered. They made my mouth turn inside out.

CHAPTER
Nineteen

lk Heart's scouts had gone as far south as the desert that lay on the other side of the Great River. There they had seen the Spaniards, wearing suits of metal, riding like gods on their huge beasts. We fell down before them, said Mud Goose. Those great kachinas. They were not happy to see us. The chief's men bore many scars; they had lost their war clubs, their spears, and their medicine bags. It was only by luck and deception they had made it back to Arenal, where they were given a dance of welcome. What they had seen during their long journey required two nights in the kiva to tell. Two warriors from the Feather Clan had been killed by the invaders, another man captured. Only four men returned safely to say that the enemy was approaching.

The land resists them, said Fire Dog, who had lost an eye during an encounter with the army. I saw a great boulder roll down and crush a soldier.

Lightning struck a man who was pissing, said Mud Goose. All that was left was a pile of ashes. He laughed hysterically, unable to control himself.

Goes-Far-to-Kill had a deep wound in his chest from a cavalryman's lance, but Kobili had drawn the poison out on the warrior's return and now he was recovering. I saw for myself how the river rose up when they were crossing it, he said. A great wave bore down on them. Three men drowned.

I, for a short while, had use of one of their horses, Quick-to-See offered. I went as fast as the wind, up one mesa, down another. But then I fell off.

The scouts described the conquistadors exactly as the Aztecs had described them. They added one detail: war dogs, who could tear out a man's throat in one bite. Two of our brothers met death in this way, said Fire Dog. Wise and courageous leader, he said to Elk Heart, the Spaniards speak of something called gold. We heard them talking in their tents before we sneaked in and killed them. Gold is dearer than life to them. They said so.

Elk Heart stood up. I have never seen gold, he said. Except in the sky, when the Sun Father rises, and in Corn Ripe Moon, when leaves turn a golden color. He stared into the fire with melancholy eyes. The Time of the Great Goodness is passing, he said. Even Sayah cannot prevent it. Because it is supposed to pass. Do you know that? The scouts dropped their heads. Birds are flying backward, they said. That tells us something.

Early one morning Deer-He-Becomes began to prance around the plaza. Then he ran full tilt toward the wall and knocked off his latest set of antlers. Bent Oak picked him up from where he had fallen and said: Will you give your life for the people of the village? I will, said Deer-He-Becomes. Bent Oak drew a perfect arrow from his quiver and walked to the other side of the plaza. He took careful aim. His arrow pierced the heart of Deer-He-Becomes, and he fell to the ground. Blood spurted out. The elders rushed forward to cut a long incision in his belly. They took out his liver and sliced it up and ate it. They removed his heart and shared it. Later, when the last of Deer-He-Becomes was used, for meat and hide and tools, Lizard-Goes-Forth returned. At least he looked like the warrior he had been many years before. No one asked where he had been or what he had learned on his journey. He appeared larger than they remembered.

Your task is to speak the language of the deer, Kobili said. It's universally understood, from one end of the land to the other. No other humans will understand what you say except those who believe in animal power. Lizard-Goes-Forth said he accepted his responsibility. He practiced shooting poison arrows at a target made of straw and hide, though his arm, which had been a leg for so long, was no longer able to pull the bowstring. Lizard-Go-Forth kept practicing until at last his arm grew strong and his aim, as it had been long ago, was deadly.

CHAPTER
Twenty

The warriors of the Seven Wise Villages of Tiguex, twelve hundred in all, gathered to be blessed by Kobili and rubbed with magic potions that would keep them safe from harm. Elk Heart donned his feather robe and spoke to them from the rooftop. In one hand he held an eagle feather wand, in the other a gourd rattle. By now another band of scouts had gone out and come back. The Spaniards were approaching Hawikuh, a village six days journey to the west. One of the scouts, named Black Knife, had joined the Spanish army and was now chief lookout for Coronado's approaching men. Elk Heart had ordered him executed if he ever returned.

Some of us must go to meet the army and offer them peace, Elk Heart said. We must talk to them, persuade them to turn back. He looked around. I will go, for I am your chieftain. I will take no more than six warriors with me. And my painted shield, my sharpest spear, and my best points, he added. I will impress them.

I will go, a voice said. They turned. Sayah was walking toward them in a beaded dress, wearing pumpkin-seed earrings and bracelets made of sweet grass. She wore a spiked headdress with tiny ears of corn hanging from it. Her eyes glittered with the power Elk Heart knew she had. The Grandmothers followed, singing softly, carrying bunches of kinnikinnick. They looked at the vast assemblage of warriors, waiting quietly. They looked at the women with babies in cradleboards. A terrible fear swept over them.

Elk Heart descended to the plaza and looked into his daughter's eyes. He saw the fiery burst of her origins and the shadows of what she would create and the terrible energy of her desire. He took a deep breath. Sayah is a woman warrior, he said, just as we are men warriors. She has power the rest of us do not. She will go forth on our behalf. Kobili and the Grandmothers will go with her. And me, Macaw piped up. He did not want to miss anything. And you, the chieftain said, also Coyote and Raven, because you will have need of them.

From a basket he took turquoise beads. Salt. A sharp knife. Corn seeds. Gourds for water. A beaver skin. A red cedar flute he had made himself. Are you afraid? he asked.

No, Father, she said. She felt many pairs of eyes upon her. Some of the warriors looked at her angrily. A few threw their bows to the ground and walked away. They would not become her slaves.

Then you must leave tomorrow at dawn. The Grandmothers will help you prepare.

The Memorizers blew smoke in her direction. Forgive us, they said. After you were born, we wanted to kill you. We were cowardly and mean. They gave her a tiny alabaster deer head, which symbolized the Sun and fire. Forgive us for being suspicious old men.

I forgive you, she said. In the days to come, your wisdom will be tried again and again. Your power as elders will be endangered. Are you strong enough to survive?

We are, they said. Sun Mountain Shining, who was more than one hundred years old, felt his strength beginning to wane. He leaned on his stick and begged the Sun Father for help. If we die, we die as warriors, he said. Do I fear them? He spat on the ground.

Macaw spoke up in a voice that sounded exactly like the shaman's. On the Night of Sorrows, so many died that Moctezuma swam across the city in a lake of blood. His children swam in blood. His wives turned the tide of blood and made dry land. They buried themselves to keep from being violated by the enemy. A parrot I knew tore out her own feathers.

Brother Macaw, the chieftain said gently, will we tear out our own feathers?

All will die, Macaw said. Except some will live. A thousand pairs of eyes were on him. Macaw buried his head inside Kobili's armpit. He was afraid he had said too much.

Sayah thanked them, then turned to the Grandmothers. We have the hunger of wolves, they said. You will be satisfied, she told them. She embraced her father and ran to her house. That night, she lay awake, listening to the elders singing verse after verse of the Creation Song. The song made her weep. The gentle sound of the river caressed her. She was homesick before she even left.

Early the next morning, Sayah walked away from the village with her little entourage. She did not look back. She walked beside Kobili, thinking how handsome he was and how much she had grown to love him. The Grandmothers dragged a travois on which was piled what they would need on their journey. Food. Hides. Clothing. Pieces of cotton cloth. Yucca sandals. Sacks of turquoise to trade for necessities. Dried corn. Meat. Blankets. Baskets. Pottery. The load was heavy. They took turns pulling it.

Macaw clung to the shaman's shoulder. He hardly dared look at the passing landscape. So big. So barren. So much sky. Where were they going? Suppose there was trouble? Suppose he did not get enough to eat? I want to go home, Macaw shrilled. You have no home, Kobili said.

CHAPTER

Twenty-one

The Mystical Beings had been walking for several days, speaking to lizards and rattlesnakes, scorpions and javelinas along well-worn paths made by the First People during a ten-thousand-year migration. Kobili walked lightly, feeling younger than he had when he was truly young. Sayah loved him. Last night, when they were camped, she had come to him and lay beside him on his blanket, watching the great rotation of stars overhead. She had put her head on his chest and let him touch her. It was enough to make any man happy.

You did not forget our time in the Universe? he had said.

No, I did not forget.

Did you make me wait for you on purpose, Sayah?

Yes. So you would remember I am equal to you.

The shaman knew she had tricked him, had made him wait and suffer and think he had lost her. I will never understand you, he'd said, and kissed her. He noticed Spiderwoman had spun a web around him, and he knew it meant she had chosen him to become Sayah's husband.

Now she walked beside him, enjoying his closeness. He had acquired gifts she had not noticed before. Tenderness. Passion. Playfulness. She put her hand in his and felt his strong fingers close around her own. I have loved him since the Beginning Time, she thought. I will love him when time ends.

Macaw whispered into Kobili's ear. She thinks you are young, Old Man. See the way she looks at you! Moctezuma's wives looked the same way at him. Quick, before she gets away, ask her to marry you.

Kobili hesitated. It's not time.

It *is* time, Macaw said. Pretty soon it will be too late.

When they stopped to rest, Kobili went off to ask a family of skunks what they thought. Do you love him? the Grandmothers asked. Yes, she said. I love him.

Then it's time you married him, the Grandmothers said. He has waited forever for you. They nudged her toward him. He was sitting on a rock, consulting one of the skunks about what to do. Hurry up and ask him, the Grandmothers said. Go on. We haven't got all day.

A man is supposed to ask a woman, Sayah said.

There isn't time, the Grandmothers said.

Kobili got up from the rock. In his hands was a bouquet of wildflowers. Remember when you made flowers? he said. Remember how hard it was to get the smell right? The first flower you made smelled like excrement. He roared with laughter.

Remember the waterfall I made for you? It was perfect.

I have gone there in my mind ever since.

She put her arms around him. He looked away and began to tell a story about Coyote Boy, long and drawn out, as all of Kobili's stories were. Macaw could see that Sayah didn't want to hear it. He jumped onto her shoulder; his tail feathers hung below her waist. Kobili takes too long to say anything, he said. He loves you. He wants to marry you. Yes or no? Macaw shed two tail feathers, one for each of them.

Yes, Sayah said. She felt her face grow hot.

The Grandmothers took her hand. Come, they said. In the privacy of some trees, they combed her long black hair and wound it into two butterfly wings. They dressed her in a deer-hide wedding dress they had made, with tiny shells sewed around the neck. They adorned her with turquoise. They painted her cheeks with two bright red spots.

Go now, whispered the Grandmother-from-the-East, giving her a shove. He is waiting for you. See how handsome he is.

Sayah put her hand in Kobili's. If you were still an old man, I would love you nonetheless. You are neither young nor old.

Kobili was dressed in his best buckskin shirt and beaded moccasins. He summoned Bear to perform the wedding ceremony, witnessed by two deer, four badgers, six skunks, three bison, sixteen rabbits, nine rattlesnakes, twenty antelope, nine elk, four mountain lions, two beaver, a tarantula, four hundred spiders, three turtles, fifty-eight crickets, forty-two bats, two pairs of golden eagles, red-tailed hawks, spotted owls, and one turkey buzzard. Songbirds furnished music. Everyone danced until the new moon set. Stars tumbled this way and that. New ones appeared, brighter than the last.

He made a bed of feathers left behind by the migrating geese. She provided a blanket made of rabbit fur. It's good to be young again, he said as he lay down beside her. Sayah remembered that faraway look. He'd worn it after he'd created the constellation Sea Spider and spread it out across the southern sky the first time he'd made love to her. She remembered her gift to him, an earthworm he hadn't liked at all.

What would she make this time? She blew into the palms of her hands. Ladybugs appeared. He liked them enormously. He gave her a fish scale, from one of the original Fish People. It was a large fish scale, colorful and clear. She held it up to the moonlight. The world looked as green as the day she created grass. I love you, she said. She slept in his arms all night. She dreamed of the tropical seas, where they swam for a thousand years.

In the morning, they resumed their journey. The Six Grandmothers followed at a respectful distance, thinking of the men they had loved. The children they had borne. How the earth expanded from the fullness of their hearts. It is a perfect world, they said. They turned their heads. In the distance, the sound of guns echoed across the vast and beautiful land.

PART FIVE

The Time When Our Hearts Were on the Ground

NUEVA MEXICO 1540–42

THE SIEGE OF HAWIKUH 1540

Heathens,
> *I called them, savages*
> *worshiping animals, naked*
> *as babies, deadly as snakes.*
While the Knight of the Plains begged
> *those beggars of Hawikuh*
> *for allegiance to Nuestro Rey Magnifico,*
I bade them embrace Nuestro Salvador.
> *Gloria Patri, et Filio, et Spiritu Sanctu.*

Pater Noster must be obeyed.

Pagans soon to become Christians,
> *I addressed them as they fell on their knees*
> *to kiss the holy crucifix. I was repulsed*
> *at how they rubbed against our horses and*
> *pushed their bare-breasted women toward us.*
Niños de Dios, I implored, pobrecitos, as the holy water
> *of baptism trickled down their sinfulness. They,*
> *being weak of mind and spirit, licked*
> *the droplets with coarse tongues,*
> *then laughed at me. Madre de Dios!*

Pater Noster must be obeyed.

Those wretched pagans of Hawikuh
> *Ketchipauan*
> *Halona*
> *Matsaki*
> *Kwakina*
> *were all the same.*

Living in sin, in filth, in pure contentment,
*   they pretended to embrace*
*   Pater Noster*
*   La Madre de Dios*
*   Nuestro Rey Magnifico*
*   Omnipotens Deus et sanctis apostolis Petro et Paulo.*
But I, having gorged myself on God, knew better.

Orate, fratres, I prayed in the midst of that dismal land. Dust
*   answered me,*
and scorpions, and dry lizards with forked tongues. Kyrie eleison.

Our weapons must be obeyed.

The General, in gilded sallet, feather-crested, crossed
*   the cornmeal lines put there to deter us. He said*
*   violence is often necessary so the jefes will recognize*
*   authority. Por Dios! Por Nuestro Rey Magnifico!*
The Santiago was given and our horsemen stormed
the walls of that sorry mud village. The savages rained
*   their arrows down. We responded with our crossbows and*
*   our arquebuses, our humble will and might. Por Dios,*
*   por Nuestra Madre España. Our weapons must be obeyed.*
*   Pater Noster must be obeyed!*

Los niños nuevos de Dios poured out of their mud houses.
Los niños nuevos de Dios were forced to repent.
We took their food because we were hungry. We forfeited
our charity for the sake of our honor as men.

*   Jesucristo saves sinners.*
*   Deo gratias. Amen.*

CHAPTER

Twenty-two

wo hundred exhausted cavalrymen of his Holy Catholic Caesarian Majesty rode on slobbering horses across the wind-blasted desert toward the peaceful mud village of Hawikuh. The animals were thirsty. There had been no water since a muddy, bug-infested stream the day before. Their masters pushed them so hard that one old stallion fell dead and an armor-plated conquistador crashed with him, a heap of shining, dented metal upon which great swarms of black flies lighted. Five months of hardship and they had not found gold. They were sure they would find it now in the wasteland called Nueva Mexico.

The General rode at the head of the column, glittering like the sun in his gold-plated suit, a symbol of his high military position. A plumed sallet, or helmet, covered his head. His eyes peered out of a slit in the visor. He did not like what he saw. Endless desert. Strange animals. Dreadful snakes and lizards. He did not even like his own soldiers. They were nobodies, illiterates, mercenaries. Francisco Vásquez de Coronado belched. Forced to eat grease and dust and rancid meat for many months, he had become dyspeptic. In the distance lay Hawikuh, the Cibola of his dreams. After a long and arduous journey, glory was finally at hand. Gold was piled in those houses, buried beneath the floors. His mouth watered. With gold, his discomfort would vanish. He yearned for greatness. A coin to bear his likeness. Vast lands. A title worthy of his name.

The fiery summer had descended upon the conquistadors during their long journey. Their metal suits were as hot as bake ovens. Inside them, their flesh was slowly roasting. Their veins were clogged with dust. Arteries coming unwound like snakes. Blood congealing. With a moan, two men fell from their saddles onto the blistering sand. They cried for water. Eyeball to eyeball with tarantulas and rattlesnakes, they thought of sangria. The sweet taste of oranges. They longed for beautiful Andalusian women to comfort them. Mother of God, do not let us die like dogs.

A blue-robed friar, bloated from too many beans, had insisted upon walking the whole way in his sandals. He hurried to see if the fallen men required last rites. He wore no armor, only a heavy woolen cassock made in Madre España. Inside it, his flesh crawled with lice. He resisted the impulse to scratch. He had not bathed in months, and

he smelled his own ripe odor. No matter. He would suffer, as Jesucristo intended him to suffer, as proof of his worthiness. A silver crucifix, worn through to the copper by years of rubbing, hung from his neck, a symbol of what he meant to do among the heathens.

Fray Marcos crossed himself and invoked the names of Jesucristo,

Maria, and the principal saints. With great effort, he stretched out the unconscious conquistadors on the sand and pulled off their sallets. He poured warm holy water from a flask and gave them last rites. Not dead, but surely succumbing to heat and exhaustion. The priest looked up at Raven, circling ominously overhead. The bird opened its beak as if to say something. Coyote drew close enough for him to see its yellow fangs. Nervously, the friar rubbed his crucifix. Other animals ran past. Antelope. Deer. Badger. Skunk. Coyote. Cougar. A large, furry bear. He rubbed his sand-blasted eyes. I am hallucinating, he thought. Wild creatures are meant to be killed. Man shall have dominion over every living thing. Genesis 1:26.

Fray Marcos squinted into the white-hot orb of the sun. He glared at Francisco Vásquez de Coronado, who waited impatiently on his horse for the cavalrymen to revive. Bless our noble General, the padre intoned to his ever-present God. He nearly choked when he spoke the General's name, for they had become mortal enemies. The General did not trust the priest, and the priest did not trust the General. As Fray Marcos struggled to his feet, he heard the rasping sound of locusts. Millions of them, making a filthy, disgusting noise. He covered his ears. Kill them, he shouted at the General.

Coronado had had enough of the padre interfering with his mission. He would find gold in Hawikuh, if it was the last thing he did. He spurred his horse and rode confidently toward the pueblo, the twin banners of church and king flying in the wind. Behind him marched three hundred soldiers and a thousand Aztec slaves. Three dozen high-strung war dogs strained against their tethers. Coronado farted inside his hot cocoon.

At that moment, something in the padre's blood boiled over. He began to run across the desert on short, muscular legs strengthened by a thousand miles of walking. Sweat poured from his two round melons of buttocks and ran down his hairy legs in which a family of ants was traveling. He waved his crosier. I am coming, he cried. He overtook Coronado, the foot soldiers, the war dogs. He did not know how he managed to run so fast, but with the help of God he did it. He stumbled into the plaza, breathing hard, and turned his face to the village. In the name of Jesucristo, I bring you salvation, he cried. Come out, come out! The people of Hawikuh drew deep breaths. Behind the walls of their houses, they wept, softly. It was a moment of decision, and the priest knew it.

Do not be afraid! he shouted. I am a man of peace. From his cassock he extracted a little flask of holy water. He grabbed a small boy and baptized him. The boy licked the droplets as they ran down his face to his arm. A hundred warriors crouched on the rooftops, bows drawn. The priest banged the end of the crosier in the red dirt, but he could not plant it. The ground was too hard. Two elders stepped forth to examine the oddity of a full-grown man behaving in such a manner. They did not plant sticks in the earth except when it was time to plant corn.

The friar crossed himself, indicating to the men they were to do the same. The elders, decorated with paint and feathers, wearing warbonnets stolen from the Apaches, reached out to touch the hot metal crucifix with the miniature man fastened upon it. They wanted to see if he was real. The padre shook the War Chief until his warbonnet slid down over one eye. If you repent of your sins, we will spare you, the priest said. He knew he must convince them of his sincerity.

The War Chief freed himself. He could not understand a word the priest said, for he spoke in Spanish, but the War Chief could tell by his expression this was not a friendly visitor. Come and eat some meat, he said. Afterward, you may go home. The padre did not understand a word the War Chief said, either. In a sudden dramatic gesture he flung himself facedown on the hard, red earth, the way he had done at his ordination long ago in España. The people of Hawikuh stared. They thought the Blue Robe had died.

CHAPTER

Twenty-three

lat on his face, Fray Marcos inhaled the red dust of Hawikuh. His eyeballs, seared by the sun, were irritated by the fine-grained dust. He was sure his intestines were filled with dust, which was why he remained constipated. He heard hoofbeats approaching and lifted his head high enough to see a commotion. Here came the callow General, who had encased himself in gilded armor hot enough to cook meat upon, his captains and his lieutenants, whose mortal sins he would rather not have heard in the makeshift field confessional. Merciful God, a man becomes a monster in the wilderness, he thought as one of the savages pulled him to his feet. The chubby priest blinked. The natives had made a circle around him. They were giggling. He brushed himself off. See here, he said. Jesucristo is no laughing matter.

The General reined in next to the padre, barely giving him a glance. He hated the meddlesome priest, with his superior ecclesiastical air, his disgusting manners, and avaricious bent. The priest wanted the glory for himself, when it was the General who had done the work, taken the risks, planned every move. He waved his hand imperiously. A dozen half-naked Indians marched out to meet him, their shields in front of them. One man carried a human skull mounted on a pole. Another wore the head of a mountain lion. Dead weasels hung on strings around their waists. Around their necks they wore beads of every description. A turtle-shell breastplate covered one man's chest. They had long, tangled hair. The smell of rotten meat. Filled with misgivings, the General and twelve of his men rode toward them. A gray desert mouse followed and stood on his hind legs in the midst of the royal army, listening intently, nose twitching, eyes as bright as stars.

Read the Requerimiento, the General ordered from the safety of his saddle, his right hand hovering over his sword in its scabbard. The Requerimiento was the prelude to conquest they carried along and read to the natives, demanding allegiance to King and Pope. Coronado forced himself to look at the Indians. Faces like monkeys. Eyes like beasts. Behind them, the cunning of snakes. We will find the gold that Fray Marcos says is here, he thought. He could not imagine how, without considerable bloodshed, he would lay claim to what the crown had decreed was rightfully the property of His Majesty, the King of España. The Aztecs had resisted mightily. But in the end, their gold had gone to España. The same with Hawikuh, he thought. He blinked in the bright desert sun.

The interpreter took a deep, nervous breath. He read the document entirely in Latin.

On account of the multitude that has sprung forth from Adam and Eve in five thousand years since the world was created, it was necessary that some men should go this way and some another, and that they should be divided into many kingdoms and provinces. He stopped and looked around at the savages. He'd heard they enjoyed scalping white men. He was sweating profusely.

If you do not yield to the mighty authority of Church and King, he went on, *we certify that with the help of God we shall forcefully enter your country and shall make war against you in all ways and manners that we can, and shall subject you to the yoke and obedience of the Church and of their Highnesses.* He expelled his breath, aware of half a dozen spears poised at his head. The interpreter was an educated man from Seville, unaccustomed to hardship or threat. He understood only a few words of the Keresan language. He smiled, bravely.

We shall t-take you and your w-wives and your children and shall make s-s-slaves of them, and as such shall sell and d-d-dispose of them as their Highnesses may command, he stammered. The parchment shook in his hands. *W-we shall take away your g-g-goods and shall do you all the harm and d-damage that we can.* His knees buckled, and he sank to the ground.

With great flourish, the Aztec slaves captured in Mexico removed large flasks of holy water from the pack animals and laid them at the padre's feet. The holy water had been blessed by the archbishop in Mexico City and had traveled all this way; algae now grew in it, also generations of bruise-colored worms. Kneel, ordered Fray Marcos. He demonstrated how it was to be done. The half-naked men fell to their knees without complaint. They enjoyed the feel of holy Mother Earth against their knee bones. The friar poured warm holy water over their heads. Ah, how good it felt, and they did not have to go all the way to the river to bathe. They caught the worms between their fingers and ate them. The mouse watched intently. His whiskers twitched; his beady eyes focused on the padre's nose.

You are now Christians, Fray Marcos said confidently, casting his eyes toward heaven. The holy water is magic water. It has saved your souls for Christ. Before anyone could stop them, the Hawikuh took the remaining flasks of water and poured it over themselves, laughing hysterically. They splashed one another with glee. They covered one another with algae. They caught more worms and draped them on their tongues. The padre was aghast.

The General offered shiny beads, red caps, and tinkling bells. They put them on, laughing merrily. Ah, the Hawikuh thought, these strangers come as clowns. Let's prepare a great feast to welcome them. We will exchange presents. One woman for one horse. Two women for one horse. Their eyes grew moist. Two or three horses would change their lives forever. Twenty-five horses would mean superiority over their enemies. They would cost only fifty women.

The War Chief's mouth watered. Welcome, he said, running his fingers over the flank of the nut-colored mare. He touched the coat of mail that the horse wore and reached toward the General's stiff metal legs. We will deceive you in every way we can, he said in the ancient language of his ancestors. The War Chief smiled a toothless smile and bowed slightly. We want these horses for ourselves. If we have to kill you, we will. We are afraid of nothing. He spat on the ground.

Coronado leaned from the saddle toward the interpreter who was standing weakly against the wall. What did he say, Salazar? Be quick.

They welcome us to their village, General, the interpreter said, not having the faintest idea *what* they'd said.

The desert mouse darted away. He ran back to where Sayah was waiting with the Grandmothers. Around her neck, on a narrow strip of elk hide, she wore the tiny alabaster deer head. She looked down. The mouse became Kobili. What he had to say amazed them. Dear Sayah, wife of one day and one eternity, are you ready? he said. Yes, she said. Her body became strong and the spirits of everything she had ever made went into her consciousness. The Grandmothers prepared her for battle. They gave her the bow and magic arrows that Elk Heart had made. Each of them knew, because she had done it herself, that women found unusual strength whenever it became necessary.

Macaw rolled over on a rock, his feet straight up in the air, his long, colorful tail feathers dragging the earth. He pretended to be dead, for he imagined that would shortly become his fate. Kobili placed him gently in the branch of a tree. Stay there, Brother Macaw, and think of ways to defeat the enemy. Macaw's voice sounded submerged. It was filled with longing for a life that would never come again, though he dreamed it would. The enemy will defeat *us*, Macaw said. Moctezuma said—

Hush, Kobili said, placing two strong fingers around his beak.

CHAPTER

Twenty-four

*T*he deceptive sound of laughter reverberated across the plaza. Dogs barked an exchange of their own interpretation of events, and it was not hopeful. Fires crackled. Smoke drifted up and formed into sky rings. People moved about, cautiously watching the officers who had slid off their horses and were eating a succulent roasted deer with their fingers. The padre had not converted anyone. Bare-breasted women flaunted themselves at the Spaniards. Lecherous savages scarcely covered their private parts. Filth and degradation everywhere, Fray Marcos thought.

The priest had witnessed the bloody fall of Tenochtitlan twenty years before. On the altar of the Templo Mayor he had interrogated a dying Aztec priest about the sacrifice of human beings to the gods. He had uncovered the remains of a human heart in a jewel-studded case. Fray Marcos had vowed to stamp out paganism if it was the last thing he did. Los Indios must wear sufficient clothing and not those flimsy skirts, he announced to the General, resting in his tent after a hearty meal, a cool cloth pressed across his forehead. They must learn morality. We shall start by depriving men of more than one wife. We will send the leftover wives to Mexico and sell them as slaves. Do you wish me to start the purge now, General?

Coronado was in no mood to be addressed by the priest. There is no gold in Hawikuh. Is there? He jumped up and grabbed the padre by the throat. You made a foray to this miserable country last year and came back to say there were cities made of gold. Everyone believed you. It's why the Viceroy mounted this expedition. There *is* gold, Fray Marcos gasped. Farther east, along the river, at Arenal. To the west, the villages of Hopi are pure gold. I have seen them. The General shoved him rudely to the dirt floor. Get out of here before I order my men to kill you.

In the plaza, the celebration continued. The Hawikuh showered the Spaniards with gifts of corn, hides, and women. They brought out jugs of the Elixir of Dreams, which Kobili, during a cultural exchange, had taught them how to make. The conquistadors sat on the ground and drank the sweet, brown liquid until they were giddy. When no one was looking, they shed their uncomfortable armor, their soiled uniforms, their itchy woolen underwear, and made quick love to the women who waited on the other side of the wall. The warriors threw themselves down in front of the Spaniards, drooling at the sight of the horses. You are our long-awaited kachinas, they said, draped in the silk ribbons the Spaniards had given them. We gave you our village, our food, our women. What more do you want? Much of what was said was lost in translation.

The General stumbled from his tent and mounted his horse. He rode toward the celebration and singled out the War Chief, who looked as if he knew something. With signs and gestures, he indicated his desire for gold. We have no gold, the War Chief replied with similar signs and gestures. We will search your homes, the General said, issuing the order to tear down the walls. Thirty soldiers rode toward the houses with their lances, their arquebuses, their swords. A barrage of poison arrows flew through the air. Two soldiers fell from their horses.

The Hawikuh held a hasty council. Outside the walls, the Spaniards held their own council. All that day and into the next, men from each side went back and forth, relaying messages. The warriors wanted their gift-women back. They wanted the conquistadors to leave them in peace. With great solemnity they drew a cornmeal line across the entrance to their village. No one was to cross it. A time-honored custom, as old as the village itself.

You must leave our village immediately, the War Chief said, trembling in front of the mounted General. He had only his war club for defense. He inhaled the acrid smell of gunpowder, sensing that arrows and spears would be no match against the deadly arquebuses. Turning his face to the East, he saw, hurtling through the air, a mysterious barrage of river stones. They smashed four weary infantrymen into the ground and killed them. From her hiding place, Sayah smiled. A cloud of hummingbirds rose from where the soldiers were pinned, arms and legs sticking out. Allies, said the War Chief, smiling. He knew more would come. He began to sing an old kiva song. Other elders joined in, singing and beating their drums. Soon, eagles and hawks and ravens filled the sky. Bears, deer, antelope, coyotes, and buffalo ran from the mesa tops in a thick, red cloud. Snakes and lizards grew to enormous size. When they saw these allies, the people of Hawikuh breathed a sigh of relief. We are safe, they said.

The Spaniards drew back. The mud village suddenly looked formidable. Coronado could still take it perhaps, but with difficulty. Before the General could utter the call to war, the friar did it for him. *Santiago and at them!* He waved his crosier through the air like a lance. With a roar and a great clattering of hoofbeats, the booming of firesticks, and the shrill warning blast of the flageolets, the Spaniards charged the plaza. Poison arrows flew from the rooftops. Sacks of stones were unleashed at their heads. The soldiers fired back. Heavy crossbows found their mark. A dozen warriors toppled from the rooftops. Two women and one child died from the same blast as they ran

screaming across the plaza. The War Chief and his son lay dead. An elder from the Red Crane Clan put himself in front of an artilleryman. Kill me, he said, for he had no further wish to live.

Sayah emerged from the stunted grove of juniper trees, a bow and arrows in her hands. With her gaze she moved certain objects into place. She made a deep cleft in the earth into which three of Coronado's men fell, horses and all. She shot her magic arrows, carefully. Because she had been taught by Elk Heart, her aim was true.

The General, wilting inside his armor, paused to catch his breath. He heard a rush of wind. A waterfall crashed in his ears. Birds and flowers floated above the village in concentric rings. Even small orange fish, and butterflies with iron wings. He giggled uncontrollably and threw his sallet to the ground. His hands, once steady enough to balance a goblet of claret in their palms, shook as if from palsy. He blinked. Standing before him was the most beautiful woman he'd ever seen, dressed all in white. Her eyes were on fire. The imprint of a jaguar on her cheek gave her the look of eternity. Who are you? he whispered. He raised his sword from habit, though what he really wanted was to kiss her firmly on the lips, then to make love to her with a passion she would not forget.

Sayah drew her bow and let a magic arrow fly. Straight at him. With the force and speed of one of the King's own weapons! The General froze and watched it coming. He could not utter a word. The arrow bounced off his breastplate and fell harmlessly to the ground. Who are you? he repeated, entranced by her audacity. Come here. I will not hurt you. He dropped his sword. Maldonado, his most trusted captain, rushed to retrieve it from the ground and placed it in its scabbard. He gathered the gold-plated sallet, noticing the dents. He whispered to the General that the earth had swallowed up three of his men. And that an assortment of wild animals had destroyed their campsite. The General wasn't listening. He held out his arms to the beautiful Indian girl. He wanted to lift her onto his saddle.

Do not touch me, she said. An apparition, there one moment, gone the next. In her place was a rabbit. A bush. A turtle. The girl again. Who are you? the General shouted for the third time. Suddenly his hands and feet felt numb. He nudged his horse. The animal would not move. His men were watching him. You tried to kill me, you shameless girl, he said loud enough for them to hear. I could have killed you, but if you lead us to gold, I will spare your life. The intensity of her look made his head ache. He closed his eyes. When he opened them again, she was gone.

Sayah went into the ruined houses and comforted the people. From her eyes she took a handful of star pieces and inserted them, one at a time, into eyes discouraged by defeat. She helped bury the dead, and she taught children to make baskets and pottery as a way of preserving sacred knowledge. Kobili gave the clan leaders Songs to Sustain Weakened Spirits. He took them into the nearby canyons where they drew their recollections on the sandstone walls. The Grandmothers brought their own gifts as the spirits they were. Macaw, when he overcame his terror, recited another verse in the long history of Tenochtitlan to comfort them. We killed them, the bird said. The conquistadors and their horses. Tanned their skins and put their skulls out to dry. He glanced at the people lying on the ground. I will show you how it's done. The shaman whisked him away.

Before she left, Sayah wound the Thread around the Hawikuh and breathed into their mouths. She stayed with them until they were strong, though the Spaniards, who spent many months there, saw only the Whirlwind People moving across the ground with unusual velocity, sucking up anything the Spaniards dropped on the ground and carrying it away. Sayah's was the angry spirit behind the Whirlwind People. When the General set a gold-framed picture of his mother beside the crucifix he kept near his bed, the Whirlwind People tore through the tent and removed both objects. They flew through the sky and crashed near what would become Oklahoma.

The General was never quite the same after his encounter with Sayah. He wore the dazed look of a zealot. His mind wandered. Later, he would think it was fatigue. Perhaps loneliness. Or the girl herself. Butterflies poured from her mouth when she spoke to him. The scent of honeysuckle filled the air. She became transparent the more he looked at her until at last she faded away, like mist. I was having visions, he thought. Thinking about a woman when I should have been thinking about my mission. But he often stood looking eastward, the direction from which she had come, longing to see her once again.

Francisco Vásquez de Coronado was a distinguished soldier from a noble line, but he was also a man who loved women. They were his weakness. He could not stop thinking of the girl who had tried to kill him. She had a mystical quality, like the Blessed Virgin. He sensed a vicious determination in her, too. Could she really have opened the earth which swallowed three of his men? Never had the General felt more lonely. Or afraid. He fell to his knees. Holy Mother of God, I need your help if I am to survive in this god-forsaken wilderness. Send me the glowing girl before the next full moonrise so that I may teach her the fine points of civilization.

Coronado sent a detachment of men east to Arenal, to check the padre's story of gold. At the head of the main army, he rode west to the Tusayan pueblos of Arizona and the Grand Canyon. The spectacular land moved him to tears, but the poor mud villages of the Hopi yielded no treasure. Quivira was not there, either. Everywhere he went, the beautiful face of Sayah followed, as haunting as the image of Our Lady of Sorrows that Fray Marcos carried along on a gently furling banner. Everywhere he went, he killed the natives who opposed him. With sword and crossbow and arquebus, he killed them. He knew, by now, that killing pagans was not a sin.

The Office of the Holy Inquisition was behind him.

CHAPTER

Twenty—five

*T*he ancient footpath along the river had been
worn into the earth by a slow nation of turtles,
who had climbed up the steep embankment and
made their way, heads held high, toward Arenal. After turtles came
ants, then lizards. Deer followed, then coyotes, rabbits, and foxes. But
turtles had been the first, and so the path was named *Hehy ty-tsitetphy*,
for them. Many generations of turtles followed, taking their slow,
sweet time, withdrawing into their shell houses at the first sign of danger. The turtle path was the one every child from the Seven Wise Villages knew from infancy; Sayah remembered taking her first steps
there, with the turtles watching.

Now she hurried along the same path toward home. The events at
Hawikuh had unnerved her completely. She could not reverse the flow
of history, could not give them back what they had lost, nor prepare
them for the future. She who had created beauty and order and balance created nothing here on Earth. I will teach them magic, she

thought. The dead will live and the living will become invisible in their sacredness. She rounded a bend where several turtles were sleeping. They woke up long enough to share their thoughts. There in the distance was Arenal. Smoke curled from the chimneys. Dogs barked faintly. She drew in her breath. Coronado's army was already there, camped in the cottonwood grove. She saw their banners flying. Tents dotted the meadow. The soldiers were making a great commotion. She ran faster. In her womb was a tiny Being, no bigger than one of the corn seeds she wore in her hair. In less than eight moons, the child would know the Earth. She wanted to give birth at Arenal, among people she loved. Elk Heart. Dawn Giver. High Cloud. Bird Wing. Sun Mountain Shining. One Fist. Deer-He-Becomes. She had missed them. Hurry, she called to the Grandmothers and to Kobili, who had stopped to talk to the fish. She could not get there fast enough.

Kobili ran along on his new, youthful legs. What will we find, Brother Macaw? Moctezuma said test the wind, the bird replied. He did it with doves. If the enemy came from the East, the dove brought back a tiny shell. From the West, an ear of red corn. From the North, a piece of walrus tusk. From the South, the serpent's tongue. Test the wind, Old Man.

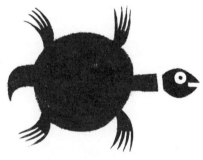

The shaman looked ahead. I do not need to test the wind, he said.

Out of breath, her mouth dry, Sayah pressed against a tree, watching the army. They had the air of conquerors. Fast horses. Heavy armor. Deadly weapons. The soldiers themselves, trained in a kind of warfare that the Clay People would be helpless against. She squinted. Three warriors from Arenal slipped among them, speaking the language of horses, until at last one of the creatures followed them to the river. Then another and another. Sayah watched her people stealing horses, and she smiled. But then One-Eared-Gopher was caught by a guard who ran him through with the point of his lance. He fell with a moan. Kobili touched her elbow. Arenal is stronger than

Hawikuh, he said. More people. More weapons. They will fight for the village. They will not give in. She turned to him. Her cheeks were streaked with tears. How do you know? You have been wrong about many things. She ran over the hard earth. Pebbles cut into her feet through her moccasins.

The village dogs were speaking their frantic canine language. They had seen the Spanish war dogs, restrained on strong leather leashes by eager guardsmen. The village dogs did not like the foreign ones. Saliva ran from their mouths. Incisors bared. Ears laid back. Killer eyes. In one gulp the war dogs devoured a cowering village dog. A hapless rabbit. A baby carelessly left hanging on a tree branch in her cradleboard. The dogs of Arenal slunk off. They were not popular dogs, alternately beaten and praised by the villagers, but they had grown accustomed to their fate. Scraps of food hurled at them and an occasional bone when they sounded the alarm at the coming of enemies made life worthwhile. Using their extraordinary senses, the village dogs had detected the royal army long before it arrived. They had tried to tell their masters. Their reward was a kick in the stomach. If we can sink our teeth into one of these soldiers, it will be worth it, the village dogs said.

The kiva drums kept up a steady beat. Women hurried back and forth to the river, water jugs on top of their heads, seemingly unconcerned, but their movements were nervous. The Memorizers stood on the rooftops telling warriors to prepare their poison arrows. They were determined not to let the soldiers bother them. Four days had passed, and there had been no sign of trouble. A supply of new arrowheads and spear points was ready. Lengths of deer sinew were stretched low between two trees to trip the horses. Sun Mountain Shining sang his Death Song in his high-pitched voice. He had had a dream his people were floating in the river, bleeding out their ancestral blood. He put his ear to the floor. The sleeping locusts say they are ready, he said. He painted his face. He had one great battle left in him.

Coronado's army waited. Where was the captain? We must have food. Warm clothing. We are freezing to death. Our balls have turned blue. The padre shivered. He would rather freeze than complain. See here, Maldonado, he said to the captain, I insist on baptizing these natives now, when they are quiet. Go to the devil, the captain said.

Above the village the shaman stood beside Sayah. Do not go down there, he said. I will go first and come back for you. He turned himself into a mouse and scurried among the soldiers, listening to everything that was being said. He jumped on the back of the captain's saddle and heard him say to his men, we want meat and clothing. If they resist, kill them. Those are the General's orders. The horsemen raised their faces to the cold, gray sky and crossed themselves. Then the visors on the sallets went down. The lances became horizontal. The soldiers of his Holy Catholic Cesarian Majesty fell into two lines, spreading halfway around the wall. There was a terrifying urgency to them.

Elk Heart walked bravely toward the advancing captain, armed only with his war club. He forced himself to smile and extend his right arm in greeting. He was dressed in an ermine robe, a magnificent plumed headdress of cardinal feathers and eagle bones. Welcome, the chief said. He did not trust these metal-covered Spaniards, yet what could he do against so many? The army swept past him and surged into the plaza. The warriors of Arenal reached up to touch the magical, long-toothed horses. They flung their bows to the ground. For such animals they would trade anything. They looked around, trying to decide which of their women they would give up. Feather Keeper hunched his shoulders and did a little dance to impress the horse. Everyone laughed. The tension was momentarily broken.

The captain was not amused. The visor was down on his sallet, giving him an insect look. Leave your village, he said to the chieftain, so that we may occupy it for the winter. The main army is not here yet. When they arrive, they will need shelter and special quarters for the General. Go now, before we change our minds and kill you. He said this in a pleasant, scarcely audible voice. Elk Heart bent his head to hear what the translator said. You cannot have our homes, the chief said. We will show you how to build your own. A lanceman struck him on the side of the head, and he fell to the ground in pain. A war dog rushed to open his throat, but with one blow of his war club, Elk Heart killed it.

CHAPTER

Twenty-six

ayah slipped into the plaza and ran toward the terrified Clay People. They had the diminished look of refugees. With their useless stone weapons clutched tightly in their fists, they recognized the inevitable. The captain watched, trying to decide who among them wore the warmest clothing. The old man in his fur parka? The warrior in his beaver hat with flaps? The bowlegged man with a rabbit-skin robe wrapped around his frail shoulders? Maldonado conferred with his men. Sayah moved among her people, whispering encouragement, repeating the names of ancestors and sacred animals. She took slivers of the star pieces from her eyes and folded them into their hands. Shifting from one cold foot to the other, Sun Mountain Shining said, I say we kill them. He had twelve sharp arrows in his quiver. His arm was strong. He was certain his arrows could penetrate the metal suits. If you make war on them, Sayah said, the blood of our people will flow as deep as the river. I will not die a coward, the old man said.

High Cloud held a small boy by the hand. Send them away, dear Sister, she said. I will give you strength, Sayah said, looking into the frightened eyes of her friend. An infantryman pulled High Cloud toward him. He sought her mouth with his. She dug into his cheek with her fingers. He pushed her beneath the hooves of a galloping horse. Sayah pulled her bloody body from the ground up and gave it to the Grandmothers. Give her life, she said.

The captain shouted an order. Gunfire blasted through the air. People fled in terror, many falling, mortally wounded. The first to die was Snake Eyes, who happened to be walking across the plaza, thinking about the battles of his youth. That was a warning, the captain shouted. He glanced around with demented eyes. Line up and give us your clothing. You with the rabbit-fur shawl first. You with the fur parka next. The soldiers seized the warriors and pinned them to the ground. They tore the buckskin shirts from Feather Keeper, Blue Water, Flute Singer, Brave Bear, though each man fought mightily to keep from becoming naked. Sun Mountain Shining was stripped of his ceremonial furs, the ermine and red fox that befitted his position. His flesh turned blue. His wives ran out with a blanket but that too was confiscated. One Fist and Lizard-Goes-Forth ran to the tunnel they had dug into the riverbank and burrowed in with the hibernating moles.

Elk Heart gave nothing until he had to. By then, one eye was swollen shut from the beating he had received. His arrows and his war club were yanked from his hand, his ermine robe was stripped from his back. Except for a loincloth, his well-muscled body was naked. He shivered, bleeding from many places. He could scarcely stand up. Sayah ran to him and threw her arms around him. Dear Father, she wept, tending to his wounds. She gave him a shirt made of rabbit fur that she had made herself. Now you will be warm, she said, as he tried to comprehend the terrible scene before him. Naked men and women. Shrieking children. But then he saw Buffalo, Bear, Coyote, Wolf, and Lion coming toward him. The furry animals lay beside the naked people and warmed them. The captain teetered precariously in his saddle. Kill the animals, he roared.

The arquebuses would not fire. The crossbows fell uselessly to the ground. The lances flew off on their own, over the walls of Arenal, and fell on a family of turkeys scurrying to escape. As the soldiers retreated, the people fled to their homes. They drew their ladders up and rummaged through their bundles to see what medicines would force the enemy from their village. Turn them into stones, they begged Sayah. She held them in her arms and reminded them of their origins.

I made the Star People to give you courage. Remember? Sometimes, a star fell to the ground, they said. It became an ally. From a star I made a woman, she said. What of mountains? they said. I pushed mountains out of the deepest part of the earth. They are its backbone.

Macaw, resting on a ledge in the room, became thoughtful. Moctezuma wanted a smart and beautiful bird, he said. So Sayah made me. The people laughed through their tears. The bird had wisdom almost as great as a man's.

Kobili appeared out of the smoke. I made Earth, he said. From the marrow of my bones, I made it. Earth was so hot, nothing lived. Then Thunderwoman and I sent rain. I came up with lightning, and she made thunder, from which she took her name. For ten thousand years, it rained. Then Turtle poked his head out of the water, looking for dry land. He climbed out. His mate was already there, so they made a turtle family.

What about the Fish People? a woman asked.

Kobili looked at Sayah. Ah, that's where we disagreed. After she left, I made those Fish People myself. Put them in an Underground lake until they learned to live in the dark. Then I made a giant cornstalk that reached up through a hole. The Fish People shed their fins and tails and fish scales. They developed arms and legs and heads. They climbed out. They found their way to Arenal. The Six Grandmothers made a cornmeal path. Everything was in harmony, then.

An old man spoke up, reverently. Our Creators are here among us. It is a great honor. All this time we thought you were our chief shaman. The Clay People gathered closer. They drank the Elixir of Dreams and beat their drums and sang their songs. Tell us more, they said.

CHAPTER

Twenty–seven

The Spaniards regrouped in the cottonwood grove. Their food supply was running low. Take what you need from the miserable Indians, the captain said, bitterly. Nothing would be easy from now on. Storerooms were soon emptied of grain. The fresh carcass of a deer was ripped from a ceiling beam, roasted, and eaten by the officers while the enlisted men ate a thin corn gruel. The soldiers did unspeakable things while they waited for the General. Blue Duck complained to the captain that his youngest wife had been raped by a soldier who owned three horses, one coat of mail, one buckskin coat, and pieces of armor. Maldonado was busy writing a report. Find him and I will kill him myself, he said. But Blue Duck took care of this soldier in his own way and rolled the body into the river.

The Aztec slaves, sick and starving, blew the conch shell. It meant that deep inside the earth, new life was forming, as it had in Tenochtitlan, where their slaughtered relatives were already fat ears of corn.

Sayah and Kobili gathered their people under the stars. The night was very cold and clear. The Star Beings looked down. You cannot save us, can you? the Clay People said. No, Kobili said. Life must follow its given path. Do not fear death, Sayah said. It comes as a friend. She wrapped the Thread around their shoulders, then went to her old house and blessed the place where No Name had died. It was filled with bluebirds.

One blustery afternoon the General rode into the village in glittering splendor, flanked by his silken banners and his entourage. There was an unnatural inflexibility to him, a stiff-legged demeanor that made the people laugh. He asked about the girl he desired greatly. Her eyes glow like stars, he said to some women. Upon her cheek is an animal mark. The women told him nothing. The General ordered the village turned upside down. But Sayah came to him on her own. His heart nearly stopped. He had not forgotten her beauty! Her sparkling eyes. Her ethereal quality. He would give her a horse. A mandolin. A fine tapestry. He went into his tent and motioned her to follow. She was close enough for him to touch her skin, as soft as the blue velvet jacket he had brought along to celebrate his imminent victory. What is your name? he whispered. The translator stood nervously in the shadows, sensing that something momentous was happening.

I am known as Sayah, she said. Her black hair shone.

An interesting name, Coronado said. I have thought of you often.

I do not think of you at all.

I bring peace to your village. Where is the gold?

I have never seen gold, she said.

He reached into a pouch and took out a moth-eaten velvet-covered box. Inside was a golden necklace taken from Moctezuma's palace. He draped it around her neck. This is gold, he said. Is it not beautiful? Fit for a queen, which you will become. He touched her skin.

She ripped the necklace off and threw it to the floor. Take your gold, General. And leave our village. We have nothing of use to you here. The General examined his carefully trimmed nails. Much is of use to me here. He caught her by the wrist. I can make a slave of you, you stubborn girl. I can sell you in Mexico or keep you for myself. Either way, you will obey me. The General stared. He no longer had hold of Sayah's wrist, but a dead mouse. He flung it into a corner and screamed for his captain.

The faithful Maldonado stood, his legs slightly apart. Because we are good soldiers, the General said, we will give them an opportunity to surrender. History will judge us fairly, Maldonado. We must not appear to be harsh or unjust. He unfolded his bold plan. The captain gasped. Coronado smiled. Why are you shocked? It is the Holy Inquisition. I am within my rights, as decreed by the Holy Father in Rome. Give the men their orders. Ask the padres to set up a field confessional. We must prepare ourselves according to the articles of war. Maldonado went out of the tent and told the padres, who said, It is the will of God.

As night fell, the soldiers clinked their great roweled spurs and asked forgiveness for their sins. The padres had improvised confessionals out of canvas and tree limbs. They shivered in the bone-cutting cold as they listened to the men confess to stealing, swearing, bestiality, fornication with Indian women, with one another, with themselves. Hardship did that to men. *Martyrs non facit poena sed causa.* Not the punishment but the cause makes the martyr, the padres said as they granted absolution. A deadly black widow spider, unnoticed in the shadows, crawled deliberately, first one place, then another. She bit one soldier on his hand, another on his leg, another on his private parts, so he would not be able to use them again. The man was the one who had violated an Indian maiden. Another victim was the younger priest, whose leg expanded to twice its normal size. Blood streamed from his pores. He breathed his last into the ear of a lieutenant from Seville, then fell on top of the crucifix and died.

CHAPTER

Twenty-eight

obili looked older now, not like the young man
Sayah had married earlier, but like the ageless
shaman he still was. As the Sun Father waited
for the Bear Twins to shove him into the sky, Kobili appeared on the
highest rooftop, where he used to live, decked out in an antler headdress and a white fur robe. He raised his arms to the East. Give us
strength, oh, life-giving Sun Father, mighty and forever, who alone
has power over food and animals and birds, he chanted. For what
is about to unfold, prepare us. Blind our enemies. Let corn grow now
in winter so we will have something to eat. He sprinkled his medicines
in every part of the village, singing his ancient, reassuring songs.
The Clay People followed him, silently. He will not let us die, they
said.

In the plaza, the freshly absolved General was arguing with ancestry. Surrender, he pleaded with Elk Heart, and no harm will come to
you. This is your last chance. The chieftain touched the General's

horse, his armor, his splendid sword. First you must give me this horse, said Elk Heart.

I will give you a horse, the General said. But you must surrender first.

We surrender nothing. You are the ones who must surrender. You can start by giving me this fine horse. For two hours the argument continued. Then the General returned to his mounted column and said something to them. One horseman after another detached from the column and formed a circle around the village, alive with shouts and warnings and incantations. The ladders were drawn up. Roof openings covered. From the small windows, spears protruded. Warriors placed poison arrows in their bows and drew back their bowstrings. Others were ready with war clubs and scalping knives. Sayah helped the women gather grinding stones and pile them on the rooftops. They would hurl them down on those enemy heads and crush them. They would help themselves to the fine metal clothing the conquistadors wore and check inside them for fleas.

We can do it, Sayah said, taking up her bow and extracting from her quiver a poison arrow made from rattlesnake venom. Then she tried to do what she had always done as an abiding force in the Universe. Her gaze, always so powerful before, failed to move anything, even when she willed a cavalryman out of his saddle or a boulder from the riverbank. Because she had come to earth as a human, she *was* human. She feared it would destroy her. She took a deep breath and aimed her arrow at a soldier who was violating a woman against the side of her house. The arrow struck where she intended. The soldier fell, mortally wounded. Sayah moved on. Another soldier ran toward the General. In his fist he carried the gold coins the children of Arenal had thrown into the corners of their houses years before, when they had dropped from the sack the traders brought from Mexico. Look, he said, and poured the coins into the General's open palm. From over there, General. Suddenly, Coronado knew what he must do. He gave the order for full-scale attack.

The siege of Arenal lasted fifty days. Finally, thirty warriors threw their weapons down and hid in a well. It collapsed on top of them. Others ran to the river and jumped in through the ice. Arenal was destroyed. The wounded staggered forth. And stared. Coronado's men were driving stakes into the middle of the plaza. Around the base they put armloads of dry grass and kindling on top of that. They dragged big logs up from the river and chopped them into smaller sizes. With their knives they cut leather into strips.

Now, the General said, we shall see who is master.

CHAPTER

Twenty-nine

Absolution and memory collided along the Great River that cold winter day, when the Sun Father stopped on his journey across the sky and went back down again. Something ancient yielded to something new that would defy comprehension, though history would soften the edges a little as time went on. People screamed as flames devoured them. They absorbed memories of corn tassels and bluebirds, the silvery tongue of the river, the magical shapes of clouds, the happy expression of children, and the flower-petal skin of women. Some managed to sing a few words of the Yellow Corn song. The people of Arenal released their breath with a great *whoosh*ing sound. They fixed the expressions of their executioners in their memories. We will never forget you, they said.

Relatives of the burning ones, terrified to the roots of their being, called upon the sacred spirits of their religion. Where was Bear Brother? Eagle Father? The Corn Mother? They groped toward

Sayah, who moved swiftly among them. Some of the relatives shot arrows at the soldiers. They pelted them with rocks. Women hurled their grinding stones. Children wandered about aimlessly, screaming with the hysteria of the doomed.

Around the rows of charred bodies another group waited, tied together with stout cords. They looked at the earth and saw all that had happened there: the gray, cooling ash that fell in the Beginning Time. The salty sea that had washed over it. Unborn mountains, deciding where to rise up from the backbone of the buffalo. Infinite generations of people sprouted before their eyes as cornstalks. They saw the sweat of their endurance. The blood of defiance. Tears of loss and tears of happiness. Rain falling into seeds. Sun blessing the Earth with goodness. Footsteps going on. The Thunderbeings created us, they said. They will help us die. The tied-together people sang of wondrous things, even as their turn came and they were tied to fresh stakes and the fires were rekindled with fragrant juniper which they themselves had cut for their executions. They sang their final songs and said good-bye to the world of spirits.

One of these martyrs was Elk Heart, with a gaping lance wound in his left side. Pain consumed him as two soldiers tied him to a stake and lit the brush at his feet. He looked around at everything he held dear and tried to move his bound arms to embrace the world. He looked up. There was his beloved daughter. With her knife she slashed at the cords that bound him. Father, she cried as she set him free. Elk Heart toppled to the ground. She pressed her face to his. No breath came out. Kobili laid a gentle hand on her shoulder.

A young infantryman bent over to light the brush under Sun Mountain Shining, dragged from his house, where he had spent his last hours praying to his fetishes. The soldier wore no armor, only the hide shirt he had ripped from a warrior's back. With a deep cry, Sayah cut through the hide and parted his ribs in two. Soon he breathed no more. Come, Grandfather, she said, but Sun Mountain Shining was already dead.

Through the smoke the General saw the girl who called herself Sayah kill one of his best soldiers. He drew his sword and spurred his horse. He would cut off her head and impale it on a stick. But she quickly vanished in the smoke. The cries of Coronado echoed across the plaza. Find her, he shouted. He felt foolish having lost his heart to an Indian girl when he had a wife at home.

Sayah embraced her childhood friend, Dawn Giver, writhing in the orange-colored flames. Smoke enveloped Dawn Giver like an anesthetic. Her tattered dress burned slowly. Bluish smoke poured from it. Dawn Giver looked down at her flaming moccasins. Her head fell to one side. Her swollen lips parted. Remember when we gathered green willows along the river? she whispered. Our grandmothers taught us to make baskets.

Take this with you, Sayah said and inserted a sliver of star piece in her eyes. You will bring light to the next generation. That's how our people will survive. Remember my name, Dawn Giver whispered. Then the flames devoured her.

Sayah embraced Bird Wing and High Cloud, who broke the stout cords that bound them to the stakes. They held one another's hands tightly. We taught you how to make pottery, they said. We gave you a brush made of yucca and showed you how to decorate your bowls. Remember our names, they cried as flames tore into their dresses.

Sayah moved between the rows, choking on the smell of charred flesh and human hair. Blue Cedar, the War Chief, with his tattooed arms and pierced ears, raised his head and sang his way to the Underworld. He was clad in a ragged cloth that covered his private parts. With a hoarse cry, Blue Cedar turned his head. His smoke-filled eyes fell on Sayah. You brought my son home from the dead. Blessings on you, Daughter. Remember my name.

Snow Bird was barely alive. Smoke poured from her mouth. Her flesh fell away in pieces. Sayah kissed her. Dear Sister, she said. In you lie the seeds of the next world. Snow Bird tried to reach out. Remember my name, she said.

Sayah looked around. A young infantryman, who had stepped out of his breeches that morning long enough to spend his passion on a woman named Bent Twig, leaned forward. In the palm of his hand lay a piece of silver. He had won the bet that Snake Eyes would die first, then Blue Cedar, and after him, Seven Trees. With this money he would buy Bent Twig from among the Indian women captured today. She was beautiful. With her he would sleep better. He would bathe every month or so. He would beat her regularly, and when he grew tired of her company, he would kill her. He was thinking of Bent Twig's dark, liquid eyes when all at once he felt an arrow in his back. Looking down, he saw that it emerged on the left-hand side of his jacket, where his heart was.

Sayah stood in the midst of the rows of burning people and the dense, acrid smoke, quite close to the flames herself. The bow that Elk Heart had given her was in her hands. The quiver of poison arrows was empty. Her dress was spattered with blood. She dropped her bow. Kobili moved swiftly toward her and led her through the carnage. Macaw trembled in terror. His eyes were glassy. The bird feared he would be roasted in a human bonfire. The shaman patted him, then put him inside his shirt with his tail feathers hanging out. I accept this woman called Sayah, he thought. Times are different now. She has become a woman warrior. Come rest awhile, Kobili said. She shook her head. I cannot rest, she said. These are my people. For them, the world has ended.

Suddenly, the Whirlwind People ripped across the plaza and created a thick dust storm. No one could see more than an arm's length. A foot soldier from Granada, busy tying a warrior to a stake, felt a hot knife slice his neck apart. He ran through the dust and smoke into a rain of arrows that came from the part of the village that was still occupied. The Whirlwind People gathered intensity, sucking up dirt and small pebbles, ash and cactus spines. They hurled them at the

Spaniards, who fell backward into the dirt. We are blinded, they cried, rubbing their eyes. The Whirlwind People suffocated the fires and tried to revive their dead. They cooled the charred flesh of whole families. The Cloud People sent rain to wash the sullied earth clean. When the smoke and dust cleared, Eagle dipped lower for a better view. So did Hawk. The scene was worth telling about. They flew over the land with their stories. Badger, hiding in terror, emerged from a hole and shambled eastward. He had a different story to tell.

The friar could not stand the stench of burning flesh, so he had waited inside his tent. Now, as he watched the flames hiss and go out, he stirred uneasily. He wiped his lips with his sleeve, fighting nausea. He fell back against a supply wagon the Indians had set afire, tripping over a dead horse. Three dead infantrymen lay on the muddy ground. He uncorked a flask of holy water and knelt down to administer last rites. *Barbarus hic ego sum, quia non intelligor ulli,* he said wearily. Here, I am a barbarian, understood by nobody.

The Six Grandmothers were exhausted. Never did they dream of such carnage. Two hundred people had been burned at the stake. People they knew and loved. The Grandmother-from-the-West ran toward the smoke. She would comfort those still alive. The other five soon followed. They took out their sacks of cornmeal, pollen, and sage. They had bird's eggs and corn tassels, corn seeds, feathers, and fish scales. As the old women went about their work, the soldiers observed six white doves flying gracefully through the air. Kobili sprinkled his medicines on the dead and dying, singing softly to comfort their departing spirits. He went around the blood-soaked plaza, where the fires of human flesh still sizzled. He gathered up the unfinished stories drifting in the air and left some of his own. Sayah watched as if in a trance. When she went to bury Elk Heart, all she found was a pile of stones where his body had been lying. She laid the alabaster deer head on top of them.

CHAPTER

Thirty

$\mathcal{T}$he General and the padre had become allies, aligned in common purpose. All those months of deprivation, they had been at odds, the padre in search of souls, the General in search of gold. There was something else now. Indisputable authority. They would make an example of these rebels. Word would spread. By the time they reached Quivira, there would be no resistance. The General mounted his horse, refreshed from a sound night's sleep, a bath, and a change of underwear. He knew his men admired him; they would not desert, though many had voiced strong opposition to the burnings. He had not been able to find the girl again, but no matter. He had a final job to do. Proceed, he ordered. His fine metal suit glittered in the sun.

Twenty exhausted soldiers dragged six protesting warriors into the plaza. These were the final rebels who had eluded capture by hiding in the hills, subsisting on bark and roots. One Fist and Lizard-

Goes-Forth had been dragged from their hole along the river. The General's men had finally caught them. Forced to their knees before the heavy cross, hands tied behind their backs, the warriors looked to the sky and drew deep breaths. Beloved Sun Father, they prayed, make our journey swift and painless.

Behind them stood the General's hand-picked executioners. *Gloria tibi, Domine*, the friar said as, one after another, the warriors were beheaded. From their necks a gurgling sound arose. Swords dripping, the soldiers drew back. The severed heads lay on the ground, staring at them with shocked expressions. The war dogs surged, restrained by the leashes that tethered them to their masters. The warriors' eyes were as bright as when still alive. Their stiff lips moved: *Upon you and all your children, we leave a curse.* The soldiers gasped. *You have swords, but you will never kill us*, said Lizard-Goes-Forth. Exhausted from the ordeal, the soldiers crossed themselves. Nothing had prepared them for such a sick feeling in their stomachs. *Mea mihi conscientia pluris est quam omnium sermo*, the Portuguese soldier wept. My own conscience is more to me than what the world says. No more than seventeen years old, with yellow fuzz where whiskers should have been, he dropped his bloody sword and began to run, despite threats to shoot him. Into the night he ran, and all the next day, until he reached a northern village, where he spent the rest of his life with a native woman twice his age, who protected him from nightmares from then on.

The friar knelt on the soggy earth, careful to avoid the coagulating blood, wondering which part of the bodies to baptize first. Thought and reason were contained in the head, so he blessed the severed heads, one at a time. They glared at him. They sounded like fish when they spoke. *Water does not make us share your beliefs*, One Fist said. The padre gave him final absolution anyway, trying not to look at those accusatory eyes. *Sui cuique fingunt fortunam*, he said. Character fashions fate. When he finished, he struggled to his feet. Are they

Catholics? the General asked. He wanted the record to show his compassion.

They are, the friar said. Bound for heaven at this very moment. The General put his hand to his mouth. If they do not have souls, as you suggested to me at Hawikuh, how can they be in heaven? The padre shrugged. All is possible under God, he said.

Suddenly, the bloody heads began to roll across the plaza. They bumped against a mud wall and lay there, looking out, eyes like hot coals. They were trying to speak. Bury them, the friar shrieked, lifting the edge of his long blue robe as he hastened away. The soldiers were immobilized. Bury them! the General commanded, wondering how the incident would look on his record. The soldiers sat, dumbfounded, in their saddles, staring at the heads, who stared back.

Very well, the friar said, I will do it myself. He asked for a shovel and began to dig. He dug and dug, but the ground was frozen, and all his efforts yielded one small hole. It will have to do, the padre said. Gathering his skirts in one hand, he chased the rolling heads from one end of the plaza to another. Back and forth he went, but the heads eluded him. He heard the General laughing. Then a number of his men. It is God's punishment, General, he said as the heads glared at him from the far end of the plaza. He threw the shovel to the ground.

The heads, as impudent as thieves, rolled away from the village, across the hard red earth. A young lieutenant mounted his horse and rode after them. Six human heads were not hard to keep track of, eyes staring blankly as they rolled, black hair gathering dirt and pebbles. He drew his sword. He would skewer them one at a time. The heads rolled down an arroyo, faster and faster. He rode hard, but he could not catch up. The heads bumped up one mesa and down the other side. The lieutenant galloped after them, but after a while he lost sight of his quarry. The heads rolled on. They had a long way to go before they reached their destination.

In the shelter of a yawning cave along the frozen river, Sayah wept herself dry. The Grandmother-from-the-East rocked her gently back and forth. Spring will come before long, Sayah, she said. You'll see. For me, there will be no spring, Sayah said. The Grandmothers stripped away her clothing and rubbed her all over with sage and tobacco so the spirits of those she had killed would not enter her body and kill the son she was carrying. The baby was beginning to grow. They could see the outline of him through her skin. Arms. Legs. Head. A tiny body attached to the long umbilical cord.

Coyote licked her hand. Do not be sad, he said. New life comes out of the old. Raven sat on a log, warming himself by the fire. A few people survived at Arenal, he said. They are getting ready to migrate to the west. Already, there are stories of you. Sayah was not comforted.

The wind howled a mournful, defeated song. Sayah moved closer to the fire. They are men without hearts, she said. Do you know what

Dawn Giver said as she died? The look on the Sun Mountain's face! She wept so hard that her tears flowed out into the snow and made an enormous ice crystal. When she was cleansed and dressed, Kobili embraced her.

Tears will not bring our people back, he said. Long ago, your tears made stars. You will not make any more stars, Sayah. This is the beginning of a new circle, one we must accept. She looked at him. I cannot accept what I have just seen. Our people are dead. Our village is destroyed. I thought we had the power to prevent such things. Kobili shook his head. Our power is different now, Sayah. He took her hands in his. In the Beginning Time, we created many aspects of life. Lessons are in everything. Pain is part of the lesson. Also death.

I remember when nothing died, she said.

Ah, but it did. Stars died. New stars were born. Animals died. Others came along. The shaman walked to the opening of the cave and looked out. There are Two Worlds of Being, he said. One dark. One light. One teaches. The other destroys. People have to choose. Sayah stood beside him. Elk Heart died in my arms, she said.

You will see him, Kobili said soothingly. You will see everyone.

How?

Because you believe you will.

When?

When the times comes. He looked at her. Everything changes. Nothing changes.

Sayah covered her face. I am no longer the woman who holds up her half of the sky.

You are, you are, the Grandmothers said in a chorus. Women must learn to be warriors. They made crooning sounds the way they used to, when Sayah was small. Rest awhile, they said. Then we will go to the next place. People are waiting for you there.

I dream of the dead children, she said. I see their faces.

They are not dead, the Six Grandmothers said. Believe us.

Macaw spoke up. There was a battle before the last battle, he said. La Noche Triste. Women drove the Spaniards out. Killed them and piled their bodies up. Took their swords. Their clothes. Locks of their pale hair. Metal hats. Leather boots. Women outfitted themselves like men. I could not believe the things I saw.

Sayah smiled. Macaw always made her feel better.

In the morning, Kobili lifted Sayah onto the back of a wondrous creature he had stolen at Arenal. It was the General's horse. The shaman called him Horse. He was white with black glassy eyes that he rolled around so he could take in much of the landscape at a single glance. The saddle with its high-rolled cantle and dangling stirrups was uncomfortable. But by making himself part of Horse, Kobili was able to anticipate what he would do next, when he would turn, when he would run, when he would jump an arroyo. Kobili loved everything about him. His long braided tail. His sleek, strong legs. His long back, capable of carrying two people at once. The way he blew through his nostrils, but most of all, his great speed. At night, when they were resting, Horse spoke of how he had survived a long journey across the ocean in a stinking cargo ship loaded with other creatures. Sheep. Goats. Cattle. Civilization is the coming thing, Horse said. No one will be able to resist it. Macaw disagreed. I can resist civilization. It will do nothing for me.

I do not like the looks of civilization, either, the shaman said. He connected Horse with a new world he only dimly understood. He would fight this world forever. Now as they sped along, Sayah cling-ing to his waist, the shaman thought he could accept so much of civilization and no more. Where did the the spirits of those dead children go? she asked.

I turned the children into hummingbirds, the shaman said as Horse jumped gracefully across an arroyo. He pulled on the reins to make him slow down. Sayah hung on, watching the earth spin past. Macaw dug his talons between Horse's pointed ears, trying not to fall off. I changed the dead women into butterflies, the shaman said. The men are Four-Legged Animals. See, there is one already. He pointed to a deer nibbling the dry grass. Blue Cedar, my old friend. He greeted him warmly.

Sayah felt as if she'd died with her people. She rested her head on Kobili's strong back. She was as old as the universe, but the universe had not prepared her for such misery. There are too many soldiers for us to kill, she said. What shall we do?

There is another way, Kobili said. Several ways, the Grandmothers said. Coyote said, I too have a plan. Macaw said, Moctezuma knew how to make the enemy think you're dead. First, you stretch out on the ground. Learn not to breathe. Close your eyes. Lie still. When the enemy goes by, grab him by the ankles and take a bite. He will bleed to death.

They pushed northward until they reached a sprawling village where Kobili had friends and where Coyote and Raven had children and grandchildren. The Grandmothers saw there was plenty to do at Cicuye, a fortresslike village that lay between plains and mountains, beside a river. They were welcomed warmly and given rooms on the upper floor. News of the fall of Arenal had reached the village. The chief spent seven nights listening to his guests tell about it; he examined the drawings Kobili made in the dirt; he heard Sayah's lament as a woman who loved children. During the festivities of the summer solstice, she was inducted into the Bow Society and given special arrows and a bow inlaid with turquoise. Her brave deeds were recounted and turned into legends that would be passed down.

They have come to fulfill our prophecy, the people of Cicuye said. As her time to give birth drew near, the Bird Women made Sayah a bed of softest goose down and found a star she was familiar with and brought it down with a yucca-fiber rope. There, they said, now you can rest until your time comes. The Sign of the Jaguar was blazing on her cheek. Sayah lay down, exhausted, wondering what had happened to Coronado and his men.

CHAPTER

Thirty-two

On the wind-lashed plains, the four principal chiefs of Quivira sat in their houses, listening to the tale of Raven, who had arrived with a piece of charred clothing in his beak as proof of what had happened at Arenal. From high above, through a blanket of falling snow, he had witnessed the destruction of the Seven Wise Villages, where members of his own family once lived. People were burned alive, Raven said. Their blood froze into ropes. The ropes became circles. The circles became new trees. You know how it is.

The chiefs nodded. In their country, slaughtered warriors became buffalo and the greatest among them became a sacred White Buffalo, though one had not been seen for many years. We felt the wind with our fingers, the chiefs said. It was thick with pain.

Coyote and I wrapped the dead warriors in blankets and dragged them to the river, Raven said. They became rocks. Some turned into fish.

The chiefs nodded. We have had our visions, they said. Men with pale skin are coming. The Father Sun will turn black before it ends. Is it true, Brother Raven? Raven had gazed into the powerful eye of the Sun all his life. He was not afraid of it. The Father Sun went back to its home, Raven said. Far beneath the Earth. It stayed there for a while. He moved closer. The enemy rides huge beasts called horses, he said. Four legs. Long tails. The enemy carries long firesticks that kill from a great distance. Everyone was killed. Some were burned alive.

The chiefs thanked Raven for his news and watched him disappear into a snowy sky. The plains chiefs had a belief in the natural order of life and in the balance necessary to connect people to animals. From the vast, rolling land, they summoned visions when they needed to. They cried for a vision and, at last, one came. It was of a single long tooth on which was impaled all the people of their tribe. What does it mean? they said. One of the scouts, named Gifted Buffalo, offered his own report. He had been gone for many moons, observing everything that Coronado's army did. He had hidden in the granary at Arenal and watched the spectacle unfold.

The day of understanding is past, Gifted Buffalo said. He carried a small drum, which had belonged to Elk Heart, and he began to beat it and to sing some of the songs he had learned on his journey. Gifted Buffalo also had picked up a small wooden cross from the ground, where the friar had dropped it. The four chiefs of Quivira examined it carefully. Their sacred symbol was the circle, which united and combined all the tribes everywhere on Earth. But this cross was a symbol of separation, a map of the four directions, which were never united. The chiefs had their answer. They would split into four groups and follow those four sacred directions. They set out through the tall grass with all of their bearers and women and children with them. Each headman went in a different direction, taking with him the powerful medicines of his clan.

The chief who had gone West was watching the returning meadowlarks and snow geese and cranes that spring when the General came riding through the tall grass with his men. The chief stopped to look at him, resplendent in his suit of armor and plumed helmet from which the dents of Hawikuh and Tiguex had been hammered out. The chief fell to his knees in front of the mighty horse. Gold, the chief said, puzzled. What means gold? I have never heard of King Tatarrax either. *I* am Chief of Quivira. You will pay homage to me. His mouth watered at the sight of the beautiful horses running through the tall grass. They were of every color, with long teeth and big heads, faster than the mighty buffalo. A horse could make him stronger, braver, and more feared than any other warrior on the plains. What did he have to do to obtain one? At first he offered a buffalo robe. The General shook his head. You know what I desire, he said. The visor was down on his sallet.

The interpreter stepped forward and read the Requerimiento.

 By now he read with much more confidence than at Hawikuh. Give us everything you have, he said. If you do not, we will kill you. We will steal your women and children and make slaves of them. They will never see their homeland again. It is the will of God. The interpreter looked around. The full army had not come. Some had stayed at Cicuye, others remained at Arenal, awaiting orders.

The padre erected a heavy wooden cross in the moist earth of Quivira. The weight of it nearly pulled him down. Splinters embedded themselves in his fingers. The chief hung a prayer plume from it, then reached toward the splendid horse and raised his war club toward the metal head of the rider. The horse meant everything to him. Everything. The rider toppled to the ground. For one glorious moment the chief gazed lovingly into the great glassy black eyes of the horse and saw himself reflected. Horse, my brother, he cried, before he felt himself impaled at the end of a cavalryman's lance.

The severed heads of Arenal now numbered four. Two others had rolled into coyote holes and were unable to extricate themselves. No matter. The remaining heads rolled on, covered with dust and cockle-burrs. Their eyes, though glazed by dirt from traveling so close to the ground, saw everything. When the heads rolled into an encampment of Quivira along a shallow river, they paused to straighten them-selves. Their hair was matted and dirty. Their skin blistered. They were afraid they would not be taken seriously. That they would frighten whoever saw them. So the heads rolled into camp during the night and found an elder sitting in front of the fire, smoking his clay pipe. He did not seem surprised to see them. Welcome, he said, and moved over so they would have room. When the four heads finished telling their story, the elder got up. He called for fresh warm water to clean them with. A fine buffalo robe for them to rest upon. He won-dered if they wanted food and drink. The heads declined. We have a great distance yet to travel, they said.

They crossed the Great Plains and floated across what was to be-come known as the Mississippi River. They alerted all the tribes they found there. They rolled northward to the Great Lakes and alerted the people there, too. On they went to the Narragansetts, who eighty years later would befriend the Pilgrims during a harsh winter, and the Pilgrims would kill them in return. Finally the four heads rested on a rock overlooking the ocean. They had come a long way. They were worn out. Their hair had vanished into the earth they rolled across. Their eyes could no longer see. But they had visited several hundred tribes and told their stories. The four severed heads of Arenal lined themselves up like penguins on an Antarctic ice cliff. One by one, they rolled into the ocean and drifted out to sea. By this time, they had ac-complished their mission.

CHAPTER

Thirty-three

he asthmatic padre, wheezing hard, offered an open-air mass in the plaza of Cicuye. It was a chilly Christmas Day, and his heart was filled with love. The red-skinned natives climbed through the rooftops to listen to him sing Latin hymns in his gasping voice. They inhaled the fumes of incense and listened to the tinkling of little brass bells and watched a newly converted Cicuye warrior waving a cross overhead. Who is that little man fastened to that stick? a white-haired old man asked, fascinated by the spectacle of a tiny human being attached to a metal cross.

Your savior, Fray Marcos said. *Jesucristu*. He crossed himself. The old man did likewise.

What means *savior?* the old man said.

Christ, Our Lord, who died to redeem the sins of mankind, the friar said. *Per omnia saecula saeculorum.* A cold wind whipped across the plaza and blew his skirts upward.

The old man touched the edge of the padre's sleeve. What means *sin?*

By now, the padre had survived two years among the savages. He had endured every hardship. He had witnessed torture and sacrilege. But God commanded his heart. *Sin* is what you pagans commit through your godless ways, he said. But not for long. We will bring you to salvation.

What means *salvation?* The old man was more than a century old, and he felt happy with the time he'd spent on Earth, admiring its beauty and loving all its creatures.

The padre raised the improvised host to the sky. It was made from a piece of blue-corn flat bread one of the Indian women had baked for him on a hot stone. He'd rounded it out with a flint knife. *Salvation* is the pathway to heaven, he said. He grabbed the crosier from the acolyte and waved it at the old man, who toppled backward. I do not need salvation! he cried. I have the Mother Earth.

The Cicuye moved toward the plaza where the Deer Dance was soon to begin. Men and boys retreated to their kivas to prepare. The padres had shown great interest in these kivas, inviting themselves down the ladders to the smoky interiors. They had grabbed the stone fetishes and smashed them. The Indians did nothing about this assault on their religion, but it had bored a hole in their memory. The drums began to pound. The singing awakened the sleeping bears who came out of their caves to watch. When the men of the Red Moon Clan emerged, they were painted with white and black diagonal stripes. They wore clay bells around their ankles and headdresses of pine boughs and antlers. Eagle-claw necklaces indicated their high position. Two young men carried the fresh carcass of a deer and laid it at the padre's frozen feet. They blessed him with burning cedar branches, singing softly about the spirits of deer and elk, turtles and porcupines, birds and insects. They hoped he understood.

This is what we believe, they sang. The Great Spirit is our Father, the Creator, the Source of Everything Good. Here on Earth and up above, all is in harmony. They offered a slice of the deer's rough, black tongue as a gesture of peace between them. It looked like a grotesque communion. Fray Marcos shrank from the sight. He pulled his thin cape around his shoulders. Where would he begin? A bead of foam appeared on his lips. He helped up the old man he had knocked down. You are no longer Fast Dancer, he said. You are Juan.

The old man had lived long enough to know he was immune from authority. Goddam Juan, he said. Goddam horses. Goddam everything. With that he walked away.

A bonfire roared in the plaza. The friar hurried toward it, anxious to warm himself, inhaling deeply. He imagined he smelled orange blossoms. Sweet almonds. Honeysuckle. He was filled with longing for the civilized country of his birth, for music, wine, and the intelligent conversation of learned men. Quite inexplicably, he began to cry. The natives looked at him with puzzled expressions. They must not think me weak, he murmured. He sniffled into his sleeve and looked around. The pagans were up to something. The sound of drums exploded. A wild, uncontrollable dance began as men, heads draped with the carcasses of freshly killed deer, threw themselves into a frenzy. The earth shook from the impact of so many pairs of feet. The padre pressed against the wall, breathing with the deep rasp of his asthmatic condition. Suddenly, the truth dawned on him. With a hoarse cry, he ran toward the animal-men, his long skirts flapping. Stop this barbaric rite, he shouted. Derisive laughter arose. The Indians shouted epithets that would have seared his flesh had he been able to understand their language.

Kobili had been watching from the terrace of the uppermost house, where he had been living for some time. The Cicuye had not resisted the Spaniards, so they were spared the fate of Arenal. Besides, Coronado needed the village as a base, the Indians to gather meat for his troops and to provide them with furs. The shaman had seen this friar many times before. The man annoyed him. Kobili made his way down the ladders, Macaw clinging to his arm as they entered the plaza. The bird was nervous. His voice was piercing. A magician tied a round mirror to my chest the day we went to see Moctezuma, Macaw said. Moctezuma looked in the mirror, and he saw the future. After that, everyone looked at my mirror to see what would happen next.

I do not need a mirror, Kobili said. I already know what will happen next. He tore the cross from the convert's hands and smashed it to the ground. In the priest's arrogant face, he saw an authority that did not impress him. In the shaman's impassive face, the padre saw a natural force he both feared and hated. They looked at each other for a long time. Then the friar called for the interpreter. I am your friend, Red Man. I can save you. But one word from me and those men over there will kill you. Accept the word of God, and I will spare your life. The priest recognized Kobili, an important shaman. All this time, he thought, and I have not been able to give Jesucristo to this pagan. I shall have him hanged. Several hundred soldiers had crowded into the plaza and were watching the spectacle. Their swords were drawn.

Kobili looked up at the layers of gray sky. He saw an eagle flying past. He understood what was in its heart. He pushed his face against the padre's pudgy one. Very well, he said. Accept the word of that eagle up in the sky, and my life is yours to do with what you please.

The friar drew in his breath. Do you think I will listen to a bird? he said.

Do you think I will listen to a man fastened to a stick? Kobili said.

The padre gestured wildly and wiped the little bead of saliva from his mouth with the back of his hand. Ten soldiers surged forward on their mounts. Do you see that insolent man? he sputtered, pointing to a figure that seemed to be receding. Arrest him. I want him hanged by nightfall. He turned. The shaman was gone. A wisp of dust whirled in the plaza where he had been standing.

CHAPTER

Thirty-four

uch was Quivira, the General said listlessly. He had spent Christmas Day riding through a snowstorm to Cicuye, eating dried meat and pine nuts. His main army had been waiting there almost a year, strangely disturbed by the attitude of the natives, who practiced witchcraft at every opportunity. We must destroy this village, they said, but the General disagreed. He was weary of destruction. Weary of the savages. Weary of this hostile land. He sat before a campfire, sipping the last of the fine *aguardiente* he had brought from New Spain. He spoke to his disgruntled troops about all he had seen and done. To them he seemed much older now and somewhat dazed. Mutiny had been discussed among them. They were sick, tired, and discouraged. They wanted to go home.

King Tatarrax was a naked old witch with white hair and a copper bangle around his neck, Coronado said. That was his whole wealth. The canoes with golden eagles? The gold bells in the trees? The wagons full of gold? The General's laugh was bitter. I ordered the execution of the miserable Indian called the Turk, who told me these lies. I had him garroted while he slept.

What was the Kingdom of Quivira like? the General went on, warming himself by the fire. Immense flat plains, as far as the eye could see. Grass taller than the horses. The native wretches live in grass-roofed huts. They eat raw meat, like animals, chewing it for hours. They carry a freshly butchered buffalo gut around their necks, from which they drink blood and stomach juice instead of water. They carry little flint knives which they sharpen against their own teeth.

What did we have to eat? the General said, helping himself to some flat bread. The large animals we could not catch, but with our lances, we killed rabbits. Stringy, tough rabbits. We cooked them over a fire made of buffalo dung. That was Quivira, my friends. There was no gold. Just this. From his hand fluttered a fistful of dry yellow grass.

The General had a deep sense of failure. What would he tell the Viceroy about the pitiful condition of Nueva Mexico? The mocking, dirty savages who refused baptism? The absence of gold? The destruction of the villages and all the lives lost? He needed to calm his nerves. Come, Maldonado, let us race our horses, he said to the captain. His aide saddled his horse and helped him on. The General was more than a little weary, his bones stiffer than usual. As he rode off, the silence of the immense land unnerved him. Waves of silence crashed in his ears. The clouds had an ominous look, as if they could devour him. He was a fearless man, but he found himself suddenly afraid of clouds. Faster, Maldonado, he cried, digging his spurs into the horse's belly. Faster. He felt himself ascending to the sky. For a moment, he felt pure, simple joy.

A field mouse, who had seen the fall of Tiguex and, before that, the carnage at Hawikuh, sat on his hind legs and watched the General race the captain across the hard ground until they disappeared in the distance. Mouse was full, having eaten much of the General's saddle girth. The girth was bound to break when the horse strained to reach his greatest speed. The General was bound to fall off and be run over by the captain, who could not veer his horse in time.

I am sorry, Mouse said as he watched the unconscious General being carried back to camp on a litter. He scampered away. At the edge of the clearing Mouse materialized into Kobili, who mounted the General's horse and swiftly rode away. That made two horses now, both of them donated by the General. Inside the shaman's buckskin shirt, Macaw was tightly pressed against the cold wind. Only his head peeked out. In my day, the Jaguar Warriors flayed the enemy, he whispered. Peeled their skin off from head to toe. They wore their enemies' skins, just like Earth covering itself with new springtime vegetation. If you like, I will show you how it is done.

I will flay no one, he said. Least of all my enemies. He had more important things on his mind. Kobili urged the animal, whom he decided to call Son-of-Horse, across the hard, snow-spotted Earth, where already he could hear the roots of springtime stirring. The buds on the trees, though tightly closed, promised the new life of the Leaf Tender Moon. Turquoise Boy, his firstborn son, was waiting for him at Cicuye. Though in human time he was not yet a year old, in mythical time he was already partway grown. Kobili had promised to teach him how to set a snare. He had already cut the rawhide strips and made webbing out of sinew. Turquoise Boy would become a great hunter. The best in all the land. The elders would tell stories about his bravery and his accuracy. The great impregnable village came into view. There, inside the Sun Clan kiva, Turquoise Boy had been born. As Sayah's time grew near, Kobili had spread out buffalo robes for her to lie upon. The Six Grandmothers attended this birth, along with Coyote and Raven. When the child came into the world, Kobili drew a mythological history on the kiva walls, so the infant could see it the moment he opened his eyes. When Sayah saw her son for the first time, she cried a mother's tears for his innocence. She knew his way would not be easy. When she breathed on him, hawk feathers appeared all over his body.

With the two horses, the Mystical Beings set out. For the next four hundred years, they would scarcely rest. They would wear out many pairs of moccasins, the travois would be exchanged for carts, other horses would join them and fall by the wayside. But the two mythical horses would not. From east to west, they went, to the wildest reaches of the cold north country, where caribou shared their secrets. They traveled into bug-infested swamps, where Hernando de Soto had murdered the Timucua, Apalachee, Kasita, Mobile, Natchez, Chickasaw, and Coosa. The villages were silent. Vines and muck and rotting trees slowly covered them. Turquoise Boy heard children's songs rising from decay. The lament of women rose from the mouths of alligators. In each of these dead villages Turquoise Boy left a hawk feather that he took from his own body. Before he was finished, he was down to his bare skin.

The purpose of the long journey was to comfort and instruct. To warn those who were sitting happily in their homes, unaware that life was about to become interrupted in unimaginable ways. The Thread traveled with them, hovering just above their heads. The Thread pulled them across rivers. It covered them on cold nights. It provided food when there was nothing left to eat.

PART SIX

The Time When Feet Became Whole Beings

SANTO DOMINGO 1599

WHEN JESUS CAME

THE RULES

In an old, old time, before the white man
  gave us regulations, we adhered to reason.

In an old, old time, before language was contaminated
  with noise, all was orderly in our village.

In an old, old time, we were connected to Eagles and Corn.
  Our hearts were in the right place.

When Jesus came with men of opposite minds, we tried to escape.
  Our lives were cut in two pieces. We lived
  in a rain of confusion. It was the beginning of sickness,

the beginning of debt,
the beginning of falsehood.

Now Jesus is in our midst forever, spinning webs of vexation.
  Por Dios we pretend to embrace regulations.
  Por Dios we remember those old, old days
Of connections to Eagles and Corn.

THE NAMES

They infected us with their names. Martínez. Lujan. Gómez.
Names of the padres who bathed us with holy water
to wash away our sins of innocence.
They tamed us with their names. Concha. Sánchez. Trujillo.
Faltering names of conquest
meant to teach us
the rewards of civilization.

They diluted us with their names. Montoya. Mondragon. Romero.
Heraldic names of conquistadors
unknown to us until they stole our women
and turned our people into corpses.
Our names have always been dear to us.
    Lion Dreams and Dog Star. Trembling Leaf
    and Red Willow. Gray Thunder and Flower Sister. Names
    blessed with the teachings of our ancestors.

Our names have always given life to us.
    Wind Hollow and Walking Rain. Pipe Feather
    and Spotted Pony. Blue Elk and Eagle Rock. Generous
    names borrowed from the bones
    of our beloved teachers. These names are mirrors
Of our long history, falling like leaves within
    the contracting circles of our dreams.

CHAPTER

Thirty-five

on Juan de Oñate, Governor, Captain General, and Adelantado, arrived in Nueva Mexico one hot summer day with one hundred and thirty families, two hundred and seventy single men, eighty-three wagons and carts, eleven Franciscan friars, and seven thousand cattle herded by drovers on foot. The caravan stretched as far as the eye could see. It wore two ruts in the earth where none had been before. The animals watched uneasily. Buffalo knew that even animals as great as himself would be overpowered. Bear and Elk and Antelope wondered if they would be called upon to give themselves to this strange new tribe. They looked permanent and weary. The Franciscans chanted their somber prayers to the heavens and looked around at the unforgiving vastness. How many souls? In their minds they saw churches rising out of the barren land, virgins becoming obedient wives, and warriors forfeiting their spontaneity. They rang little brass bells as they shuffled

 along. The sound was pleasing, and from their outposts along the way, the Indians sang to its little music.

Don Juan de Oñate had spent most of his personal fortune on this expedition, and he could not stop now. His mission was different from Coronado's. By now, the civilized world realized that Nueva Mexico contained no gold. But something more. Limitless land which could be divided up among men like himself. Pagan Indians, whose conversion meant more *reals* for the mission churches and the kind of glory that had eluded Oñate until now. In full armor he rode toward San Juan de Los Caballeros, where the chiefs, recognizing hopelessness when they saw it, swore allegiance to God and the King of Spain. *Del rey abajo ninguno*, Oñate said as the people of San Juan fell to their knees before him. Between us and the King, nobody. His mission was clear; he would claim the land, introduce civilization, punish those who did not obey. He had little softness in his heart for the natives who worshipped birds and animals and held wild dances, half-naked, in the plaza. He both feared and hated the power of the kivas. Like Coronado before him, Oñate was a devout Catholic, a trusted servant of the King. The proclamations he carried with him at all times made clear the sovereignty of his master. The first few months were spent reinforcing this truth.

So it was a personal insult to the Governor when his nephew and sergeant major of the colony, one Vicente de Zaldivar, was murdered by the Indians on the towering rock fortress of Acoma that first winter. One thousand Acoma warriors fell upon eighteen Spanish soldiers on the high island of dusty red rock and killed them. Let it be a lesson to you, the Acoma said, stripping the corpses of weapons.

Zaldivar rose and fell three times, one hand trying to keep his entrails from spilling out, the other making the sign of the cross on his bloody face and chest. *Los Indios diablos!* He saw their dark faces and burned-out eyes, rotten teeth smiling behind set lips. Then he saw nothing. The third time he rose, the warriors cut off his private parts and threw them to the dogs. Let it be a lesson to you, the Acoma said, dressing themselves in armor.

Four soldiers survived to ride to San Juan to tell the Governor what had happened. Don Juan de Oñate erupted in ice-cold fury. When I am finished, there will be nothing left of Acoma, he said. There will be war, but it must be waged with good faith, and without covetousness, malice, hate, or ambition for power. This oath, sworn before his absent King half a world away, made him feel better. Governor Oñate was not an unjust man, merely an unforgiving one.

Seventy men, each with his coat of mail, double strength, set out from San Juan one bitter cold morning with their shields, lances, halberds, arquebuses, a petronel, and two brass culverins with the Spanish crown engraved above their touchholes. They also carried fixed maces and morning stars with spiked balls which hung by a short chain from the mace staff. They scaled the walls of Acoma with a vengeance, though one soldier drew back long enough to say his rosary.

Deep inside the village, Sayah and Kobili helped the people to prepare, she with the same foreboding she had had at Arenal nearly sixty years earlier, he with the growing acceptance of a wise man who understood that nothing at all could be done. Turquoise Boy hid the children in openings in the cliff; he rubbed himself with sage and applied hawk feathers to his body. He stationed himself at the highest point.

For weeks, the visions of the doomed Acoma had been of cornfields eaten by huge worms, of women set afire by the tongue of the enemy, and of children roasted slowly over the fire. The medicine men listened to the ancestors and hid in their kivas. Chief Zutucupan fortified himself inside his house and began to pray, hoping his medicines would save him. But Oñate's medicines were superior. Two brass culverins, loaded with two hundred iron balls, blasted into three hundred advancing Indians. Seven hundred more died during the fierce battle. The village was leveled, a cross raised at the smoldering site. Our towns, our things, our lands are yours, said two old medicine men when they came out of the kiva. They accepted the ropes that

Oñate's men offered and hanged themselves from a tree. Turquoise Boy cut them down.

When the people of Acoma died, a giant arrowhead formed in the sky, its tip pointed at the blood-soaked village. It pierced a knot of soldiers ready to enter a house where three terrified young sisters were hiding. The pent-up soldiers yearned for release, for they had left their sweethearts behind in New Spain. They unbuttoned their breeches. One soldier was cut in two, horizontally. Another said good-bye to his head as it rolled away. The rest of the soldiers fled down the cliff in terror. Evil spirits abound in this hellhole, they said. They described seeing a young woman, starry-eyed in white ermine, move one of the heavy culverins over the cliff without touching it. A man in an antler headdress, with half his face young, the other half old, summoned a huge flock of ravens from the sky. He told them to peck out the eyes of eleven wounded soldiers as they lay on the ground. A young man covered with feathers rose from the ground with a fierce look. He killed two Spaniards with his turquoise-studded arrows.

Macaw hid behind a wall, summoning his courage. Listen, you mighty soldiers of the King, the bird said in the perfect Castilian Spanish that don Juan de Oñate used. Lay down your arms and jump off the cliff. His laughter was like the General's, too. Crazed with victory, incoherent with what it meant, with blood-stained hands, frozen feet, and hallucinating about the ravens that filled the sky, and the coyotes running everywhere, four soldiers dashed to the edge of the cliff and jumped off as they were told.

Macaw half flew, half hopped to the edge and looked down. He stared at the snow-covered boulders. There lay the King's unfortunate men. Dead, he said.

The survivors of Acoma were dragged from their village in chains. As they went along the well-worn trail, the conquistadors sliced off a captive's ear, or nose, or fingers. They threw these bloody parts into the river. The Indians would not see their home again, nor would spring come to their hearts the way it had for centuries, nor would eagles lead them to elk and deer. They sang to give themselves courage. It was the time of year when dances for Turtle, Deer, and Buffalo were held. As they went along, the warriors danced these dances in their minds. Soon they did not feel pain or cold or hunger.

Oñate donned a full suit of armor and rode southward toward Santo Domingo, thinking about suitable punishment for the captives. A flock of ravens flew overhead. They called his name. Across the river, a herd of antelope thundered past. Fish rose from the frozen river and stayed there, captured in the ice. A White Buffalo stood in his path, staring at him with glassy eyes. Move out of the way, Oñate shouted. The buffalo charged straight at him, then veered off. The Governor galloped on, his captains struggling to keep up. He hated Indians. Reports of what had been done to them in Mexico and Peru and Florida appealed to him. I will preside over this trial myself, the Governor said to his aides as he rode into Santo Domingo. He glanced at the prisoners huddled along one wall. They stared back. Unkempt, filthy, with the look of animals. Oñate felt a sudden, inexplicable anger.

The Mystical Beings had gone into the desert to rest. As the days passed, Kobili was the first to sense that something was wrong. We must go to Santo Domingo right away, he said when he got up one morning. I had a dream about it. The people there are calling to us. Sayah had also had a dream. Terrible things were in it. She climbed on a sleek white mare. The Grandmothers rode their own horses, holding on to their manes for dear life. The Grandmother-from-the-South had found a pair of silver spurs, and these she strapped to her moccasins. When she spurred her horse, he outran all the others. They rode steadily toward Santo Domingo, where aged cottonwoods guarded the dark memory of the ancestors and the people blew sickness into the sky through a reed.

CHAPTER

Thirty-six

he General sat at a table, resplendent in his gold-trimmed uniform, presiding over his open-air court. His sword lay in its hand-tooled leather scabbard on the table, along with his books and writing materials. The prisoners were pushed forward, hands tied behind their backs. For two days they had been fed wormy bread and muddy water and slept on the frozen ground. Many were sick and feverish. They gazed at the fire, dreaming of its warmth. They yearned to lie down, but each time one man dropped to the ground, he pulled the others with him. Raven flew down and spoke comfortingly. My friends, think of your loved ones. They are praying for you. They send courage. Coyote pressed against their bare legs. Do not give up, he said. Show them what you are made of. The prisoners nodded, thinking of All Ripe Moon, when crops and women were ready for harvest. Gradually, they thawed out.

The shaman slipped into the plaza as a yellow village dog, sniffing each soldier, then sniffing Oñate, who kicked him harshly. As the Governor read the charges, Sayah drifted into their midst with pieces of dried meat in her bundle. She broke them off and fed them to the prisoners. They ate, hungrily. Step forward, the Governor shouted, pointing a long finger at Xunusta, who had killed many conquistadors. The warrior looked at the thin-lipped Governor. I am not afraid to die, he murmured. He had said good-bye to everything. His heart was at peace. If death came, he was ready.

The Governor pounded on the table. The Court of the Holy Inquisition is hereby convened! His leg muscles twitched. He felt unusually cold. Face me, he said, calling for a fur robe to be draped around his shoulders.

The Acoma did not need a court to tell them how things would go. Dreams were maps to future events, and in their dreams they had seen themselves dead. Caoma was dragged forward first. Why did you kill Captain Zaldivar and his men? Speak up.

Because they asked for such large amounts of maize, flour, and blankets we killed them, Caoma said evenly. Xunusta spoke up. The Spaniards first killed an Indian, and then all the Indians became very angry and killed them. We did not want them there. A soldier punched the warrior in the stomach. He did not flinch. He thought about his wife standing naked in the moonlight.

Taxio stood before the Governor, his hands tied behind his back. He would not look at his accuser, but kept his eyes on the sky. Why, when the village was ordered to surrender, had the Indians refused? Oñate demanded. Taxio replied, the old people and other leading Indians did not want peace, and for this reason they attacked with arrows and stones. We wanted to live as we had always done. We do not like your ways. He lifted his head and tried to find compassion in the Governor's eyes.

Our ways will become your ways, the Governor said. Royal authority commands you to give up whatever we need to establish communities. The Holy Father commands that you become Christians. His fingers curled around a quill pen and broke it.

We do not want to become Christians, Xunusta said. You call yourselves Christians, and look what you do. He gave him a dark look. We do not want to become like you. A number of soldiers fell upon Xunusta and beat him until he dropped.

Coyote saw what was happening. We must help them, he said, certain that he could become a war dog. Wait, Kobili said. Sayah slipped among the troops. She took a star piece from her eyes and inserted it into each prisoner's eyes. Thank you, they said. The Governor removed his sword from its scabbard. He bent so he could see himself reflected in its shiny blade. You are guilty of treason, he shouted. You are guilty of murder. The Court of the Holy Inquisition finds you guilty as charged. Here is my sentence. Every man, woman, and child over the age of twelve, and under the age of twenty-five, will give personal service to our brave colonists and holy missionaries for twenty years. At the end of that time, we will set you free. He smiled weakly. If you are still alive. He tried to cover up his laughter but could not.

No one moved. They were stunned. The Governor came around the table with his sword. He was not a tall man, but to the Indians he looked enormous. Their life of slavery was about to begin. That much they understood. The women wept softly, knowing they would be separated from their children and husbands forever. The men wondered if their new masters would beat them. How would they survive without their families?

Courage, Sayah said. Into their hands she slipped corn seeds. Arrowheads. Small clumps of red earth. They clutched these things fiercely. Face death as you did life, she said. Go deep into the roots of a tree and stay there. Do not look up. She motioned to Turquoise Boy. Rub their heads with ash, she said. On their tongues place juniper berries.

Step forward, Taxio, the Governor said. Put your foot on this block of wood. That's it. Two soldiers sprang forward to hold the foot in place. Then Oñate raised his sword above his head. With a deep expulsion of breath, he brought the blade down on Taxio's foot, above the ankle. The foot dropped to the ground with a huge burst of blood. The prisoners gasped. Taxio was a courageous warrior and hunter who could run as fast as an elk. He drew in his breath, but he did not cry out. He thought of his homeland, which he would never see again, and his young wife, Spring Bird. He hopped back to his brother and tried not to pass out. How could a man work or fight or make love with only one foot? He fought to keep tears from forming.

Xunusta, you are next, the General said. But the warrior saw what had happened to his cousin, Taxio, and he started to run away. The General would not cut off his foot or any part of his body. Creator, give me wings, he cried, reaching upward toward the sky. Just when Xunusta felt his feet leave the ground and wings begin to form, a soldier shot him in the back. His last thought was how beautiful his wife looked the last time he made love to her.

The pile of feet grew larger, twenty-four in all. The men screamed in agony. The women cauterized and bound their ragged stumps as best they could so they would not bleed to death. Sayah comforted the women, the amputees, the children who huddled in terror against the wall. One woman screamed, The blood of innocent people is on your hands.

When all the feet were amputated, the Governor called forth two Hopi men who happened to be at the village during the worst part of the battle. Hold out your right hands, he said. The men knew what was coming next, and they tried to resist. Two soldiers wrested the hands from behind the men's backs and placed them on the wooden block. The hands which had planted corn and shot arrows from bows and made love to women were quickly severed from their strong brown wrists. The Governor gave them back their bloody hands with the blade of his sword. Take these home, he said. Tell your people this is what will happen to them if they question authority. Go, before I cut off one of your feet as well.

Turquoise Boy recoiled and ran to offer assistance to the Hopi. No one saw him moving through the smoke except the Indian people. They had prayed to him all their lives, just as they prayed to his parents, the Thunder Beings. The young woman and the old man, kneeling on the ground, their mouths on the bloody stumps of the Acoma feet, sucking out the poison, no one had seen before. Yet they recognized them. Is it possible our sacred spirits are here among us, they wondered, we who do not always live up to our old ways, who quarrel among ourselves, and let jealousy and hatred interfere? They felt both humbled and afraid and looked to the elders to tell them the truth about themselves. It is Thunderwoman, the War Chief said. And that is Thunderman, her husband. I am certain of it.

Do not think I am an unreasonable man, the Governor went on. He collapsed in his camp chair and called for water to quench his thirst. I have spared your life. The Hopi shrank away. They still had feet. They ran back to their mesa-top village, thinking of ways to destroy the enemy.

CHAPTER

Thirty-seven

The agony of Santo Domingo held the Sun Father in place. For a few minutes, his westward movement ceased. Don Juan de Oñate stared blankly at the sky. The Six Grandmothers encircled him, though he could not see them. They sang songs that Thunderwoman had taught them, deep in the abyss of time. They called for Coyote and Raven. There was the sound of wings, the thump of huge paws. Lightning struck the plaza and made a deep gash in the earth. Oñate fell backward with a cry. Something was lodged in his throat. He spat it out. A bluebird! A sharp pain ran up his calf. He looked down. A rattlesnake coiled around his ankle, its fangs darting out with cool malice. He tore it away and hurled it to the ground. He felt a piercing pain in his chest and groped beneath his woolen jacket and underwear. Spiders, he screamed. The amputees smiled.

A baby lion bit him. He kicked it away, feeling its sharp little teeth. For the first time, he felt fear. Fear of the unknown. Fear of the savages, whose power he had underestimated. Fear of the land itself, filled with murderous creatures. Fear of what might happen to his reputation as a just and peaceful man. Help me, you useless eunuch! he called to the priest. Remove these spiders from my person!

I see nothing, Governor, the friar said. You are mad. He walked away, resolving to make his report to the Holy Office of the Inquisition. Oñate has overstepped his bounds, he thought. What good does it do to cut off a man's foot? Then he cannot work.

The sickly smell of coagulated blood filled the air. Though the amputations had stopped, the elders saw the terrible scene clearly in their minds. We will never forget this day, they said. We will make stories so they are not forgotten. They met secretly in their outlawed kivas, talking about everything they had seen. Sayah helped with firsthand description. Kobili provided detail; Macaw drew his usual comparisons with Tenochtitlan, where, he said, the Spaniards had amputated *both* feet of the warrior Aztecs. They learned to make the best of things, Macaw said. They learned to walk on their hands. Turquoise Boy said, The feet deserve the best we can give them. What can it be?

As they spoke, the crippled men were hobbling toward Mexico, to live out their days as slaves. They minced along, supported by relatives on either side. A lament arose. We are half-men, half-warriors, half-husbands to our women. Still, we are functioning through the sacred world of our ancestors. The enemy will never take what we hold most dear. Reaching up, they grabbed hold of the Thread. They spoke to one another in their native Acoma language, unintelligible to their captors. They made disparaging remarks about Oñate and his mother and his relatives. The journey passed quickly.

CHAPTER
Thirty-eight

he swollen, bloody feet, purple in color, lay where they had fallen in a pile beside the amputation block. No one dared touch them. Soon Sayah came, carrying a large deerskin sack. So did Kobili, the Six Grandmothers, and Turquoise Boy. Working quickly, they gathered up the feet and took them to Acoma, where they belonged. They buried them in what was left of the demolished wall and patiently covered it with a new layer of mud. People came out to watch. They had been crying so long their tears had worn pathways down their cheeks. Now they began to smile.

Ah, there is the right foot of Taxio! We would recognize it anywhere because of his crooked toes. And Xunusta! See how he is still able to wiggle his big toe. Caoma's foot we could never forget. It has claws like a bear's foot. It is furry like a bear's, too.

Those feet were magical. One got loose and walked across the plaza all by itself. Then another came out. Ah, how good to see them again! Winter Buffalo with only four toes. Long Knife with the fallen arch. Little Thunder with his foot mangled by an Apache spear. The people talked to those feet like long-lost relatives. They were, after all, part of their one-footed fathers and husbands, uncles, sons, and brothers on their way to becoming slaves in Mexico. Only a few Acoma remained in the village, but with the feet returned, it was as if the men themselves were there.

The feet became sacred. People decorated them with feathers and shells. They painted them with the bright colors of their clans. As Acoma faced more difficulty, people prayed to them. Whenever there was a matter to be resolved, the feet came out to lend support. They were present when women and children were forced to build the first mission church, urging them to insert fetishes behind the thick adobe walls so that when they appeared to be praying to the white man's God, they were actually praying to their own. The feet appeared when starvation swept the village. They directed the people to a secret store of corn hidden among the rocks of the cliff. The feet climbed onto the roof of the new church and stayed there. The Indians realized this when one morning they noticed that the cross erected by the padres was gone. In its place was a row of corn. From that day on, a row of corn grew on the church roof, no matter how many times the padres tore it out.

Those feet are like whole men, the Acoma said in amazement. They can do anything. The feet helped escort don Juan de Oñate out of Nueva Mexico after his sins became known to the Viceroy, who removed him from office in disgrace. The feet walked from village to village, telling people to resist. The sight of them caused legends to grow. People attempted to capture them with snares. They invited them to fiestas. They erected shrines to the valor of the feet and left offerings of what they thought they might like to eat: cornmeal cakes, roast duck, a sweetish dessert made of nuts, berries, and thick, dark honey.

For several years, until they became tired, the feet marched with Kobili, Sayah, Turquoise Boy, and the Grandmothers. They visited the Secotans in North Carolina, the Apalachees, Coosas, and Mobiles in the swampy southern regions, the brave Plains Indians who believed themselves invincible, the frost-covered Inuit, who spoke to them through walruses and seals. The feet danced on icebergs. They traveled southward to the jungle and danced with Mayas, Zapotecs, Mixtecs, and Aztecs. Macaw, though he'd been born to those kinds of spirited dances, could not keep up. Sometimes the feet rode on the horses, right between their ears for the best views. Most of the time they preferred to walk on their own. Those strong Acoma feet, conditioned by hardship and great valor, could outrun a fast horse.

Kobili gently washed the feet whenever they became dirty. He helped them over difficult terrain. He sprinkled them with magic potions to keep them safe from harm. He wrapped them in deerskin to keep them warm and to protect them from cactus and pebbles. Throughout the wounded land, the legacy of the severed feet was one of hope and conviction. In the pueblos ravaged by the Spaniards, stories about the courageous feet of Acoma were told and retold until they reached mythic proportions. The feet glowed with the luminosity of stars. They sounded like hoofbeats clattering over the hard ground. Sometimes they could be seen marching single file up to the doors of the churches and going in. The padres fainted against the altar at the sight of them. Soldiers tried to shoot the feet, to pierce them with swords, to trample them under their horses' hooves. The feet were spat upon and kicked like dogs. Settlers' wives shrieked at the sight of the feet walking about their gardens, ruining the squash, frijoles, and chilies. Mothers locked their children indoors and watched fearfully from their windows as the feet ran wherever they pleased. At night the feet climbed the walls and danced on the rooftops, *rat-a-tat*, until the unnerved settlers begged for relief. The feet became the collective consciousness of Nueva Mexico. Whenever the Pueblos saw the feet dancing, or running, or marching without legs or arms or bodies, they believed they could become free men and women once again.

CHAPTER

Thirty-nine

Not long after Oñate was dragged off to Mexico City to face the Court of the Inquisition,
Nueva Mexico was divided into twelve enor-
mous parishes, with a Franciscan assigned to each, one exhausted
padre having as many as sixty pueblos under his jurisdiction. A thin,
nervous Basque, trembling from the wild animal sounds that kept him
awake at night, commanded the old village of Hawikuh, which was
part of Zuni. Far beyond that battle-worn pueblo, a weary, dyspeptic
Franciscan assumed control of the ancient mesa-top villages of the
Hopi, noticing the burning hatred of the people toward him. No matter. The will of God was being served; those who disobeyed felt the
wrath of the Holy Inquisition. With a fervor as hot as the sun, priests
built sturdy mission churches with the forced labor of Indian women
and children. The Spaniards did not know how to hunt game animals.
The Indians did it for them. Strange new crops soon grew in the pueb-

los—apricots, apples, chilies, wheat. The Indians learned how to tend them.

Horses were gods, but the Pueblo people did not own them without sacrifice. One man traded a cornfield for a horse. Another his wife. Whenever Kobili wanted a horse, he stole it. He had nine horses now, though the Grandmothers did not entirely trust them. Feet are better, they said. But the shaman noticed that more and more they rode their horses with glee and fed them fresh grass and combed their manes. Horse, Coronado's old steed, had outlived his master by more than fifty years. The General had died in a dusty Mexican village, left with only his membership on the city council, comforted by the exoneration of all his crimes and errors.

PART SEVEN

The Time of the Great Revolt

NUEVA MEXICO 1680

ENCOMIENDA: LAS HUMANAS

When the Spaniards arrived, demanding wheat and hides and corn,
we satisfied their hunger as our own began. We were slaves
to misfortune and while the enemy slept, bellies filled with wild meat,
we were too hungry to sleep. We dreamed of our children growing
strong enough to become hawks. Our women,
whose dead babies watched them from the grave, did not dream.

We were emasculated warriors, too weak to resist
the invasion of our hearts. The encomienda meant
our land became divided, crops were not ours to eat, and animals
were killed without ceremony. When we fell, the enemy

Cut the backbone from our flesh. From our homes and fields
a great wailing arose. Our people became so dry they resembled
mantises. Our prayers for rain were not accepted, and, with a moan,
the land contracted. In our stillborn fields,

The corn of our grandfathers withered. In the mountains,
heartsick animals departed before they said good-bye. Not a morsel
remained as far as the eye could see. Without food,
the enemy boiled cowhides and ate them,
until their stomachs filled up. In our aching village,
children died first and we could not save them. Women
collapsed among landslides of oppression, as warriors

Fell upon the earth and embraced its emptiness. A lament for
families rose to the sky, where corn blossoms sang

for rain and moths waited to become new butterflies.
Ancestral voices said: strangers have raped your women,
stolen your land, your right to live in a sacred way. Your hearts

Are strong enough to resist tyranny. The ancestors
pulled themselves up from their graves until at last
they faced the horizon. They marched eastward
to the buffalo prairie, where they begged the animals
to come home with us, so we would never go hungry.

What we had and did not have, what we were and never
could be, collided in buffalo memory. The animals discussed
endurance with the ancestors and when they were done talking,
the secrets of the buffalo became our path of honor.

C H A P T E R

Forty

he Place of Dreams collapsed. Hardly anything of it remained anymore. Kivas were filled with sand, shamans hanged for witchcraft, including two of Kobili's best friends. Soldiers were quartered with their families inside the villages, keeping an eye on the slaves who toiled in the fields, with not a moment to pray or dance or observe the path of clouds. Slavery had been upon the Pueblos for eighty years. Little by little, the ways of a spirited people had been eradicated or changed by the conquerors. People wore clothing now; men had but one wife. They attended Mass and fell to their knees before Nuestra Señora, Jesucristo, and all the principal saints. The Pueblos had their heads filled with dogma about sin, guilt, and redemption. If they went to heaven, would the animals come along? Would there be room for the sacred buffalo? The Corn Mother? The Rain Spirits? No, the priests said, and gave the baptized children their own last names. Martínez, Romero, Sánchez. Kiva boys became altar boys. Girls just learning the secrets of the Bird Women Society donned white dresses and became the brides of Christ. In the pueblos, Latin hymns drowned out harvest songs. Cornfields withered. The churches grew strong.

We have been away too long, Sayah said as she tried to find the old villages along the Great River. Many had fallen, the people killed or escaped to distant villages. Kobili admonished the elders. Have you forgotten your old ways? The people wept. We have entered the Christian hell, and we are dying, they said. Sayah looked at the emaciated faces, the swollen lips that scarcely moved. One old man sat in the sunlight, chewing on a piece of bark. He was so thin his bones danced beneath his skin. She took his hand:

> *Never shall we leave the places that we love,*
> *even though our eyes are somewhere else.*

Sing it, she said, and taught the old man and his people one hundred verses in all. The Spaniards demanded, Why are you singing? Do you not have enough work to do? We will give you more. Fifteen hours a day the Indians worked, then twenty. When they dropped from exhaustion, the animals took up the song.

> *We are but a footprint on the earth*
> *A wing against the sky*
> *A shadow in the water*
> *A voice beneath the fire*
> *We are one footstep going on.*

Along the banks of the Great River, where soldiers and missionaries watched for some deadly infraction of the rules, the Pueblos whispered their mutually incomprehensible languages. The Spaniards perked up their ears. What are you saying? Are you disputing authority? No, master, we are speaking of rain clouds. See how they move in the shape of buffalo and sheep? At the slave markets they encouraged one another before they were sold to one of the great haciendas, causing mystified looks. We must kill the Spaniards before they kill us, the slaves whispered as the whip cut into their flesh. Have you spoken to Brother Eagle? Yes, and to Bear. They are ready to help us.

Around the campfires, in the outlawed kivas, or in musty houses where people clung to the comforting darkness, the Indians prayed. We cannot go on much longer. Sayah and Kobili appeared to them in the night. She inserted slivers of stars in their eyes. He gave them the Thread. You are still strong, they said. There is one great battle left in you. We are never far away.

The Indians shook their heads. We are trying to become civilized men, they said. Is not a Bible better than a spruce tree?

No, Macaw said, it is not.

CHAPTER

Forty-one

he survivors of Las Humanas stumbled along a
narrow path, fighting nostalgia for a life that
existed only in their minds. Before they left, the
group had blessed the village of their ancestors, bade farewell to
the sacred bones lying in the burial place, dug their fetishes out of the
walls where they had hidden them, and said good-bye to the elders
who tottered off into the desert to die on their own terms. The traces
of smallpox were on some of their faces; children walked with the
bloated stomachs of starvation; the breasts of women hung empty for
babies who were hungry. Two kiva leaders were among this group,
Old Axe and Running Bird, who was the Sun Chief. They carried
their medicines in a bundle on their backs. They trudged along, calling
to one another like birds. They had different-looking grandchildren
now. Those light-skinned babies of the padres and the soldiers would
learn the ways of their bear and eagle ancestors, just as they'd been
forced to learn what the padres knew. The elders would teach them

the old ways. They would carry on, despite the fact that tribal blood was becoming diluted.

The Sun Chief, too old to become a slave, urged the people forward with a soft branch he'd cut from a fir tree. It is coming, a place to lie down, he sang. It is coming, meat for our bellies. It is coming, cool water to drink. It is coming, freedom from our enemies. In his renovated kiva he had listened to an impossible plan. I give you my blessing, he'd said to the San Juan sorcerer, Popé, who, along with forty-six other sorcerers, had been jailed in Santa Fe for witchcraft. Popé had escaped by turning himself into a wasp. Another became a bat. Another a butterfly. Popé was mad and the Sun Chief knew it. He laughed to himself. It would take a madman to save the pueblos.

Everyone's feet hurt. They wondered if they would be killed by Apaches, for they were deep in Apache territory. They came to the edge of the desert and went up into the mountains. When they came to a stream, they fell into the tall grass. Ah, dear Earth. They looked up. A procession was coming down the slope. Six old women. An ancient white horse. A handsome boy. A young woman riding behind a man in a feather cape. A macaw. A raven and a coyote. They rose to welcome them and offered to share their food.

Food? What kind of food, Macaw said, thinking about the mangoes and bananas he used to eat in the jungle. Here he had subsisted on dried fruit for a long time. Whatever you like, the Sun Chief said. Bananas materialized. Then mangoes. Macaw ate himself sick. The Sun Chief carried a drum on his back. I will play you a traveling song, he said. Several women began to dance. Sayah and the Grandmothers danced with them, singing the Yellow Corn song. They carried bunches of sweet grass and juniper branches. The stream sang merrily. The wind extended its long arms.

Coyote entered the circle and danced on his hind legs with Turquoise Boy. Macaw sang with the Sun Chief. The Six Grandmothers made soup from dandelions and wild onions. They roasted a porcupine by burying it underground on a bed of hot coals until the quills pulled off. They made a thin flat bread from blue cornmeal and cooked it on the hot rocks. A delicious pudding emerged from cornmeal, dried fruit, and pine nuts. Kobili produced a magic tobacco he had traded and put it in his pipe.

I see my old village, the shaman said. Still strong. People everywhere.

The Sun Chief felt a pleasant tingling extending through his head. A long time ago, we had harmony. Our kachinas protected us. They brought rain. Now everyone is sick and dying. It has not rained for twenty years. The Spaniards demand our crops, but there are not enough to go around. With the magic tobacco, he felt he could touch the Moon.

Go back to your village, Kobili said. Rebuild it. We will come along and help. You can make it like new again. Your fields will ripen. Rain will come. Rid yourselves of the Spanish demons. They have brought misery to our people.

I met Popé, the Sun Chief said. He says we outnumber them.

The revolt must begin with you, Sayah said.

Old Axe got up. Who will be our allies?

Close your eyes, Sayah said. He heard the sounds of village life and saw the plaza clearly in his mind. A procession of painted men was going to the kiva, and they looked the same as they always did. The ancestors formed a circle in their minds.

The enemy has many guns and horses, Running Bird said.

Kobili touched his shoulder. We have guns also. Metal suits, like the Spaniards wore long ago. Horses are hard to get, but we are trying.

If they learn about our plan, they will kill us, the Sun Chief said.

The villages will rise up on the same day, Sayah said.

The Sun Chief looked into Sayah's glowing eyes. Will we live as we used to?

No, she said. But we can make a new life out of the old.

Popé is at Taos, Kobili said. Find him. Tell him we are ready to fight.

The Sun Chief looked dubious. Great distance separates our villages, my friend. But he began to feel hope surging through his frail, old body.

Sayah beckoned to Turquoise Boy, who had been sitting under a tree, listening. Take Son-of-Horse and ride like the wind. Tell the people what is happening.

Turquoise Boy put eagle feathers in his hair. He packed his medicine bag. Sayah looked at him. He was tall and handsome, tough-minded, with the strong features of Kobili and the gentle, inquisitive nature of herself. Will you come back? she said. He shook his head. My work is at hand, dear Mother. He embraced her. For the roots you have given me, I thank you. For the knowledge I have received from you, I thank you. She noticed, though he turned away quickly, that tears stood in his deep-set eyes. I do not want you to go, she said. Though she was one herself, Sayah knew better than to argue with a spirit. With a little cry, she let go of her firstborn child.

CHAPTER
Forty–two

obili led Turquoise Boy to the edge of the cliff and told him to look down. A man is never alone, he said. Fear is his companion. The task ahead is difficult, yet you must do it. The people are counting on you. He pointed to the rocks. If it became necessary for you to jump down into those rocks to save your people, would you? Turquoise Boy moved closer to the edge. Yes, he said. He was not afraid to give his life. Another life was waiting. He was certain he would be the fleet-footed Antelope next time.

Turquoise Boy had been instructed by his parents and the animals all his life. He knew about the secret Universe. Time had no beginning and no end, and he himself had no origin, for he began in the sky, which was limitless. The boy closed his eyes and drank from a gourd the shaman offered. The liquid tasted bitter and burned all the way down his throat. Then a pleasant feeling spread over him. He left his body and drifted out over the land. Back he went to a time of shimmering yellow light and warm water in which multicolored fish lived. The Earth contained no animals, though birds with long tails flew gracefully through the air. People emerged on a cornstalk and built mud houses and planted corn. So they lived for a long time. Then swarms of huge insects stung the Clay People and killed them. He saw in his mind how strong they were, metal-plated and ferocious.

Dear Father, he said, I thank you for giving me wisdom. Through you I have become strong enough to kill the enemy. Kobili touched his shoulder. What happens must happen together with our Pueblo people and the animals, he said. Our blood has flowed together across time in a pattern so old that I myself don't remember when it began. He cut his middle finger and smeared the blood on the boy's forehead. He gave him certain medicines to protect him, also tobacco, eagle feathers, a turquoise necklace, and a bear fetish. Turquoise Boy jumped onto Son-of-Horse's back and rode swiftly down the mountain. Sayah shaded her eyes against the Sun and watched him go, then she went into her Memory Basket and found her stories. Whistling between the gap in her front teeth, she gathered the women of Las Humanas around her. She told about villages deprived of children who were sold as slaves. These slave children did not want to leave, she said. As they were being dragged along, they turned into bluebirds. They flew back home. See, there they are, waiting for you. Bluebirds chirped noisily in the trees.

The women smiled. They were grieving for their children, who had been torn from their arms. They had never seen them again, though they visited them in their dreams. We have seen the dark side of life, they said. It comes with more tears than a river. We lost our children to men without mercy. We survived because we had to.

Sayah said, It's up to you to drive the Spaniards out. For what they did to your children. If we do not do this, children will always be afraid of men. From a dilapidated cart, Sayah took the upper half of a suit of armor and put it on. She had found a battered sallet that had belonged to a conquistador, and also his sword. Kobili rubbed himself with a white powder and put on his elk-horn headdress and his feathered robe. Long ago he had fallen in love with this headstrong woman preparing herself for battle.

Borrow the names of the great warriors, Kobili said. Slow-Eyed Bear. Cedar Boy. Star-Gains-Position. Long Eagle Plume. These are your ancestors. They died fighting.

Don't forget White Feather. Cradle Rocker. Salt Woman. Spirit Walker, she said. These are your ancestors, too. They died believing the peaceful way of women was better than the warlike ways of men. The shaman shrugged. She had always drawn a line between them, and he supposed that men and women fell on either side of it. Some things could not be helped. Give us courage, Sayah, he said. That is what men will need. And gentleness, he thought, though he would not say so.

Give us wisdom, Kobili. That is what we women will need.

We need your sense of purpose.

Your persistence.

We need the ancestors to guide us. I will pray to them, Sayah.

And the animals. Let us pray to them together.

The Six Grandmothers went off to find suitable weapons. Then the little party walked down the mountain, as silently as cougars, inhaling the fresh, clear breath of morning. The Thread went with them, billowing around their eyes and mouths and feet.

CHAPTER

Forty-three

he animals gathered to talk about the task that
lay ahead. They had performed amazing feats
that formed the basis of countless stories. But
this plan to rid the land of Spaniards was beyond anything they'd ever
done before. They were frightened.

Brother Antelope, said Bear, you are the fastest. Run to the villages with Turquoise Boy. Help him if he gets tired. Bear stood on his
hind legs and looked around.

I am the fastest, Eagle said, flexing his enormous wings. I can fly
from Taos to Zuni in no time. He launched himself from a tree and
circled overhead.

Bear sniffed the air. He had a keen sense of smell. People were
nearby. Not the kind of people he preferred, either.

I have a sense of direction, said Turtle, though it takes a while for
me to arrive. She was not afraid to travel, for she had her own shell
house to protect her.

Very well, said Bear. Start now. In a hundred years, you will reach Zuni. They will welcome your stories, even then. Bear dropped down to his four legs. The people that he smelled were not friendly people. Last year he had lost his mate to their muskets.

Skunk raised her dainty tail. You know what I can do when I'm angry. I'll slip into their houses and awaken them the way I do best.

Bear had had an encounter or two with Skunk. Sister Skunk, take your family with you, he said. Now you, Brother Cougar, carry these knotted yucca cords in your mouth. Tell each headman to untie one knot the moment the Sun Father rises and to keep on doing this until all the knots are untied.

Cougar took the knotted yucca cords that Bear had prepared and ran with them, as fast as his legs would carry him. He moved only at night, across the lonely land, to one isolated village after another. He found the headman and explained the plan. He dropped one yucca cord at each village, then moved on. Cougar's jaw grew sore and the bottoms of his paws became lacerated. At each village, he saw Turquoise Boy making weapons and describing an elaborate plan.

Meanwhile, Eagle flew to Hopi. Wolf ran to Acoma. Deer bolted for Hawikuh. Raven flew to Jemez. Coyote raced to Taos and Picuris. At the edge of the plains, Buffalo ran to alert the people of Pecos, San Marcos, Galisteo, and San Cristobal. Owl warned Santa Ana, Sandia, and Zia. Elk arrived at Tesuque, Nambe, and Pojoaque. Antelope darted to San Juan, San Ildefonso, and Santa Clara. Hummingbird arrived at Socorro, Teypana, and Senecu. Cougar dragged himself into these villages carrying the knotted yucca cords. You mean, the headmen asked, this is how we revolt? Yes, Cougar said. But tell no one. The Spaniards are looking at us. They do not understand a headman talking to a cougar.

CHAPTER

Forty-four

$\mathcal{I}$n the occupied villages, the Spaniards were nervous. Something did not feel right. Lightning struck two padres dead as they returned from matins. The earth cracked open and swallowed a guardsman squatting to relieve himself. A howling wind tore the roof off a hacienda and blew away a family sleeping inside. Bats came down chimneys and sucked the blood of babies. Nine women died of snakebite. In the dusty village of Santa Fe, Governor Otermín heard rumors about a plot to revolt. Huddled inside the fortified Casas Reales, he learned that the Indians outnumbered his soldiers twenty to one. To be on the safe side, he hanged the suspected leaders. Locusts began chirping, louder and louder, in the courtyard. The Governor began to go deaf in one ear.

Shortly thereafter, the high-strung friar at San Juan fell to his knees at the altar, admiring the beautiful *retablos* and *bultos* and *santos* hauled over the Camino Real in an ox cart. There was reassurance in these holy relics, the guttering candles, the scent of incense. Sixteen hundred years of flawless faith, of pageantry and holiness, of absolute authority and reverence, thought the priest, who had survived an attack by a foul-smelling Indian the week before. He touched the sacred statue of the Blessed Virgin Mary. Nuestra Señora, in her blue robe, standing on a nest of snakes, the infant Jesus in her arms, was as dear to him as his own mother. The priest was devout and sincere; sometimes he felt great pity for the Indians. At other times he wished them dead. They will never become wholly civilized, he thought. Educating them is a waste of time. He rose to go to supper. A little bread, a little wine, some frijoles, and the Indian boy, Antonio, to stroke his brow, and he would be fine. As he struggled to his feet, the Virgin toppled from her niche and broke. An omen, the padre thought apprehensively, sweeping up the splinters with a sense of bereavement. The statue *was* Mary; it spoke to him; it shed real tears. Now it was shattered. The snake at her feet had only its head intact. From it protruded its forked tongue. The snake hissed its displeasure. The padre clutched his heart and fell backward to the floor.

A mouse scampered down the nave and out the heavy wooden door. It had caused Nuestra Señora's fall to the floor, the first of many such warnings involving the idolatry of the Catholics. In the plaza, Mouse materialized into Kobili, who climbed onto Horse and hurried away. The stricken padre was standing in the doorway, blinking in the sun. He stared at Macaw. More than anything he wanted the bird's bright blue, orange, and yellow feathers to brighten his cell-like room. Macaw seemed to read his mind. In his best ecclesiastical voice, similar to the archbishop's, he said: Take up thy cross, Brother Lazarus. Take it to the top of the mountain and nail yourself in place. The priest ran after him, blue skirts flapping. Impudent bird! You are not long for

this world. By this time, Horse had taken Kobili beyond the village of San Juan and they were headed toward a safer place.

CHAPTER

Forty-five

o one slept the night before the revolt. Not one
animal. Not one bird. Certainly not Kobili and
Sayah, who managed to be everywhere at once.
In the ruined kivas, elders did not build fires, did not sing songs, did
not beat drums. We cannot risk it, they said. They met in the ripe
cornfields, their faces illuminated by moonlight. The village dogs, accustomed to bearing the brunt of their masters' anger, slunk around,
listening to what was going on. Soldiers roamed the villages with the
uneasiness of victims. They detected blanketed figures hurrying to
and fro, but just as they were ready to shoot, clouds covered up the
moon. Along the Great River, animals stationed themselves beneath
the trees. Warriors stole more horses. Gunpowder. Uniforms with
shiny brass buttons. They said good-bye to their Spanish lovers, but
said nothing about what was to happen in a few hours. We will remember you, the warriors said to the tearful señoritas.

.   .   .

When the Spaniards awakened at dawn on August 10, 1680, they were faced by a bizarre array of animals: eagles, hawks, ravens, vultures, owls. Snakes, giant lizards, bears, mountain lions, coyotes, elk, deer, and long-toothed beavers who smashed down the doors and entered the haciendas, destroying everything in sight. Those who survived the carnage said the Indians had ghastly painted faces. Knives and war clubs. Arms and spears. They killed all who resisted. Animals and Indians seemed to work as one. We saw a warrior riding on the back of a bear, they said later. An eagle armed with a long knife. A raven who flew from the trees and killed a man by pecking him to death. A coyote who tore the throats from soldiers, just like old Spanish war dogs.

When the revolt was over, no one could say who was responsible. The elders in the kivas? Women who had lost their children to slavery? Or the birds and the four-legged creatures, who were perfectly aligned with humans that day? As stories grew, elders said that the Sacred Beings had planned the whole thing. Thunderman and Thunderwoman. Turquoise Boy spread the word on an ancient horse; he shot three men with one arrow. The reports to the Viceroy contained no evidence to support such fantasy, for they were written by frantic, retreating men, determined never to set foot in that barbaric province again. The legends grew. That day, the animals took over, the survivors reported from the embarrassing safety of their exile. A common language existed between them and the Indians. A bear told a warrior to kill a priest, and he did so. A warrior told a lion to tear the heart from a soldier, and he did. When we opened our eyes, there was a little mouse, of which much has been written, the refugees said.

The creatures had worked quickly. One padre, who had been teaching the children of Santo Domingo how to read and write, was attacked by a grizzly as he was about to say his matins. His blood splattered against the plaster walls. He believed he'd died a martyr's death, his breviary clutched in his hands, embracing his Blessed Savior. He murmured his last words. *Nil non mortale tenemus.* We possess nothing that is not mortal. Snake Sister slithered up and swallowed whole the statue of the blue-robed Virgin that the priest kept on a shelf beside his bed. Bear ran outside with the crucifix in his mouth. The plazas of every pueblo were filled with dead and dying Spaniards. Their moans rose to the heavens. Their blood disappeared into the hard, red earth.

At Taos, one wounded officer crawled toward a stream on his belly. He clutched the crucifix of his faith, stopping every now and then to kiss the metal savior. A shadow suddenly loomed over this officer. He looked up. A huge elk rose, its forelegs high in the air. Its sharp hooves dropped swiftly on the officer's neck. The elk saw the man's blood spurt out.

The officer screamed. *Jesu,* deliver me from this holy hell. Amen.

CHAPTER

Forty-six

obili found himself standing amidst the smoldering ruins of the mission church at Taos.
The heavy beams, erected by slave labor, had
crashed to the nave. Only one thick wall was left standing. Splinters of
wooden saints lay amidst the rubble. Over everything, a fine red dust,
the finality of retribution. The pock-marked priest from Seville lay
dead on the altar, a golden crucifix protruding from his chest. Other
Spaniards lay in the nave, throats slit ear to ear. The armor which had
protected them from spears and arrows was now worn by warriors on
top of their wildly painted bodies. They danced among the wreckage
and sang the words of the Latin Mass, for they had served the priest as
altar boys. *Gloria tibi, Domine. Pax vobiscum. Ete, missa est.* After this
day, priests would preach no more. They would whip no more. They
would take no more liberties with children and women. The books
they brought from so far away were burned. Apple and apricot trees
had been torn up, also grapevines and cantaloupe patches. Nothing

Spanish would be grown, only the traditional Indian food of corn, beans, and squash. Popé had decreed it. The warriors bent over the body of the fallen priest. His wooden rosary beads would make a fine necklace. One man reached for it. Leave it, Kobili said.

The shaman took a small feathered Kachina from his pouch and placed it on the altar. It had a ferocious, warlike expression, but it was the manifestation of a god the people believed in. Left in the church long enough, its ancient magic would remove all trace of the foreign religion forever. Macaw stared at this effigy. Don't leave it there, Old Man. After Moctezuma left a stone image of Thaloc, the war god, sickness came. After that, destruction. I know what to do, Brother Macaw, the shaman said.

Kobili, great friend! The Acoma feet skipped across the rubble and perched on the altar rail like birds. Free at last, those incomplete old warriors said. Eighty years had passed since their humiliation at Santo Domingo, but they had been busy all this time, going from one village to another, telling of their ordeal. They had become legends as far away as the Arctic Sea. Look at us, the feet said jovially. Pieces of the men we used to be. Yet we have learned to adapt. Our limitations are a blessing. We are not easily spotted down here. Very few people believe in us. But there we are, rushing out of our wall to help people. Our task is not to stop the flow of progress, but to point out its path. They began to dance along the altar rail. Kobili noticed they had shrunken in size and that they were the color of ripe plums. But they were still useful. He told them to comfort the wounded people.

The shaman went outside. The bloated corpses had begun to rot with a hideous smell. Flies buzzed. Vultures circled overhead with a sinister look. In their beady eyes he saw his own reflection. What have I become? he wondered. Macaw pushed closer to the shaman's ear. Moctezuma told me to expect bad things. But I never did. Hush, you tiresome bird, Kobili said, too exhausted to listen to any more of Macaw's endless recitations.

A black ring closed around the sun, until at last only its fiery inner eye was seen. People ran from their houses wearing the blue-hooded robes of the padres. One elder wore a mitered hat; another carried the golden shepherd's staff that the priest carried on feast days. Their faces were painted in black and yellow diagonal stripes. They carried daggers. They did not recognize the Acoma feet, but chased them until the feet climbed to the top of the wall and stayed there. These are our brothers, Kobili shouted. Do not harm them. The elders opened their arms. The feet jumped into them.

Popé, with live snakes dangling from his mouth, was dancing wildly in the plaza, arms outstretched to the blistering sun, praying in a high, reedy voice to the god who had brought him the fruits of victory. His eyes rolled back, and the whites filled with the fire of zealotry. His arms and legs were thin, like vines, but there was animal power in them. He wore the sallet of a conquistador, but he wore his chieftain's robe of green parrot feathers. Upon his weathered face was the mouldy look of a creature who has lived underground for a long time.

All is restored to the old way because the people believed in me, he shouted. I am the great Popé. Now you will obey me. The warriors were returning from the other side of the river. Their suits of armor were spattered with blood. They looked at him dully, exhausted by their ordeal. Kneel to me, brave warriors, Popé said. Offer your allegiance to me and me alone. In one hand was a padre's scalp, in the other his obsidian knife. The padre's blood ran down Popé's arm to his elbow. While the warriors watched, he licked it off.

The warriors carried the remains of a jug of altar wine made by the priest. This wine was having a pleasant effect. They would drink the rest, make love to their wives, and go to sleep. They dragged themselves past Popé, noticing the bead of saliva that ran from one corner of his mouth. Popé is no better than the Spaniards, a warrior named Spotted Horse muttered, and gave him a dark look. Something told Spotted Horse that life under Popé would be no life at all. Kneel, Popé repeated. Spotted Horse shook his head. Popé raised his knife, then dropped it. You warriors will learn the price of disobedience, he said.

Kobili watched in disgust. He had never trusted the famous rebel during their days together at San Juan, where Popé had killed his son-in-law for some minor infraction of the rules. He believes he is a kachina, the shaman thought. That will bring the true kachinas down upon his head. He turned and noticed a black giant with fiery yellow eyes standing beside the wall, the war god who communicated with the spirits of the underworld: Caudi, Tilini, and Tleume, who had guided them through the revolt. The shaman knew these spirits well. They had taught him how to make magic from spiders and snake venom and bat dung. The war god shook his fist at Popé. Fool, he said in a voice cracking with anger. I am in command here. It is *my* war. I brought the victory spirits to you, Popé. Honor me.

Popé turned, terrified at the hideous sight. Son of the devil, he said. I will fight you with the arrows of my ancestors. Arrows? the war god said. We use guns borrowed from the enemy. From the Taos people a great cry arose.

Popé ran toward the kiva where he had spent his days and nights for many years. The people had turned against him. He who had saved them from slavery and torture. What did they know of gratitude? Despite their Christian upbringing, they were still savages. At the last moment, Popé veered toward the river and jumped in. The blood of the padre would not wash off. On the opposite shore, Bear stood looking at him with mistrustful eyes. Bear is not my brother anymore, Popé said. He wondered why he listened to animals.

Kobili moved across the plaza, leaving a trail of yellow powder meant to produce vomiting and sickness in all who came in contact with it. In this case, the defiant Popé. But his spell was not working. Dripping wet, Popé had disappeared into the kiva. The Taos were singing Christmas carols. They had smashed the sacred objects in the church and dismantled, brick by brick, what had not been burned. They had found a dozen soldiers cowering in the trees and killed them. More soldiers were rumored to be hiding in the canyon. When they were finished, the Indians would strip the corpses, then roll them into the arroyo. They would eat, for the last time, all the fruits and vegetables and bread that Popé had denied them. Then they would go back to the old ways and not be satisfied by them. The Time of the Great Goodness, which they so fervently remembered and desired, had seeped away from them entirely. They would never see its likes again.

Forty-seven

ayah sat on a tree stump, staring at a flock of birds. She was sick at heart. The blood of the Spaniards was upon her hands. She looked at them. Smelled them. Pressed her hands against her cheeks. Other women had fought beside her, closing their eyes when a soldier fell to their arrows, knives, or rocks. Revenge curdled their blood. Never again would these brave women kill, but they had done so and were not ashamed. They washed themselves in the river, but their hands were stained. A peculiar odor like almonds rose from between their legs. They would not conceive for many moons, and when they did, the babies would bear the sacred Sign of the Jaguar.

The Six Grandmothers took Sayah's clothes and burned them. They rubbed her body with sage and cornmeal and sang songs from their long histories. Now it is over, they said, soothingly. Now peace will come. Sayah wept bitter tears until she was dry inside. Her arrows had been true. She had struck her mark again and again. She had seen the startled, frightened faces of the enemy and heard them beg for mercy. Finally, she could not kill them anymore. She threw her bow in the river and broke her arrows in two. She threw away her scalping knife. The smell of death was in her hair, so she cut it and buried the long tresses. She rubbed her hands with river sand until the bloodstains began to fade. When she was finished, she ran across the plaza, her long hair shorn. She wore a simple cotton dress the Grandmothers had given her. Victory is ours, all over the Place of Dreams, she said to Kobili, who had spent the terrible day leading the warriors into battle. Tears fell from her eyes. I killed them, she sobbed. When they ran away, I killed them. Remember when I killed nothing?

Kobili embraced her. New circles are forming on top of the old. Not better circles, but still a circle. You have taken lives in order to finish the old circle. What does it matter? The people have achieved a great victory.

We should have figured out a way to stop time, she said.

But then we would never have had children. We would still be making stars and trees and skunkweed. Come, we must go to the capital city, he said. Many warriors are gathered. A new battle is forming. She shook her head. I am exhausted, she said. The berries are ripe in the mountains. I want to gather berries for Macaw. No, he insisted. There is not time. He pulled her toward him, gently. She pulled away. I always do what you want, she said. Sayah, you are needed there, he pleaded. People are depending on you. He kissed her. In ten thousand years, nothing at all had changed.

He helped her into the saddle and swung himself up behind. Horse is nearly two hundred years old, he marveled. He should have died long ago, but he is still alive. If you want something to be true, it will be. He set off at a brisk pace, the feet scampering along after them. We want our old bodies back, they said. Ah, my friends, Kobili said, looking down, then you would be no different than anyone else. Accept your fate.

C H A P T E R

Forty-eight

ayah slipped into the thick-walled Palace of the Governors and found the elegant salon of don Antonio de Otermín, Governor and Captain General of what was left of the province of Nueva Mexico. She hid, unnoticed, in the shadows of the high-ceilinged room. The Governor was sipping a fine *aguardiente* as he wrote a frantic report to the Viceroy. The invincible army of His Majesty had been defeated by a throng of savages. How was it possible? I am an educated man, he reasoned. I have the power of the Holy Mother Church behind me. They have nothing but superstition. The brandywine slid easily down his throat. Outside in the plaza, he heard angry voices rise.

A warrior named Spruce Leaf, wearing the loose cotton clothing of a Spanish peasant and the striped blanket of his Picuris tribe, stood a safe distance away from him. He was Otermín's most trusted slave. He held out two crosses, one white, the other red. The choice is yours, Governor, he said. If you choose white, there will be no war, but you must all leave the country. If you choose the red, you all must die, for we are many and you are few. His face, normally placid, acquired a dark and hostile look. The Governor dropped his pen.

He is capable of murder, Otermín thought. He wondered if he had time to draw his sword. The warrior stepped closer. Either way, we will kill you. The Governor did not move. Only a twitching eyelid indicated he had heard. Spruce Leaf felt a hand on his shoulder. He turned to see a beautiful, mysterious woman with glowing eyes, not quite human, though she had human form. Her face shifted and changed while he stared at it. Was she the Sacred Being of his kiva religion? Or was she the Blessed Virgin? From long habit, he made the Sign of the Cross. Listen to me, Sayah said. Speak with the courage of your ancestors. Do not look back, Spruce Leaf. Yes, Spruce Leaf said. I look upon now. Otermín leaned forward in his thronelike chair. Who is there with you, Juan Pedro? Come, come, man, I do not have all day.

The Indian seemed to falter.

The Governor drained his glass. You are a Christian, Juan Pedro de Martínez. For the love of God, fall to your knees and beg forgiveness. I am the Governor. My word is law. But for how long, he wondered. He poured himself another glass of *aguardiente*, but his hands trembled so badly he spilled it. His scouts had brought word of revolt in the north, the destruction of the churches, the murder of the padres, the soldiers, and the settlers. Now the murderous savages had arrived in Santa Fe, expecting him to capitulate. What arrogance! Eighty years wasted trying to impose civilization. Christianity had tried to save them. The authority of the crown had taught them the redemptive qualities of slavery. Slaves had built the mud palace in which he lived—not much of a palace, but high walls surrounded it. With only a light whip to encourage them, they had built the church, as uncomplaining as nuns.

Spruce Leaf did not move. His blazing dark eyes bore through the Governor's, to whom he was distantly related on his mother's side. The Indian had been a slave since he was fourteen years old, but something told Otermín the young man would not be a slave much longer. The warrior threw his head back. He felt Sayah's warm breath on his neck. Go now, Governor, Spruce Leaf said. I do not want to kill you. We are friends.

If you do not stop making threats, Juan Pedro de Martínez, I will have you hanged. I am still your master.

My name is Spruce Leaf, the warrior said. I am not a slave. He tore the gold cross from a chain around his neck and threw it to the floor. He looked out the small window. Waiting in the plaza, with the hurt expression of martyrs, were the incinerated people from the Seven Wise Villages of Tiguex. One hundred and forty years had passed, and there they were, speaking the language of their defunct pueblo. The severed feet of the Acoma were lined up on a tree limb, like shriveled birds. The feet said: For every Spaniard who made us miserable, who tore the life from our bodies, who killed innocent children and ruined our women for ordinary life, two must die. The martyrs of Arenal made a circle. Sun Mountain Shining, looking no different than he had before they burned him at the stake, said: Those are our terms.

Spruce Leaf jammed the red crucifix into the wooden table. There, he said, our ancestors have spoken. He left the room before the Governor could stop him. Panic seized him.

Sayah moved closer, noticing the yellow flecks in the Governor's eyes. He recoiled at the sight of her. That mysterious face, those blazing eyes. What tribe was she from? She looked young and old, both at the same time. Who are you, he said, feeling a strange tingling in his hands. He was unable to focus his eyes. Tell your people to surrender, she said. They cannot win. You are speaking to the Governor, Otermín replied. I do not take orders from you.

Waiting outside the palace walls were enough warriors to kill himself and his men in a very short time, but the Governor did not know this. Most of his army had been killed, and few were left to defend the Casas Reales. He gripped the red crucifix so hard it cut deeply into his hand. This strange Indian woman must not sense his fear. She stood, calmly examining a portrait of his family, completed in Mexico City only a few years before. He gazed at it fondly. My dear family, he said. I miss them. She nodded.

You have children, she said softly. A wife. A mother, a father. A family.

Yes, he said. But my beloved family is no concern of yours. Who are you?

Sayah emptied her medicine bundle on the tabletop. Bear claws. Beaver teeth. A rabbit's foot. Two white feathers. An eagle-bone whistle. A pouch of tobacco. Another of pollen. We also had families, she said. Before you killed them. They were dear to us.

There is no comparison, the Governor said. Mine is a God-fearing, educated, Christian family, while you worship those disgusting pagan objects. The padres destroyed them for a reason. I am here to uphold that reason. Now get out of my sight.

She held up the bear claw. This was a bear family. She held up the rabbit's foot. This was a rabbit family. And in this pouch is a baby's navel cord. A boy from Santa Clara. You killed him when he was three days old. You hanged his father. His mother was so sad she swallowed poison leaves. They were a family.

The Governor fell back in his chair. Weariness overcame him. I own great lands, he said.

They were our lands, she said.

You do not need so much land. By royal decree, you must share it.

We do not believe in royal decree.

We gave you the one true, holy religion.

We have no need of your religion. Now you must go, Governor, before we change our minds and kill you. He watched as she moved a heavy armoire from one side of the room to the other by her gaze alone. With a sweep of her arm, she filled the room with lizards. You are a witch, he gasped. I will have you burned at the stake. He rang a little bell to summon his aides. No one responded. He looked up. Sayah had vanished through the walls. He ran to the door. His chief aide, Rodrigo, lay dead, an arrow through his heart. Two caballeros were slumped against the sofa. Don Antonio de Otermín tried to compose himself. With fourteen frightened men to protect him, he marched outside with a determined air.

How many? he whispered to his captain. Thousands, don Antonio. They want us to surrender. If we go peacefully, they will spare our lives. He glanced at Otermín. We cannot win.

The Governor blinked in the harsh sunlight. He had his sword and sidearm. He would shoot the ringleaders himself. An arrow whizzed past his head. A lance embedded itself in a cottonwood tree a few meters from his left shoulder. He looked up. The sky was thick with ravens. Round and round they went, then hurtled toward him like a great arrow, beaks wide open. Had it not been for the captain throwing himself on top of the Governor, the ravens would have killed him instead of the captain. Mountain lions after that, sailing over the wall with their teeth bared. Where had so many come from? Rattlesnakes materialized. They bit two of his men on the leg. With their ghastly rattle of death, the snakes slipped inside the palace and hid inside chamber pots. Cupboards. Horsehair mattresses. Riding boots. Water jugs. From then until the capitol fell, rattlesnakes injected their venom in every possible part of human anatomy.

Fortify the Casas Reales! the Governor cried. Remove all valuables and hide them. Barricade yourselves! Secure the horses! Man the cannons! We will never give up! His hands trembled; his knees began to buckle. In the privacy of his bedroom he knelt beside his bed and said his rosary. God is on our side, he thought. There was that Indian woman with the glowing eyes, drifting above him with the false confidence of a wooden saint. He drew his sword and dropped it. An old man loomed out of the shadows. Half his face was young, with the steady ferocity of a warrior. Accept our ways, General, he said.

Why should I accept your ways?

Because they are the ways of right-minded people, Sayah said. We did not try to convert you to them.

The Governor could trace his bloodlines back to Moctezuma and

Cortés. He had great wealth, though he was debt-ridden now. Why should he talk to those of inferior class? Do you believe in God? the Governor demanded.

We believe in the Corn Mother, said Kobili.

There is only one God, Otermín said hysterically. He had a son called Jesus.

We met him, Kobili said. He thinks like us. The Old Man released a sackful of bats into the air. Filthy things with the faces of rodents. They brushed the Governor's cheek with their furry wings. The Governor jumped into bed and covered his face. He opened one eye. Macaw perched on the footboard. Your horse is waiting, the bird said. The Six Grandmothers formed a circle around the bed. If you do not leave now, we will tie you to the ant pile, they said.

Don Antonio de Otermín expelled his breath and lapsed into unconsciousness.

CHAPTER

Forty-nine

T he Governor refused to surrender. When he
emerged from his stupor, he was surrounded by
the strength of fantasy. He barricaded himself
inside his living quarters, trying to devise a way to harness the giant
wasps that had invaded the Palace of the Governors. Some were the
size of adult humans. They stung his tired and thirsty men. They
killed them. If he could harness wasps, he might increase his strength
tenfold. He poured the last of the water into a goblet and drank it.
Dead bees floated. Otermín's body was on fire. His brain was melting.
Nothing went into it, only out. The fierce sun blazed down on the
palace. The Governor would not touch his food.

In the shade of the plaza, Kobili waited with Sayah, the Grandmothers, and Macaw. Coyote licked his paws. Here is what I would do,
he said, divulging his plan. I would do the same, said Raven. Everyone agreed. While the Governor was taking a siesta, and his troops

were taking theirs, Raven flew to the mountains and talked to the biggest, bravest Deer.

Deer came down and stood at the main ditch above Santa Fe. This ditch carried water from a snowfield high in the mountains to the Casas Reales, watering farmland along the way. It had been painstakingly dug by Indian slaves, who had chipped away at the rock and the many layers of red soil until clear, cold water flowed. It was a wonder of engineering and slavery, the very finest acequia in all the territory, the sole water supply for the Casas Reales. Kobili pointed to a spot where he wanted Deer to work. Deer pawed the earth with his sharp hooves and diverted the water into some nearby fields. Water no longer flowed in the acequia. It was dry. Thank you, Kobili said to Deer. When some of the Governor's men came to investigate why water no longer ran to the Casas Reales, warriors sprang from the bushes and killed them.

Don Antonio de Otermín and his men drank all the red wine, barrel after barrel of it, which made them thirstier. The Governor, so thirsty that the inside of his windpipe erupted in sores, could hardly speak above a whisper. The cattle died of thirst. The horses died of thirst. So did dogs and pigs and goats. Their bloated bodies reeked so badly that no one inside the walls could stand it. Disease spread. Holes were dug and corpses piled into them. The days were hot. Dust and agony filled the air. Water, cried the men, hallucinating about wet beaches and the moist orifices of women.

The Pueblos quickly overran the Casas Reales. Three painted warriors, wearing partial suits of armor, rushed through the door and shot the Governor once in the face and once in the chest. His blood spattered to the ceiling and dripped from the vigas. He screamed for the doctor, who was immobilized in his makeshift hospital with half his leg blown off. God and Santa Maria are dead, the warriors said, mopping the Governor's wounds themselves. You Spaniards will worship our God, who never died. We obey him and not your Catholic God. A warrior nudged the terrified Governor with his moccasin. He had his scalping knife in his hand, but at the last minute he decided not to use it. Instead he helped himself to the prized picture of the Governor's family.

Barely conscious, suffering from the pain of his wounds, the Governor surrendered. His humiliation was great. God wills it, he said as the Spanish flags were torn from the flagpole and burned. He recognized Spruce Leaf, whose face was painted in lurid yellow stripes. Around his neck he wore a dead weasel. He had a triumphant look.

Word of the great victory spread among the Pueblos, still mounted on their exhausted horses, still carrying the weapons and gunpowder they had stolen. Popé arrived in a horse-drawn cart, decorated with skulls, and wearing a crown he had made himself. Give me all the turquoise in your possession, he said to Spruce Leaf, who had taken command. Give me the meat you are hiding. Kobili scowled. Do nothing, he said to the people. He is mad. Popé cracked a whip around the shaman's shoulders. Mad, you say? Popé roared. Kneel to me, Old Man. My power is greater than yours. Kneel! Kobili pushed him away. This is what I think of you, he said. Popé drove off, screaming the names of the saints who had decreed his position as the King of Nueva Mexico. Kobili never saw him again.

As night fell, the elders held council about what to do with their Spanish prisoners tied together inside the Casas Reales. Kill them, said the majority. For what they did to us. One warrior said, Why not turn the Spaniards into slaves? They could harvest our corn. Rebuild our villages. Weave cloth for clothing. The discussion went on all night, with the majority voting for death. Toward dawn, Owl spoke up. If we kill them, we will become as savage as they. Owl is right, said Wolf. Turtle had taken a long time to get to the site of the battle, and he was tired. How do we know they won't return?

Sayah stood in front of them, dressed in a clean white buckskin dress. On her head she wore a *tablita* as symbol of her high position. Let them go, she said. Back where they came from. Raven will go first, to clear the way. Coyote will follow along behind, to make sure no one turns around. The Grandmothers will see they have enough to eat. Some of the Two-Legged and the Four-Legged Creatures protested. We must live in peace, Sayah said, firmly.

The animals and the people gathered more than two thousand Spaniards and led them southward on the Camino Real to El Paso del Norte, where they founded a great city in the desert and filled it with the habits and the hardware of their Catholic existence. The Pueblos held a great feast that lasted many days, but even as they danced in the clothing of the dead Spaniards, something did not feel right.

CHAPTER
Fifty

hen Popé died of the disease that had consumed him, the elders began to fight among themselves over who was in charge. There was little food. Sickness spread. The villages, once allied during the Great Revolt, became as isolated as they had been before. We are no better off, the Pueblos complained. They were too weak to defend themselves when the Navajos and the Apaches raided their villages. They missed the Spanish troops who had protected them. It was as if salt were in their blood. For bones they had willow reeds. They retreated to their linguistic isolation, afraid of speaking old thoughts, old convictions. They replanted the once-forbidden crops of apples, apricots, grapes, and cantaloupes from seeds they had stored. They combed refuse dumps and found pieces of furniture destroyed earlier. They put tables and chairs together painstakingly. In the arroyos they found bedraggled chickens and restored them to efficiency. Clans uprooted themselves, cast cornmeal on their villages, and walked slowly to join other tribes.

The religion of the ancestors was still strong, yet with a difference. Though the Pueblos ran to the river to wash the accursed baptism from their bodies, they still *felt* Catholic. Some wore the forbidden crosses around their necks. Others recited prayers the friars had taught them and sang Christmas carols in place of their old kiva songs. A terrifying realization struck. We have Spanish names, along with our clan names, they said. We speak Spanish along with our native tongue. The Catholic kachinas are enjoyable to look at. The padres taught many of us to read and write. We like Spanish food. Spanish dances. Horses, cattle, and goats. Our daughters marry Spanish caballeros. Our sons fall in love with señoritas. Our grandchildren have the blood of both. They looked around. Sky and mountains had not changed. The Great River was still the same. Birds and animals had not changed, either.

The Casas Reales was a ruin, though new rooms had been added and battlements from which the Indians defended themselves. Sickness had taken many lives; a prolonged drought had destroyed the corn. Dogs walked through the refuse piled in the courtyard; maggots feasted on their sores. The ancestors spoke through rainclouds. You have forgotten the old ways. You have forgotten the names of the dead and the gods who made you. Kobili had ordered a kiva built in the plaza, and in it he told his stories; a new generation of Memorizers tried to remember theirs.

What of the White Corn Maiden, who loved the Deer Hunter, and then she died?

What of the Snake Brother with two heads, one male, one female?

Kobili took a warrior society to the bluffs west of town and showed them how to leave their history in the rock. What is history? the warriors said. We are better off without history. Listen, and I will give you history, Kobili said. Lifting their arms, the warriors did not have the strength to make the pictures in the rock. Kobili did it for them.

Sayah and the Grandmothers comforted the women, birthed the babies, buried the dead. They lifted their voices in song, and the Indian women heard them. We were victorious, they said. But our victory came with a price. Our children were born with webbed feet. Short tails. Incipient wings. One had the prongs of an antelope.

We cannot go back to the old ways, Sayah said. Here, the Thread will help you. She pulled it down. Corn was there, also sinew and bone, animal vision, raindrops, the jar where the rainbow stored its colors, feathers of every kind, and the long hair of the Bird Women of Arenal, who had been burned at the stake. The Thread had Catholic prayers woven into it, the religious dogma of the priests, and the printed word, which had come to them via educated men. The more people looked at the Thread, the more they realized its usefulness. They did not have to use all strands of it at one time, nor did they have to admit they used any part at all.

CHAPTER

Fifty–one

lory be to the Blessed Sacrament of the altar! Spanish voices rang out in the icy predawn. The Indians struggled from their beds in the Casas Reales and cautiously peeked out. A vast metallic army surrounded them, lances pointed in their direction. Glory be to the Blessed Sacrament of the altar, five more times. Be calm, an authoritarian voice commanded. I am a Catholic, known as don Diego de Vargas Zapata Lujan Ponce de León. When the sun rises, you will see the image of the Blessed Virgin on my banner. The trumpet sounded, a long roll on the military drums. A warrior named Flint Keeper cried out: Stay away, whoever you are. We are living in our own excrement. We have no need of you. He staggered back to bed and tried to sleep.

The Captain General was patient. He had time and men and heavy artillery. His orders were to reclaim Nueva Mexico, no matter what the cost, in the name of the Spanish King. And he would do so, regardless. The shameful defeat of Governor Otermín was etched in his brain. Indians did not defeat Spanish noblemen, himself included, without paying an exorbitant price. He was a high nobleman, with palaces and houses and villas at Madrid, Granada, and Mexico City. He believed from the bottom of his heart that the Indians must be restored to the holy faith, that lands now theirs must be returned to the crown, that civilization must take precedence over savagery. With his cross and his rosary in his hands, his armor sending penetrating cold waves through his body, don Diego de Vargas waited patiently, ignoring his discomfort. The honor of the Spanish crown was up to him.

Finally, something in the Captain General snapped. Perhaps the utter silence of the Casas Reales had something to do with it. Or the Sun Father, bursting with impudence right into his eyes. He was weary. The Indians seemed to mock him. He weighed his options. Then he motioned to his lieutenant. Take the Casas Reales, he said. Capture the ringleaders. The battle was fierce and lasted for days. Winter gripped his senses. It wore him out.

Hang them, the Captain General ordered.

With a detached air, he watched the execution of seventy Indians who had resisted. They swung from the trees in the plaza, not far from the kiva Kobili had ordered built. Vargas watched the bodies swing stiffly in the ice-cold wind, stripped of all but their underwear. Then he drank a cup of hot chocolate, seeing in the bleak, frozen landscape a mirror of his own soul. Seventy ravens suddenly alighted in the bare-branched trees. Exactly seventy. Merciful God, Vargas said. His teeth chattered. He rode his horse to the edge of town and rested in his tent. Like Coronado, more than one hundred and fifty years before him, Vargas saw infinite possibilities in Nueva Mexico and its people.

CHAPTER

Fifty-two

reams and practicality collided along the Great River once again. Don Diego de Vargas spread out with his settlers and his soldiers, who broke the backs of the resisting Pueblos for the last time. The Place of Dreams shrank into itself once again, taking its secrets underground. In the once-thriving Pueblos, a sullen acceptance prevailed. The Indians became docile, as Vargas knew they would, for reality had jolted them into passivity. The warriors were broken men. They had failed at what they desired most, and they were never to hear the end of it. Mythic time was preserved in the kivas, where the animals were encouraged to speak of all they had done since the Time That Fish Emerged. The shock of defeat was softened by stories.

Sayah and the Six Grandmothers gathered and redistributed seeds of knowledge. The Hopi provided insight into the four sacred directions. The Keres gave knowledge of corn. The Tewa contributed stories about animals. The Tiwa gave their perceptions of the stars, while the Towa defined the nature of fire. The Zunis knew what it took to make rain. Birds came to share what they knew of distant lands. Macaw told about Moctezuma, though people scarcely remembered his name. A condor brought word of walruses and sea lions. From the plains, two crows delivered a message from the buffalo. A tortoise had crawled for three hundred years to share his knowledge of the conquest of Mexico, but by the time he got to the Pueblos, he was too old to remember anything except the way the earth looked close up. Eagle had the advantage of speed and magnified eyesight, so he brought word of what was happening from a unique perspective, high above the changing land.

By then, many of the great chiefs were gone, as were many languages, songs, and the creative imprint of generations. The stench of death hung heavily above those villages all over Turtle Island that the Memorizers used to watch as they journeyed through the sky. The silence of these villages was deep and unrelieved. Blood crusted over the land and formed a layer of resistance upon which nothing grew for many years. Just when tribes had given up hope, the Grandmothers sprinkled corn seeds inside their footprints and shed tears to make the seeds germinate. Sayah left feathers and cornmeal. Kobili found a rock wall where he etched the symbols of native peoples, forming a network of cryptic knowledge that would inspire them long after he was gone. Women encouraged the Cleansing Rain and the Wind with Four Faces to do their traditional work. They gave stories to the trees for safekeeping. Beneath the outer layer of Catholicism was a strong, resistant core.

The Spaniards, and the Mexicans who came after them, wondered why so many fires burned in the villages. Why they always heard singing, day and night. Why a raven and a coyote seemed to have so much to say. Why Macaw, with many of his tail feathers gone, barely able to hop around, spoke in perfect Spanish of his meeting with Cortés three hundred years before. Who were those apparitions floating about the pueblos? Six old crones. A beautiful woman no more than twenty. An old, old man. And those horses, surely older than any horse had a right to be, clattering past their houses, waking them from sleep.

The Mystical Beings slept in the pueblos. They went into the ki- vas. They strengthened memory. They wound the Thread from one place to another. They fortified connections to animals, to earth and sky. From a deep place, known only to themselves, they summoned the ancestors. The Pueblos realized they were not alone. Now was a time of incomprehensible change. It was, on the Christian calendar, the nineteenth century.

An army of fur trappers moved into the mountains and emptied streams and rivers of beaver. Trails opened up to join east to west, and wagon trains rumbled over them; the American government claimed mountains, deserts, and river drainages that had formerly belonged to Mexico, and before that to Spain, and before that to the Pueblos. What had been the Center Place began shrinking. The Woman-Who-Can-Stop-the-Sun could not stop what was happening. The Americans swept across the continent, killing whole villages, killing magic, killing spirit.

PART EIGHT

When Mountains Died

MANIFEST DESTINY

Up where the sky bends to catch lost sunlight,
*   our ancestors are weeping. They are watching*
*   the transformation of our people who believed*
*   that ancient wisdom was stronger than dogma,*
*   that religion amounted to reverence for all living things.*
*   The destruction of our sacred ways began*

amidst the battle to maintain dignity. Warriors died
*   defending their right to live as allies of the sun, crying out*
*   our words for corn, stars, and sunrise. Displaced*

from our homeland, damaged beyond recognition,
*   we made our way to the Center of Our Being.*
*   We did not respect the ways of our enemies, but*
*   we embraced them in order to survive. Deep within,*
*   our world grew strong, and as our villages crumbled,*
*   our prayers sustained them. We accepted*
*   the ropes that tied us to an alien culture. We wept*
*   tears enough to fill the River of Sorrows*
*   twice over. We stared down progress,*
*   but it came, defiantly,*
*   with cheap whiskey and smallpox germs.*
*   The sale of our sacred land tore our hearts*
*   from wholeness. The faces that we obeyed*
*   were imitations of those we had always loved,*

and the language that we learned contained
no pictures. You are no longer savages,
our masters said, but you are not people, either.

We are fading. We are dying. We are clinging
to straws, to memory. The inner world
is all we have, but the inner world is shrinking.

This is our Manifest Destiny.

CHAPTER

Fifty-three

For more than a century, the Mystical Beings crisscrossed Turtle Island, witness to change, to the armies of kings and mercenaries, to the anguish of native peoples besieged by hostility. The catastrophe of three centuries of assault meant the end of contentment, of unimpeded religion, of dreams of infinite possibility. Their journey took them to ice and jungle, to green oceans and deserts the color of quartz. Though wagons were common by this time, the Six Grandmothers preferred their old handmade carts. Into them they piled blankets, antlers, hides, and baskets containing corn seeds, turquoise beads, and elks' teeth. Kobili lined one of the carts with wildflowers and pulled Sayah through what had become South Carolina. She laughed as she bumped along. Giant lizards and tarantulas joined them, also alligators and foxes to discuss what was happening in their part of the world. They visited whales who told of men who killed them for their oil. Buffalo took them for rides through the plains, where the four chiefs had resisted Coronado. In Florida, flamingoes took them into the dripping, bug-infested swamps, where Andrew Jackson had massacred the Seminoles. Sayah kissed the ground where they had fallen.

In the damp forests of the Northeast, Sayah comforted Canonchet, the veteran sachem and war leader of the Narragansetts, when he was executed by the English firing squad. She hid in the dense forests of Massachusetts during King Philip's War, loading muskets for the Wampanoag, Nipmuck, and Narragansett nations to use in their futile defense. On Baffin Island, she crouched in an ice-block igloo and listened to the spirit songs of the Inuit. She wove corn silk into their hair. She paddled a swift canoe along a river, with Kobili and the Six Grandmothers following behind in theirs, to the camps of the Iroquois, the Huron, and the Ottawa. She spoke of what had happened at Hawikuh, Arenal, and Acoma. Kobili drew a circle in the dirt. One part of the circle was open. There, he said, is where you are falling out.

We trade our furs to the white men for guns, powder, balls, hatchets, blankets, combs, and brocaded clothes, Iroquois said. The Frenchmen will not harm us. Sayah knew that one day the beaver would be gone. The land would be gone. The blankets of the white man would be laden with smallpox germs. She gave a handful of star pieces to the women, also corn seeds to plant when they ran out of food. The women gave her a dress from which hung hundreds of tiny seashells. Kobili offered stories and a deer antler to the headman in exchange for a painted shield. Our history will never die, the Iroquois said. We are a people of strong belief. Kobili offered his arrows and his spears. The headman laughed. We have gunpowder. With gunpowder we can kill our enemy with lightning speed. Macaw piped up: The Aztecs thought they would never die. Then one day they died.

Now the friends had arrived at Taos, where Popé had brooded and plotted in the kivas so long ago. The kivas were given a house on the third story, from which they could see the sacred mountain and the river that ran between the two imposing villages. Taos, or Braba, as it had been called earlier, had been there ever since the First People came out of Blue Lake and followed a cornmeal path to their present site, where they'd built their village. The land of the Taos people stretched from the mountains to the Great River. Now, suddenly, the Americans were building towns and houses and roads. Hunting game. Planting crops. Desecrating sacred soil. The elders had heard rumors about what the new American governor would do. They will take our children. Destroy our pueblo. Make us vomit our convictions.

I say we kill them, said Sun Hawk, whose memory part of history was the coming of Coronado three hundred years earlier. Kobili rose from his honored position in front of the fire. There has been enough killing, he said. I witnessed the Revolt. It sickened me. On his shoulder, Macaw stirred. I could not eat for a week, he said. It was like the Night of Sorrows when Moctezuma— Kobili clamped his fingers over Macaw's beak. Not now, he said.

Memory was long, patience short. If you are our Creator, keep these American demons out, said Gray Cloud, the War Chief. He had his eyes on Macaw. With feathers like that, he would make himself a new headdress. He edged closer to Macaw.

I cannot prevent what is meant to happen, Kobili said. In this life, my power is different. He pushed Gray Cloud away from his beloved bird. Do not touch him, he said.

We do not believe in you, the elders said. Leave the kiva. Do not come back. Kobili drew his blanket around his shoulders. No, he said.

The spiral of time spun out of their anger, and they began to arm themselves. Gray Cloud stole enough horses so each kiva man had a mount. His brother, Looks-with-Eagles, stole muskets and powder. Each man sharpened his knife and found the old, discarded war clubs

of their grandfathers' time. They painted themselves for war, rubbed themselves with sage, put the heads of wolves and cougars on top of their own, sang and prayed to the kachinas, taken out of hiding to perform their holy intercession. But the Taos, because they had been Catholics for nearly two hundred years, also prayed to Jesus, Mary, and their patron saint, Geronimo. Help us, they said. Gray Cloud poured holy water over his head. Ah, now I have magic, he said. Looks-with-Eagles shoved a crucifix in his trousers. Sun Hawk carried a rosary. The warriors, along with some of their Mexican friends who had volunteered to help, assembled in the plaza as the sun came up. The day was bitter cold.

Kobili ran after them, feeling in his arthritic old legs a stiffness he had not known before. Do not do this, he said. Gray Cloud shoved him rudely into the snow. That's how much you know, Old Man, he said. With one swift movement he yanked out the last of Macaw's tail feathers and put them in his hair. He mounted his horse and rode away. What indignity! the bird cried. Kobili comforted him as he watched the war party disappear into the swirling flakes of snow.

CHAPTER

Fifty-four

The American governor had not locked the door. Had not armed himself. Had not stationed guards around his house. There was no need. He had known the Indians all his life, for he was a trader, and they liked him. The Indians appeared in front of him, painted and armed. He called out the names of the kiva men, for he knew them. Coffee? he asked. Sweetcakes? Gray Cloud, what are you doing? Put down that knife. Looks-with-Eagles, why are you not home with your family? For the love of God, listen to reason! After they killed him, they took his scalp and stretched it across a hoop in the village. People laughed at the thin hair, dirty with shallow roots. A weak white man's scalp, worth nothing. They ate and drank and danced through the night, though it was Quiet Time, when they were supposed to be reflecting on the meaning of their inner lives.

Word spread quickly throughout the pueblo. We are victorious. The Americans will not bother us again. We killed their traitorous governor, who used to be our friend. Kobili sat in his borrowed house and waited. Sayah went from house to house, urging the women to leave. The women said, The warriors have found their courage again. We cannot leave them.

Word of the massacre of Governor Bent had reached Santa Fe. An army was coming up the valley with big guns and a bad attitude. They promised to level the pueblo of Taos and hang the leaders. The troops surged up the narrow canyon with a feeling of expectation. A cold north wind blasted them in the face. The sky was dark. Snow fell softly and stuck to their blue woolen uniforms. They were mostly volunteers from the South and the Midwest who had been promised an opportunity to kill Indians. Among themselves, they had formed a pool. One dollar for each dead Indian. A man could make a month's salary in one day.

In the ancient village, people grew sober. It was Cold Moon, when the men were in the kivas, praying for wisdom and guidance. The women brought food and left it, quickly. The future of the pueblo was in the hands of the kiva men. This period normally lasted six weeks, but now the elders were distracted. They came out of the kivas and stood in the snow, wrapped in their blankets, waiting for a sign from Above. They were opposed to Sun Hawk and his men.

Soldiers are coming to kill you, Raven said. One day's journey away, said Coyote, who had run as fast as he could with the news. Deer said, The animals are sleeping for the winter, so they cannot help you this time. The elders turned to Kobili. Ancient Revered One, we should have listened to you. What shall we do? Beneath their blankets, their knives were at the ready.

The shaman had been living in the Turquoise kiva, teaching the boys the story of Creation. Go to the church, he said. You will be safe there. It is the house where their God lives, shut up in his little house on the altar. He had no use for church himself.

Clutching their fetishes, their rifles, and some bows and arrows, the men, women, and children, crowded into the thick-walled mission church that their ancestors had built more than a century earlier. The church was a holy sanctuary. The padres had taught them that. They fell to their knees and prayed to the Catholic God at the same time they prayed to Iatiku, the Corn Mother, and to the Old Man and the Old Woman, who had created them.

The army moved closer. Now they were in the narrowest part of the canyon, singing to keep themselves from freezing, discomfort mounting with each painful mile. The Captain was young and ambitious. He knew little of the history of Nueva Mexico, but as a soldier he knew that a man's duty was to his country. He felt great pity for the Indians. They were without a country.

Sayah ran headlong down the trail, straight into the midst of two hundred exhausted volunteers. She tried to turn them back, tried with all her power to make boulders fly just once, tried to cloud their minds so they fell off their horses. The Americans rode straight through her, as if she weren't there, though they saw a tongue of flame shoot out from the frozen earth. She commanded the river to rise and drown them, but the river was frozen. The army moved on.

The first cannonball tore through the thick adobe wall of the church and struck Deep Lake in the chest. His heart exploded. Ice Terrace, known for the quality of her beadwork, felt the second cannonball part her head from her body. Her oldest boy, Looks-with-Crow, glanced down and saw that his legs were gone. Gray Cloud stood on the shoulders of Sun Hawk so he could look out the small window. See what we have done, the old man said. A bullet from the rifle of a farrier from Illinois pierced his stomach. The drum carried to the church by the elders of the Old Axe kiva exploded with an urgent hysteria. Looks-with-Eagles blew frantically on the conch shell before a bullet entered his mouth and took with it his brain as it exited his neck. Black Water tied a white shirt to a stick and waved it through the hole in the wall. All day long and into the night, the cannonballs and the bullets kept coming. The people fell on top of one another, men, women, and children. Half of the village walls were gone. Through the gaping holes, people looked out. They dropped their moccasins, their turquoise, their baskets, and their ceremonial clothing through these holes. They believed the sight of so much bounty would make the Americans stop firing. The Captain sat on his horse, watching. He did not feel well. Keep firing, he said.

Sayah, standing on the frozen ground above the village, stared into the bloodred afternoon Sun of winter, saw that it had escaped from its sun rings and was falling toward the Earth. For three hundred years she had watched blood flowing across the Place of Dreams. Now the blood of the dying Taos disappeared beneath the crusted snow. Something inexplicable began to form, a certain energy or force. It went deeper and deeper into the earth and remained there until it was needed.

Until the Americans hanged them in the plaza, Sayah gave comfort to the quivering revolutionaries. She bound their wounds with her own hair and with her lips extracted the hot lead pieces from their bodies. The Six Grandmothers used the power of their saliva to cauterize their wounds. They comforted the children and gave blankets and food to the old people, whose homes had been destroyed. Kobili surveyed the ruined church, the village riddled with cannonballs, the sky thick with smoke. I told them to go to the church, and they died, he said, bitterly. I am to blame for what happened.

Macaw, who had spent the siege inside the shaman's shirt, poked his head out. Another massacre. Blood everywhere, frozen into patterns of anguish. Dying people staggering toward their homes, making terrible noises. Corpses frozen into positions of obstinacy. Moctezuma blamed himself, Macaw said. What good did it do? Kobili scratched the bird's soft head. Deep emotion came over him. You are my dearest friend, he said. What would I do without you? Macaw went back inside the shirt.

Nothing, he said in a muffled voice. You would do nothing without me.

CHAPTER

Fifty—five

aos was the last great revolt in Nueva Mexico, the last time blood was spilled in the plazas, the last time the Pueblos believed it was possible to return to an obsolete life. For the next century, the Mystical Beings did what they could to help people adjust to the inevitable. By this time, though, Coyote had white around his muzzle and Raven's vision was not as sharp as it used to be. Macaw's feathers had become dull, but he talked as much as ever about a life that no one on Earth, except himself, even vaguely remembered. Kobili's face was as deeply ribbed as tree bark, but his senses were keen. Sayah's hair had turned the color of snow. Now she looked as old as the Six Grandmothers. The old women plodded along, too stiff to ride the horses, which, except for Horse, Kobili eventually gave away. For the time that remained to them, the friends preferred to walk in their well-worn moccasins. With each step, the Earth reaffirmed them.

Now, the party moved in a westerly direction. They had heard

that some people in California were in need of them, so they would go there. Horse blew through his rubbery nostrils and thought about his life. He had not been with one of his own kind for a long time. Perhaps he could spend the afternoon with a pretty mare. Perhaps the mare could join them on their travels. Though he was fond of the Mystical Beings, Macaw, Raven, and Coyote, Horse longed for someone who spoke his language. Together he and the mare could make more horses so that when he died, Kobili would have companionship. Horse went along at a new speed, dreaming of what might lie ahead.

The friends had seen unbelievable changes. Cities now dotted the landscape. Highways bisected the land. Factories spewed out filth. Dams blocked rivers from their natural course. Fish died. In the forests, Grandfather Trees perished with a terrible shriek when the blade of a chain saw cut into them. Airplanes flew overhead, transporting people great distances in short amounts of time. What fine birds, Kobili said, but Raven was not impressed. Those birds need fuel, he said, while I can fly on my own, anywhere I want. Airplanes will never replace birds. They looked around. The buffalo were gone. So were many tribes, who had fought to stay alive. The Time of the Great Goodness had entered the realm of mythology.

In the prisonlike Indian boarding schools of California, children were surprised by a visit from Sayah, who left totems of their old lives. A bluebird feather. A colored stone. A bear fetish. An arrowhead. A pottery shard. A robin's egg. A piece of deer antler. She drew mystical symbols on a piece of paper and sang to them in a sweet, lyrical voice. She made the captive children smile through their misery. Hair shorn like refugees, mouths on fire from the strong lye soap teachers used on their tongues when they spoke their ancestral language, the children clutched the fetishes for dear life. Looking into her starry eyes, they recognized Thunderwoman. The female part of the Creator. Our grandmothers tell stories about you, they said. You created us. In another time, I created many things, she said. From her blazing eyes she took slivers of the star pieces. The children held them for warmth and light in the darkness of their cells. When the pieces began to burn the palms of their hands, they knew something outside themselves had touched them. And they went on.

CHAPTER

Fifty-six

O n the day that Sayah arrived at what used to be
Arenal, but was now the creation of dreams
and memory, Elk Heart felt great joy. For four
hundred years he had thought of her, knowing that if he believed in
her, and prayed hard enough, she would return to the Clay People.

Raven had told him she was coming after a long journey to the
coast. She had many stories to tell him, and Elk Heart was eager to listen. Wearing his finest bluebird-feather robe, he stood in the plaza,
calling up to the elders. Will she recognize us? Will she stay a long
time? We must have a dance. You, One Fist, play the drum and you,
Spotted Deer, play the flute. I will kill a deer, and we will roast it over
the fire. Tell the women to start baking bread. Green chili stew. Po-
sole. Bread pudding. Get out the Elixir of Dreams. Ah, my heart has
never been more full. For two nights he could not sleep.

Sayah rode into the plaza on Horse, who wore an ancient Spanish
breastplate, a plumed headpiece, and anklets of bright feathers. He

held his head high. The Grandmothers and Kobili followed on foot. Sayah looked around in amazement. Arenal looked the same as it did before Coronado leveled it. The same trees. The same walls. The same mangy dogs. The same sturdy women cooking over the open fires. There were the Memorizers, as implacable as ever, standing on the rooftop, looking down. And there was Elk Heart with his arms outstretched. She slid off Horse and embraced him.

Elk Heart had changed little during four centuries. As spirits go, he had survived. So had the incinerated people of Arenal, who were now part of the myth of ancestry. Those who believed, saw them. Those who did not, saw gophers, mice, and squirrels running through the ruins of Arenal, staring at the tourists who paid good money to see what had become a tourist attraction. Elk Heart hung a turquoise necklace around Sayah's neck. Welcome, Daughter, he said. We have been living as dead men who never died. Feather Keeper stepped forward, no older than he was when she'd seen him last. After they destroyed us, our spirits went into the Cave of History, he said. At the mention of this sacred site, Macaw shrieked, *The Cave of History?* Did you find the g-g-g— Kobili clamped shut his beak with a strong brown hand. Hush, he said. That was long ago.

Elk Heart continued. We rebuilt our village and resumed our old life. He looked around. We do not see the highways. The cities. The automobiles. Here is Lizard-Goes-Forth. There are Bent Twig, Dawn Giver, High Cloud, Bird Wing. Sayah embraced them warmly. Tears flowed from her eyes. She turned to Elk Heart. Father, you gave me courage for the long journey. Thank you.

We spoke of you often, Elk Heart, Kobili said. The chieftain bowed his head. We prayed to you when we were slaves, he said.

Each time they lashed our backs with whips, we thought of you. Many years ago, the feet of Acoma came to visit. They stayed the winter, telling us of events along the river. We were hungry, but every time we looked, here was a cornstalk pushing up.

A colorful procession of women crossed the plaza, singing Corn Dance songs. They danced in a circle, holding Sayah by either hand. Coyote danced with Raven. Sayah danced with the children. The Grandmothers danced with men who did not have wives. Kobili danced with Macaw. The Memorizers climbed down from the rooftop. They presented her with gifts. They stayed up all night reciting all three hundred verses of the Creation myth without repeating the same verse twice. People could hardly stay awake.

On the last day of the celebration, Elk Heart took Sayah aside. Your mother did not die when you were born. She has been with you all along. Here she is now. Out of the chieftain's house stepped No Name in a white elk-skin dress, wearing high-topped white boots, turquoise earrings, necklaces, and bracelets. Her hair was in two butterfly wings, and a spot of red paint dotted either cheek. She was the most beautiful woman Sayah had ever seen. Mother, she cried. No Name stepped back to look at her. The Sign of the Jaguar had completely faded by now, but there were the star pieces she had put there herself. You know me, No Name said. I am Iatiku, the Corn Mother. I am your Earth Mother. I am the First Daughter you had in the Beginning Time, but in this life I bore you. I have been with you on your journey, as rain and wind and fire. I comforted you at Hawikuh. Arenal. Acoma. Cicuye. Jemez. Taos. I was with you when you visited the Ponca. The Oto. The Chitamacha. The Catawba. The Cahuilla. The Grandmothers made you into a fearless warrior.

Elk Heart came forward and took her hands. I am not Elk Heart, he said. I am Shaiyak, the father of the game animals. I watch over the forests. When the Spaniards demanded meat, I gave them rabbits and squirrels. I saved the deer for us. They took our corn, but I hid most of it. The Americans educated our children, but when they came home, we reeducated them. I saw to it that the animals and the children became one, as they had long ago. Sayah had tears in her eyes. Dear Father, she said. Your wisdom is in me.

Iatiku drew Sayah close. Wherever the First People gather, they will honor you. Remember Eagle, who led you to the Seminoles deep in the swamps? Iatiku said. Sayah nodded. Bear, who walked with you when you were leading the Nez Perce northward with Chief Joseph? Sayah nodded. Seal, who guided your canoe to the camp of the dying Inuit? Buffalo, who showed you where the Sioux were ambushed at Wounded Knee? Those creatures were me. I listened to your breathing. I filled your head with stories while you slept. I kissed your cheeks so you would not forget. Now you must do one last thing. I will help you, but you will not see me. With that, Iatiku vanished.

Shaiyak came closer. Daughter, not far from here, on top of a great mesa, is a village called Tsankawie. A brave people lived there. Drought came and they left. The village buried itself in dust. The spirits of the people stayed behind to watch over it. Some of this sacred land was taken by the government during the Big War. I have seen for myself how it was. They put a high metal fence around this land. Guards everywhere. No one knew that a terrible weapon of destruction was being built up there. First the game animals vanished. Then a strange green light drifted among the trees. Birds fell from the sky, dead. Rabbits and porcupines disintegrated in mid-air. The descendants of Tsankawie were living at San Ildefonso by then. They felt odd vibrations. The bones of ancestors floated to the surface. The ones who lived closest to the fenced-off land began to vomit their insides out. One night, during All Ripe Moon, everyone had the same dream. A huge cloud, black and poisonous, towered higher and higher.

Sayah looked at him. What was this black cloud they dreamed about, Father?

The atomic bomb, he said. It can destroy the Earth. He looked down at his stone knife and his moccasins and his buckskin leggings. The chieftain belonged to a vanished world. Though many First People had adapted to the new ways, he would not.

Sayah and Kobili fell silent. They had heard of the atomic bomb on their travels. On the day it fell, birds and animals had rolled onto their backs. Waves rolled backward from the shores. Great whales rose straight up from the sea. Rain stopped midway to the earth and went back up. Nothing had been right since.

The land needs to be cleansed, Shaiyak said. Here is what you must do. Sayah bent her head to listen. She nodded as he told her. He gave her a medicine bundle which contained all the things she would need. Then she climbed on Horse's back. Macaw's beak dropped open. His dark tongue rolled out. What if a bomb falls here? he said.

Kobili tried to calm his nerves. If it falls here, you will be seeing Moctezuma in his Sun House very soon. The bird glanced anxiously over his shoulder. The Cave of History is right over there, he chirped. Do you know what's buried there?

The shaman turned away.

PART NINE

The Time When the River of Blood Washed Away Sorrow

1947

ATOMIC CITY 1947

On the dry tongue of the Southwest wind, they come,
brave Ohuwa and Kawa, warriors beheaded
by Oñate and Otermín, who saw them as obstacles
to authority. Women sing the Song of Giving Up Importance
In order to feel connection between themselves

And the lasting gifts of seasons. On the farflung mesas,
our friends are drops of disappearing water.
Agoyo and Tyugham, holy men choked
by their own voracity, redeem themselves with drink.
Their lost children
are walking with them, armed with pumpkin seeds and corn tassels,

But they are reduced to skeletons. Women dance like corpses,
remembering the blood that congeals their history
into scabs of misfortune. On the dust, they ride as specks
of flying red earth. Pauna and Fana, our hanged elders, are
Alive with news of bumblebees. In the kivas, we open our ears

To stories of ancestors still breathing truths
after all these years. The enemy must bend
in order to be useful and we must have patience
when we are starving. We will kill them with our courage.
Shame them with our pride. They will fall from too much food.

On unfurled lightning Po-towa and Kaya-towa avenge
our murdered leaders, with heat enough to melt

the righteousness of our enemies. They come with animosity,
with impotence, with twenty million slaughtered
Natives no longer in a position of respect. They are here to commiserate

With the sorrowing earth split open in violation
of her sacred dignity. The green fields tilled by
tender hands are filled with poison ash. Birds die
in heavy air not even clouds can breathe. Zealots build weapons
of destruction in the hills where we used to dance.

Our homeland moans in futile protest. Our ancestors
prowl the mesa tops, searching for a place to lie down.
We hear them singing: men who embrace destruction
Are poor in spirit. They will not see God, either.

CHAPTER
Fifty-seven

rattlesnake slithered across the sand of an arroyo. She stopped and lifted her triangular head to a dense yellow sky filled with heat rays. Snake felt strange vibrations in the ground. They shook her scaly body, accustomed to the deceptive peacefulness of her home underground. Her tongue darted at a toad and caught it. She swallowed it whole; the toad moved in her throat for some time. Snake pushed on, leaving a perfect imprint of her body in the sand.

Snake Sister crawled upward over the large rocks, the sun hot on her dry, scaly body. When she reached an open place, she made herself into a coil, listening to the flute that the Grandmother-from-the-East was playing. After the music stopped, the other five Grandmothers drifted out of the trees in dresses made of spiderwebs.

What are you doing here, Snake Sister? said the Grandmother-from-Below.

What I always do, said Snake. What are you doing here?

The Grandmother-from-the-South spoke up. The people in that village on top of the mesa are calling to us. They don't know what's happening. Only that their blood is running once again. We are on our way there. Will you come with us, Snake Sister?

I will, said Snake Sister. She slithered up the rocks ahead of everyone, bright eyes looking at all the plants she encountered. Her forked tongue darted at insects and caught them. She rattled her tail because she liked the sound it made, much like the sound of the gourd rattles women shook during the Corn Dance. Up the steep mesa they went, enjoying the view, mountains and plains, mesas and deserts, all at once. At the top they saw the ruins of Tsankawie. Dirt and grass and trees covered them. Here and there, part of a wall stuck up. Suddenly, with a deep, disturbing sound, the earth began to crack open. An ancient hand, then a moccasined foot emerged, much like a baby bird trying to emerge from its shell, a wing and a foot at a time. The Spirit Beings watched in fascination.

Snake Sister wrapped herself around Sayah's neck. I helped bring you into the world, she said. Iatiku died, but did not die. Sayah touched Snake's beautiful diamond skin. We'll go back to a time when there was no time, she said. Now I know it's necessary to live life in our minds. Snake Sister rattled her tail. Those people emerging, full-grown, from the earth, were delighted with the sound. All over the mesa top, they brushed themselves off and turned their faces to the Sun Father. Ah, they said, how good it feels. They were wearing the clothing they might have worn long ago. They stretched and felt

their bodies to make sure they were still intact. Below them were their old cornfields, but they were overgrown. Their village was in ruins. They did not know where to begin.

The Six Grandmothers remembered Tsankawie. Long ago, the Grandmother-from-the-East had taught the women how to weave cotton into cloth. The Grandmother-from-the-South had met a warrior and spent a lifetime showing him how to be gentle. The Grandmother-from-Above had learned the language of horned toads. A red-tailed hawk flew past. She recognized him as Hawk Boy, who had fallen in love with one of her daughters and dragged her through a hole in the sky. Raven had gone to get her, but from that day on, Hawk had disliked Raven for spoiling his pleasure. Now, Hawk came down to instruct the people of Tsankawie. He taught them Hawk songs. Pretty soon the old drum came out from a place in the rocks and a very old man began to beat it.

The Grandmothers and Sayah sprinkled cornmeal, tobacco, and bee pollen over the ruins. They sang the spirits into being. In the shadows she saw the flash of calloused hands. Behind a piñon tree stood a young warrior dressed in a beaded vest and buckskin leggings of the kind worn long ago. His hair was parted in the middle and hung in two long braids woven with strips of fur. A young woman carried a baby in a cradleboard. She was singing a lullaby. An old man with white hair was talking with Raven about his journey to the ocean. There are fish the size of mountains, the old man said. Birds as big as a man. I have been there, Raven said. Fish smell bad.

The people were shy and unaccustomed to strangers. The minute they saw Kobili walking toward them, they dissolved in sunlight. They left their tools behind, also burning fires, a blackened drum, water jugs, brooms, and the obsidian points they had been sharpening. Sayah sat down on a rock. She felt the people all around, waiting. She tried to coax them out. We are afraid, they said. We have seen no one in a long time.

Why are you afraid, my friends? We are here to help you.

Because of what happened not far from here, we are afraid. Because of what they are doing in Atomic City, we are afraid, the people of Tsankawie said.

Sayah sat up straight. Where is this place you speak of?

Turn around, they said. Sayah turned. Directly north of Tsankawie was a long, steep mesa, like the one she was on. Only this one had stark white metal towers and many large windowless buildings on top of it. The Grandmothers and Kobili stood in a circle, staring across the space that separated the two mesas. In one of those sterile buildings, so close they seemed almost to touch it, the atomic bomb had been built. The government had built it on top of where the Indian people had their shrines, where they'd danced for rain, where the old ones were given back to the earth. When they realized what was happening, the animals had gathered to discuss the glowing green lights and the odd vibrations in the ground. Small animals and birds soon left, followed by the larger animals, also caterpillars and earthworms. Pine trees shed their needles. Rocks broke open, and dust poured out of them. Into the deep canyons so much poison was poured that rabbits, snakes, spiders, lizards, and young birds dissolved in it.

Sayah stared at Atomic City in all its ugliness. The steel towers and windowless laboratory were not part of the natural world. The spirits had deserted it. They would never return to such a poisonous site. Nor would the animals and birds who had once lived there.

The bomb was built on the graves of our ancestors, Kobili said. Think about it. Spirits came out of the ground without their bones. He climbed inside a ruined kiva, overgrown with weeds, and sat down. Sayah sat beside him and took his hand. When the bomb fell, it turned the Japanese people into cinders, he said. A Lakota medicine man told me about it. All over the world, animals commiserated. Porcupines and rabbits, badgers and deer rose into the air, simultaneously. Fish turned inside out. Monkeys fell from trees. High in the mountains, ptarmigans shed their feathers. Polar bears hid under the icebergs. Snakes left their old skin behind. They did not grow new skin, but died in their nakedness. Kobili looked at the sky. The clouds were there. The birds he had known before. The rain was somewhere, waiting to arrive. He turned to Sayah. If we could give the Thread to the people who once lived here, they would have confidence and purpose once again. We can, she said. We've done it all along. They reached up and took hold of the Thread and wound it around the ruins, the plaza, the kivas, the stone buildings which had crumbled. They stared at the ominous efficiency of Atomic City. We must destroy it, Kobili said. But how?

The Six Grandmothers got up. Watch, they said. They raised their arms to the sky.

CHAPTER

Fifty-eight

he Whirlwind People were invisible, yet they
made their presence known all over Turtle Island, wherever they were needed. When the
Grandmothers summoned them, a cloud of red dust exploded across
the horizon. Bits of wood, small stones, and birds' nests flew through
the air. The Grandmothers hung onto the trees to keep from being
blown away in the fierce wind. They shouted: You have leveled buildings before. Atomic City is not so much to ask. At first, the Whirlwind People balked. Do you mean *everything?* they said. Everything,
Sayah said, clinging to a rock. We will have to think about it, the
Whirlwind People said.

The discussion with the Whirlwind People went on all day, then
a black funnel formed. A terrible wind roared across the mesa, the
strongest ever recorded by machines that measured velocity. A dull
pewter light pressed down. A tornado struck Atomic City full force,
just as the bomb makers were going home. They looked up and fled to

their automobiles and rolled the windows up. The Whirlwind People upended the cars; bomb makers tumbled out. The faces of the Indians who used to live there loomed before them. Elk Heart, No Name, Sun Mountain Shining, Lizard-Goes-Forth, and Dawn Giver arose and admonished them. The bomb makers were blown down as they tried to escape. The laboratory crumbled in a flash of green light. Chairs and desks and files blew apart. Scientific instruments were smashed to smithereens. Plans for the hydrogen bomb were blown to shreds and blew out over the plains.

Coyote and Raven watched the destruction of Atomic City. Our ancestors were there too, they said, once upon a time. Without another word, they went down to San Ildefonso, where the descendants of Tsankawie lived. They were the first to tell them what had happened. They waited while the people of San Ildefonso gathered their medicine bundles.

Macaw, seeing what the Whirlwind People had done, felt a terror unequaled since one of Cortés's lieutenants tried to roast him on a spit. A defeathered jay drifted overhead. The naked bird unnerved him. I want to go home, Macaw said in a hollow voice. He disappeared into a hole in the rock and looked out, fearfully. The shaman reached in after him.

Nothing is left of your home, he said. Do you want to live with a million people? Dirty air? Stench and garbage? Traffic and noise? There is nothing left of Moctezuma. Nothing left of Tenochtitlan. Time has eaten it whole. They call it Mexico City now. As he looked across to the smoldering ruins of Atomic City, the shaman saw the spirits of the ancestors begin to settle in.

My dreams are ruined, Macaw cried. His small body did not contain tears, but had he been able to cry, a whole river of them would have burst forth. He stared bleakly at the horizon. Four hundred years of hardship. Every kind of danger. Nasty people. Ruined land.

The shaman stroked him. Make new dreams, he said.

A carload of black-suited officials pulled up and got out, standing knee-deep in rubble. All their precious instruments ruined! Records and scientific measurements destroyed. They could not believe their eyes. What had caused such destruction? They sifted through the waste. This was no ordinary tornado, they said. The scientists felt something even more dangerous than whirlwinds. The whole time they were making the bomb, they had felt a supernatural force that had belied their scientific training. One expert was hurled down the mesa by what felt like an enormous pair of hands. Another expert was lifted into the sky and dropped on his head. The most delicate of their instruments rose through the roof on its own. Now, utter destruction. What had happened? They consulted their colleagues. No one had the answer. They would apply for a government grant and embark on fifty years of research in order to find out.

A strong southwest wind blew the dust from the ruins of Atomic City east to the ruins of Tsankawie. An exchange of energy took place, negative turned into positive, and time reversed itself. The Grandmother Spiders scrambled across the mesa and spun their fine silver webs over the debris of Atomic City until at last it looked ancient and immobilized. Then, elders who had died of cancer emerged from the waste of Atomic City. Here came animals who had perished of radiation. Birds whose eggs had never hatched. Deformed children and children whose brains had absorbed the invisible deadliness. Out of the dust, animals rose and made themselves at home. They had not seen one another for a long time.

Sayah sat on a rock beside Macaw. There were deer and coyotes, porcupines and jackrabbits. She also noticed jaguars, macaws, and javelinas. Where had these jungle creatures come from? Macaw fluffed himself up. I brought them, he said. He hopped on Jaguar's back and hunched his shoulders. He rode the length of the mesa and down the other side. In the four hundred years they'd been together, Sayah had never heard the timid bird laugh. But that day he laughed as he rode across the countryside at breakneck speed on Jaguar's back. She noticed he sounded exactly like Kobili.

CHAPTER

Fifty–nine

For many weeks, rain fell over the Place of Dreams, penetrating the Earth's deep pores. When the rain stopped, life took hold. Certain medicinal plants began to grow that had not been seen for hundreds of years: dayflowers for potency, jimsonweed to change the perception of reality, sunflowers to draw blisters, wallflowers to prevent sunburn. Elders from San Ildefonso, who had foretold of calamity, arrived at Tsankawie with their medicines and their fetishes. Blue Duck, Star Plucks, and Rising Eagle wore their ceremonial dress and carried a small hand drum. They sang their old songs of thanksgiving as they climbed to the top of the mesa and sat in the ruined kivas of their ancestors. Something good is happening, they said, watching green grass poke up through the white dust that had blown over from Atomic City. Watch. The old mud houses magically reappeared. The south side of the village materialized. Then the north side, complete with drying racks and fires and strings of chilies and corn hung up to dry.

The dogs were slinking around in their ancient, unchanging way. Children ran in their moccasined feet across the plaza, chasing ground squirrels.

The elders shouted with delight. Sayah stood before them. You have given us a great gift, Woman-Who-Can-Stop-the Sun, and we thank you, they said. In the end, nothing can kill our people. They made her a crown of paintbrush. New moccasins. A beautiful shawl. They held a great feast in her honor and danced with their revered ancestors. The people of Tsankawie turned their faces to the Sun Father. How good it felt on their skin, after all this time. They promised to live the ancient, indestructible way from now on. They planted the corn seeds Sayah gave them. They drew their stories in the rock, the way Kobili taught them. They brimmed with life. Happiness consumed them. Their long centuries in the grave had been worth it.

From that day on, whenever the people of San Ildefonso came to their ancestral home at Tsankawie, bearing offerings of cornmeal, sage, and bee pollen, they saw the ancient village flourishing while tourists saw only the silent ruins of before.

The Mystical Beings hurried down the mesa to where they had left Horse tethered to a tree, swishing his tail to keep the flies away. They gathered their belongings and put them in a freshly made cart. They spent a week at San Ildefonso, making their plans. They would need certain dried foods, plus medicinal herbs, corn pollen, a hand drum, beads. Hurry, Kobili said. We have a long way to go. Sayah and the Grandmothers took their time. They would not see this beautiful landscape again. They wanted to fix it in their minds. Macaw sensed the finality of this journey. He rode between Horse's ears. I don't like the look of things, he said.

CHAPTER

Sixty

orse had grown tired from the fatigue of prolonged experience. As he headed northward, his
glassy eyes had the reflection of adobe villages
in them. The image of uneasy conquistadors. The likeness of an eagle's perfect wing. His heart stirred with the sweet yearnings of an old
man trying to exceed his grasp. Horse rested often; some of his teeth
fell out; flies bore into his thin layer of flesh. Whenever he napped under the shade of a tree, Horse still dreamed of a mare's softly rounded
flanks, her perfectly shaped head, dainty hooves, a long tail that would
swish the flies from his back. One hot summer day in eastern Oregon,
as he was drinking from a muddy stream, he saw a pasture full of
mares chewing indifferently on the grass. He nickered softly. I have
come a long way, over a long period of time, he called to them. I have
many stories to tell. A strawberry roan looked up. She nickered back.
I am always interested in stories, she said.

Horse surveyed the possibilities. Fourteen beautiful mares to delight him. I must be going, he said to Kobili, who was preparing to make camp for the night. You know how it is. He lifted his head and ran toward them. The shaman watched him race through the tall grass and wildflowers, leaping a barbed-wire fence as if he were a young stallion. Good-bye, friend, Kobili said.

Horse found love in Oregon and he never left there. He lived another twenty years and then he died, having sired one hundred and fourteen children who, it was said, all had the reflection of adobe villages, conquistadors, and eagles in their eyes.

CHAPTER

Sixty-one

bove the Arctic Circle, the land began to change. Nature held her breath, time ceased, a brooding force seemed ready to strike. The frozen tundra had a bland primordial look; arctic terns spoke about loneliness; distant herds of caribou raced across the wilderness and were swallowed up. For the Mystical Beings, hunched against the strong north wind, each step became a struggle. Tears stung their cheeks. Dryness filled their throats. The land yielded little to satisfy their hunger. A few roots. Dry berries. Small, thin fish that Raven caught in the meandering river and dropped at their feet. A choice rabbit that Coyote presented. They had eaten the last of the dried meat, and their bellies raged with hunger. They imagined the taste of roasted caribou, but the animals refused to die for them. I'm hungry, Macaw said. When do we eat? He was a vegetarian, and the prospects looked bleak. He longed for the green chocolate treats that Moctezuma used to feed him.

Be patient, Brother Macaw, Kobili said irritably. We are almost there. His old legs could scarcely push through the deep snow. Sayah wore heavy fur boots and a fur-lined parka that some Inuit women had made for her when they camped together along a wide river during the summer. She felt warm and comfortable inside, though her feet were sore. The Grandmothers wore similar outfits. When the women became so exhausted they could go no farther, Kobili, dressed in a long fur robe, made camp. He found a rabbit hole, set a trap, and caught four rabbits, which Sayah roasted on a spit. She cooked the entrails in a clay pot with water. They drank the nourishing broth and slept soundly in a lean-to made of hides. The friends wondered how they would recognize the North Pole when they came to it. It cannot be far, Sayah said.

It *is* far, Macaw said. He wondered what he was doing there.

Raven turned his back to the fire. I have flown ahead. It's right up there, only a little way now. Everyone looked into the swirling whiteness. Who knew where anything was? Earth and sky looked the same, a great void like the Beginning Time.

We remember worse times, said the Six Grandmothers. Their bones ached. Their teeth chattered. Suddenly, they could not go on. They looked around, fearfully. We will die here, they thought. Away from all that we love. Only the Grandmother-from-the-North was enjoying herself. She felt right at home.

Macaw wondered why he, a tropical bird of great distinction, had undertaken such a perilous journey at this point in his life. I am freezing, he said. Cold air rushed inside his beak and chilled his vocal cords so he could not speak. He began to shiver. Finally he turned upside down on the little piece of fur that Kobili had spread out for him on the ice. The shaman became worried. With his knife, a bone needle, and sinew thread, the medicine man made him a little coat out of rabbit fur. It fit him perfectly. The bird felt warmer immediately. Moctezuma gave me a coat of woven gold, he said. And then he— Kobili clamped a hand over his beak. No more, he said. I'm tired of your stories. But he wondered what he would do without them.

The friends pushed across the vast and featureless tundra, speaking only when they had to. Each of them felt a deep and expanding wonderment at the hugeness of the land, its relentless grip, the way time faded into nothingness. The world looked new, and they yielded to its frozen magic. The Grandmother-from-the-North embraced the knife-sharp edge of the fierce north wind and danced with it around the campfire. She had not made love to this wind for a long time. When a raging blizzard forced them to stop for two days, she welcomed it. Ice crystals formed on her clothing, until at last the Grandmother-from-the-North looked twice her normal size. She spoke to Moose and Caribou, who told her everything that had happened since she had made her home among them.

Sayah paused to look at the wide, blank mouth of sky, the brown grass, and the embryonic rivers pushing southward. They oozed across the tundra like an afterthought. She had the same satisfied feeling she did when she created the world and stood back, admiring her handiwork, wondering what she had left out. Not much color, but a dull-hued lushness. No trees. She hadn't had time to make them yet. Caribou to watch over things. Always the ice-cold wind, searing the barren landscape. A pale sky filled with ice crystals. Clouds too thick to move. An ineffectual Sun Father. I should have made less ice, she thought. More color. Not so much wind. I was in a hurry when I made this place.

She looked tenderly at the Six Grandmothers. She loved them. They were part of her. They had taught her everything she knew in her earthly form. She touched the edge of the shaman's fur coat. He had become part of her in a way he had not been before, though he and she were one and the same. He looked at her and smiled a frozen smile. Our time has just begun, he said. She nodded. Her eyes were as beautiful and deep as they had been long ago. Constantly changing color. Brown. Blue. Yellow like the wolf's eyes. Always glowing with the star pieces, which were the knowledge she had given to the world. He took her mittened hand. He was the mountain, she was the valley. She was Earth, he was Sky. Inseparable. Coyote was the trickster, still teaching her things about herself she had never known before. Raven was the wise bird, reminding her of his own part in the creation of the world when he had pried open a giant clamshell full of people on a rocky western shore. Macaw, so consumed with the history of Tenochtitlan that he had not learned any other useful history, presented a different view of the world. Macaw made her laugh. She had not laughed before she came to Earth. Kobili had not cared this much for a creature before, though he'd had his choice of eagles and condors and hawks. He had chosen Macaw for his compatibility.

At last, I have become human, she said, and pressed close to Kobili. Tears formed in her eyes. The human world was the best of all. She had lived in it a long time and done what she was meant to do. She had to leave it soon and say good-bye to all the people and animals that meant everything to her. I cannot leave the world, she said in his ear.

Kobili kissed her cheek. One world ends, another begins, he said. We have left something of ourselves behind, Sayah. Many children. All the knowledge we possessed. Then, before she could say anything, a strong wind picked her up and deposited her on a moving ice floe.

I love life as I know it here on Earth, she shouted. I don't want to leave it. Do you hear me, Kobili? I don't ever want to leave.

CHAPTER

Sixty-two

hey stood on the blue, groaning ice of the
North Pole, scarcely able to breathe. The wind
seared their lungs. Was this truly the North
Pole, as Kobili had insisted? They didn't know. They had come to the
end of their stamina. Two Grandmothers collapsed on the ice, unable
to move. Sayah hauled them to their feet. Macaw, buried inside
Kobili's furry parka, had not been seen in days. Ice crystals saturated
the air and stung their faces. Time was no longer time; space was
smudged by the frozen tongue of the original cold. The devil wind
originated there, at the top of the world, formed from the icy indif-
ference of the Universe. It whirled around with disturbing ferocity.

The Grandmother-from-the-North, whose home was among the
crevasses and impermeable waves of ice, shouted instructions: Blow
the air clear. We cannot see far enough to do what we came to do. The
wind thought it over, then with a huge, throaty roar blew a frigid gust
of arctic air toward North Dakota. The sky became a clear, pale blue.
Ice crystals drifted down. Time slowed. Bitter cold crept into their

bones. The world realigned itself so that the mystical side of life prevailed. Kobili built a fire from twigs he had gathered from the last grove of stunted trees and carried in a bundle on his back. They huddled around the fire, singing in voices that seemed small against so great a vastness. Kobili beat a small hand drum. The wind suddenly stopped. The idea of a last and fitting ceremony came to them simultaneously. They arranged on a small red-striped blanket their totems and fetishes; they lit a bunch of sweet grass and sage. Its purifying smoke comforted them, though it created great homesickness. The Grandmothers sprinkled corn seeds on the ice. Cornstalks would grow where nothing had ever grown before, on a deep layer of ice. From around the world, scientists would come and study this miracle. The Grandmothers blew their noses onto the ice and watched spruce trees form.

Sayah bent her head. The last of the star pieces fell out in her hand. With a cry she scattered them across the ice. A flock of white birds rose to the sparkling sky, dipping and wheeling as they passed overhead.

Kobili stretched his neck. Ah, what beauty, he said. The white birds made him think of Sayah as she was in the Beginning Time. He looked at her longingly. The shaman had been with her many lifetimes. She was the First Woman and the Last Woman, the rising moon to his setting sun. Love never dies, he thought. It takes a new and different form each time. He had come to realize this during their wanderings, where they'd witnessed the death of people living peaceable lives. Many of the oldest Animal People had vanished. Many of the oldest Bird People, too. The Plant People were diminished and could not provide remedies for illness the way they used to. All over Turtle Island, a mutual sorrow prevailed. Out of that sorrow, great resolve. Kobili sang his innermost thoughts to a wandering polar bear who looked at him with sympathetic eyes.

I love you, the shaman whispered in Sayah's ear, but the wind tore the words from his lips. He had not spoken them in years. He knew now, when it was too late, he should have said them before.

CHAPTER
Sixty-three

acaw ventured out from Kobili's parka and looked around. The ugliest place he'd ever seen. No trees. No flowers. Too much ice. Moctezuma thought Cortés was a god because he could fart like music, he coughed. Kobili nudged him. We have listened to your stories long enough, he said. Macaw had a dreadful premonition. Well, you won't have to listen to them much longer. Is that true, Old Man? Suddenly, the friends became very still. They looked southward toward the pale ring of the Sun Father. Look, they cried. As if by magic, the sky had cleared. They were able to see beyond the white horizon the whole length of Turtle Island to Macaw's beloved Mexico. Beyond that, the length of the enormous South American continent. How beautiful it was! How still! They were not sure how far it was to the tip of South America, but they knew it was very far.

Suddenly they heard a deep rumble and looked down. Blood bubbled up through a hole at their feet. They jumped aside. Blood was warm; it made the ice melt. It swirled around and around, then became a small stream and swung southward, developing speed. They watched it become wider and deeper as it went along, over mountain ranges and down the other sides, through valleys and deserts. The river seemed to have a purpose. It curved southeast to Baffin Island, where frenzied English soldiers had massacred the Inuit. As it coursed through the villages of the Montagnais and the Naskapis, the Micmacs, the Maliseets, and the Abenakis, the river became bigger. It swerved west to Michigan, where the French had murdered the Hurons, then to the desecrated villages of the Crow, the Nez Perce, Arikira, Arapaho, Cheyenne, Sioux, and Cherokee. It gathered the voices of all who had perished there. The river flowed on.

The friends huddled together, astonished at the sight. The River of Blood coursed through every sacred village that had fallen to Spanish, English, French, American, and Dutch invaders. It stopped wherever the invaders had waged war against the native people. Where they had given them smallpox. Whiskey. Rotten food. Slavery. Shame. Flowing mystically south to north, then west again, the River of Blood touched the battlefields at Hawikuh, Horseshoe Bend, Canyon de Chelly, Wounded Knee, Sand Creek, Meeker, Tiguex, Taos, the Everglades. It bore down on ancestral lands the First People had been forced to relinquish and stained them red. The river roared southward, gathering strength until it became a torrent. Before it entered the sacred land of Mexico, where the Aztecs lay beneath the moist soil, awaiting justice, the River of Blood turned into a tidal wave. It swept through Mexico with a roar, then surged across South America, stirring the dead slaves brought to Brazil by the Portuguese, awakening the slaughtered Incas in Peru. It made a noise like thunder.

The Mystical Beings clung to one another, too shocked to speak. Two continents covered with blood! The land glowed with the color of mortality. When the River of Blood reached the southernmost tip of South America, it paused, exhausted by its long, tumultuous journey. Its purpose was now unmistakably clear. The friends joined hands and made a circle on the ice. Taking a deep breath, they recited the names of twenty million Indians killed by the Spanish, the French, the Dutch, the English, and the American invaders. The names of those burned at the stake, decapitated, raped, murdered, poisoned, ambushed, sold into slavery, ripped apart by war dogs, hanged from the trees, executed by the firing squad, and torn from their families to die of broken hearts many miles from home. While the blood-red tidal wave waited, teetering precariously where the land ran out, they spoke each name slowly and reverently. They touched every moment of shame and dishonor there had ever been in five centuries. They honored the villages that had died. The chieftains who had fought bravely. The women who had turned their hearts into shields.

When the tribute was finished, twenty million voices rose on a long tongue of wind all the way from the icy tip of South America. *We remember.* The words echoed upward across two continents, becoming louder and louder. The River of Blood wobbled. It seemed to be deciding what to do. *Now we can forgive,* the voices cried.

With a great, deep moan, the River of Blood plunged into the frigid South Atlantic. The blue-gray salt water turned the dull brown color of coagulated blood. The tide rose ten feet. The River of Blood sank beneath the thick ice of Antarctica. New species of fish emerged.

With the hems of their dresses, the Six Grandmothers mopped up the remaining drops of blood from the ice. Kobili waited for the last embers of the fire to die out, then he walked away from the group and stood alone, feeling the icy wind on his face. He removed the little fur coat from Macaw, though the bird complained. Coyote got up and, with one last look at the people he had spent his life with, headed for home. Raven could not bear to say good-bye. He lifted off from the ice without looking back. He flew southward, searching for a giant clamshell. He would pry it open. People would spill out. Mankind would start all over.

Sayah took Kobili's hand. Their circle was finally complete. But there was still much to be done in corners of the Universe she had not yet been to. Come, she said. He nodded. They rose to the blue cold of the sky and disappeared. The Grandmothers watched them go. They huddled together, singing softly. As they sang, they grew smaller and smaller until at last they were only six dark specks on the blue-gray ice. They resembled seeds. The wind blew them away.

Macaw looked around in terror. He was all alone at the North Pole. They had forgotten him completely! How would he survive in that vast and frigid land? Wait for me, Kobili, he cried, as he struggled to fly on his inexperienced wings. Suddenly, the wind lifted him off the ice. Macaw was sure he could fly, if only he put his mind to it. He flapped his wings with a determined effort. What I have been trying to tell you is—*Those Aztecs buried Moctezuma's gold in the Cave of History!* Macaw felt himself begin to fall.

A strong, gnarled hand came down from the sky, lifted him gently, then tossed him southward. The bird felt himself going higher and higher toward the pale white orb of the same sun that shone in the jungle far away.

At last, he was on his way home.

ALL IS A CIRCLE WITHIN ME

All is a circle within me.
I am ten thousand winters old.
I am as young as a newborn flower.
I am a tree in bloom.

All is a circle within me.
I have seen the world through an eagle's eyes.
I have seen it through a gopher's hole.
I have seen the world on fire
And the sky without a moon.

All is a circle within me.
I have gone into the earth and out again.
I have gone to the edge of the sky.
Now all is at peace within me.
Now all has a place to come home.

Odd Asteroid Mirrors Earth's Orbit

The Earth has a tiny companion that orbits the sun exactly in tune with our planet, astronomers at the University of York in Ontario, Canada, announced Wednesday.

Calling the six-mile-diameter rock the "Mona Lisa of asteroids" for the subtle beauty of its sympathetic vibrations with Earth, astronomer Paul Weigert said it was a "thrilling discovery," akin to "finding a diamond in your own back yard."

Similar odd couples orbit the solar system in harmonic resonances, including the moons of Saturn and Jupiter. However, out of hundreds of asteroids that orbit near Earth, only the rock called Asteroid 3753 is held captive by our planet's gravitational pull in a way that keeps it pulsing in a regular rhythmic dance.

Unlike the Earth's most famous companion, the moon, this asteroid orbits the sun—and at times is 1,000 times farther away from Earth than the moon, Weigert reports. . . . However, it is still considered a "companion" because of the exact mathematical one-to-one relationship of its orbit to Earth's.

The mystery is: How did it achieve such an unlikely orbit? The asteroid was discovered eleven years ago, but its unusual horseshoe-shaped orbit was revealed only recently with the help of powerful computers. The asteroid, scientists say, poses no threat to Earth—at least for 100 million years, when it could stray from its present path and career unpredictably.

The asteroid remains enthralled in Earth's gravitational grasp through a complicated celestial choreography. As the asteroid begins to approach the planet, Earth's gravity flings it out to a larger orbit. Since objects orbiting far from the sun orbit more slowly than objects nearby, the asteroid slows down. When the asteroid gets too far behind Earth, the planet pulls it back onto an inside track, where it can orbit faster and catch up to Earth again.

Called a "horseshoe orbit" because the asteroid appears to shift direction in mid-swing, it is a phenomenon seen only in one other place in the solar system—on the two moons of Saturn.

Just how the asteroid got there in the first place remains a mystery. Since asteroids orbiting near Earth usually hang around for no longer than 1000 million years, it is hard to imagine how 3753 could have formed with the Earth at the birth of the solar system, almost 5 billion years ago.

LOS ANGELES TIMES
May 11, 1997